MARIE D

STILL WATER, SKIN

A RECORD OF REVIVAL
BOOK 1

Book cover by MiblArt

Chapter header art by Book Brush

Formatting by Antoine Bandele

ISBN (paperback) 979-8-9999351-0-6

ISBN (ebook) 979-8-9999351-1-3

First edition: November 2025

Revised June 2026

LET'S CONNECT!

Scan to sign up for the latest updates from the Record of Revival series!

For Pepper,
Who taught me that love is always worth it

CONTENT WARNINGS & READER NOTES

This novel contains graphic descriptions of body horror of monstrous, animal-like creatures, referred to as "zonbi," alcoholism, and mentions of death by suicide.

On family members: Family members who have been adopted, whether through legal means or by simply being welcomed into a non-blood-related family, will have their relationship status capitalized. For example, an adopted sibling will be a Sister, a Brother, or a Sibling, an adoptive parent will be a Mother, a Father, or a Parent, and so on. A blood relative will have their relationship status in lower case (sister, brother, sibling, mother, father, parent, and so on).

On origins: "Having roots in" and other similar phrases indicate that the character's ethnic background is native to the stated continent. If they are mentioned as "being from," "residing in," a location being their homeland, and so on, then the mentioned location is their nationality.

INDUCTION CEREMONY

What does repression feel like? Is that a question he can answer? Does he yearn for a celebration of spirit as we do? Does he ever desire to give in to the lust of pain, even if it strains the life around him?

Foolish questions.

He is the breath of the Natural. He is the bulwark blocking us from the emotions we've silenced for generations, the emotions that sustain our spirits. He is the Saint.

But he is no Saint of mine.

Leonardo, the thirty-second spiritual leader of the Natural Plane. It only takes the sound of his name to sour my body. A young, attractive man, admired by all, his eloquence and charm have perpetuated conflicts, broken spirits, and systematically slaughtered thousands. Among the victims of his terror, my son.

I can't let my mind wander right now. He has bled his will into history. Today, I will bleed mine.

In minutes, he will bless the latest arrival of recruits, future scouts and medics who will continue to repress our true emotions. They are gathered here at the base of the Cathedral, the home of the Saint, for the induction ceremony. Their excitement and apprehension are particularly aggravating this time. Their chatter stops when the Saint's assistant appears at the Cathedral's balcony, raising a hand to command silence. He steps aside as the Saint walks forward, taking center stage. Arrogant as always, in all his bold, violet regalia, he begins his speech—the last he will ever give.

"I've done dozens of these things, and every time it gets harder to find new ways to say welcome. So I'll say thank you instead. Thank you, young adults, for giving your future to fight..."

His words fade to air as I search my surroundings. My comrade in this plot should be ready to make his move. I must admit, the anticipation is sickening. The Natural forbade me from celebrating the life of my son in the way he deserved. But he, and everyone who suffered its chokehold, will dance tonight.

An explosion on the balcony, its dim waves crackling with rage. The assistant falls to the ground below, a voiceless death. Recruits scream and scatter. Scoutmasters forge weapons, prepared to defend. The Saint grabs his chest and struggles against a force he can't comprehend. A few seconds more and he collapses. Chaos rises as more bodies fall.

"Odomi! Let's get in there! They'll need medics."

I follow my fellow medic into the Cathedral. I want so badly to give in to the satisfaction of a plan perfectly executed, but I have to keep appearances. Needing insurance, I taste the remaining waves of rage, smothering any joy that may surface.

We are victorious in the first battle against the Natural and its repression. No doubt the Cathedral will strike back with fangs primed. But let them come. Today, our people were gifted with hope. And when people have hope, their repressors can no longer silence their spirits.

PART 1

5th Month of the 801st Cycle, Era of the Saint (ES)

ONE

NIESH

Niesh feared little.

As the Grand Scoutmaster of the Scouthood, the Natural Plane's defense against unnatural threats, the woman with roots in the lands of Fa'atasi and Artemisa fought both zonbi rashes and insubordinate comrades. The former she felled with grace. The latter she brought in line with strict logic in one hand and the threat of punishment in the other.

Then why wasn't she commanding her scoutmasters to silence?

Within seconds, the most important meeting of the cycle would begin. Her scoutmasters stood in clusters in the conference hall, likely trading rumors that had surfaced since the attack on the Cathedral five months ago. Expected, but unproductive.

Niesh, a woman of considerable height with skin the intensity of hot sand, twirled drops of metal around the tips of her fingers. The rest of her body waited for her mouth to give direction. Her brown eyes watched her scoutmasters, but she also trained them on the reality ahead of her.

She was once just the arm of the Saint, the spiritual leader of the Natural Plane. Now everyone expected her to act in his stead.

"Master."

Upon hearing her old title, Niesh forged the metal into an

3

armband and synced it onto her left arm. Ignacia, a young Artemisan scoutmaster whose deep ochre skin matched her optimistic personality, looked beyond Niesh at the opening doors. Ignacia flicked her brown eyes back to her commander, wasting no time finding a place to stand along the hall's wall.

"Position!" Niesh roused herself out of the relaxed stance she found herself in and took the posture expected of a seasoned leader. She fixed the hunter green scarf around her neck, the scarf that indicated her position as the Grand Scoutmaster, the commander of the Scouthood. Then she gave her scoutmasters a sweep with her eyes to ensure they wore their gold-embroidered viridian scarves, the gold indicating they were stationed to protect the Cathedral. "Respect for our guests, the Board of the Cathedral."

Every scoutmaster, experts in eliminating the unnatural zonbi, straightened their bodies in deference to a status higher than theirs.

And that higher status entered with a soundless quake.

The four members of the Cathedral's Board, the governing body created to ensure the Saint acted within the expectations of their office, entered without ceremony.

Kaima, a man whose youthful appearance belied cycles of experience, held his sight straight. But any scoutmaster with their senses intact knew his eyes studied, judged, corrected.

The shadow to Kaima's reticence, Toiva, a brash woman, did not rein in her gaze. With an obstinance honed by age, she served her judgment saucy and quick.

Nadir, a quiet, handsome man, almost floated above the polished floor. No one, not even Niesh with all her worldly knowledge, could ever tell what the man was thinking.

And then there was Zenaida, easily the one to watch out for with her cutting edges and wry mouth.

"Salute!"

In one motion, the scoutmasters executed the scout's salute—right arm straight across the stomach, left arm diagonal across the heart. The salute signified the Scout's Word, their dedication to the tenets of the Cathedral, control of emotions and respect for all life.

"It's always so obvious when the children practice right before performing." Zenaida dripped her eyes over the scoutmasters before taking a seat at the long table. "Maybe a pop quiz would be a better assessment of their capabilities."

It took every nerve in Niesh's body to stop her from reacting to her comment. And to keep her emotions down to zero, it usually took nothing. Thankfully, the children—*scoutmasters* were quick studies and knew to hold face in front of the Board.

"Guard."

The scoutmasters returned their arms to their sides, at ease and ready to defend if necessary. Zenaida sat next to Nadir, who remained poised. Kaima and Toiva sat across from them. Toiva hung an arm on her chair's back and rested a leg on a thigh, while Kaima steepled his fingers and tilted his head toward the chair at the end of the table—the Saint's designated chair.

"It may be heresy, but these are unprecedented times," Kaima said, smiling gently. "We do require a leader to speak to."

"Of course. It would be an honor." Niesh made her way to the table's end, ignoring Toiva's magnetic glare and Kaima's smile. She also ignored the discomfort itching at her when she became aware of the difference in her dress from the Board's. The Board always wore the traditional clothing of their respective cultures, jewels and glossy fabric glimmering from their bodies. Niesh wore her uniform, a faded patchwork of brown and blue.

As soon as Niesh sat, the meeting began.

"Leaders around the Plane are concerned," Nadir stated, his voice characteristically flat. He pulled a file from under a fold of his finely tailored kaftan and set it before Niesh. "They want to know how your scouts, citizens of their lands, mind you, will protect the people when you, the scoutmasters, have failed to protect the Saint."

Niesh put a hand on the file, the Board's report. Her eyes lingered on Nadir for a second before she averted them and pulled the file to her. She knew he wasn't accusing her of incompetence, but she chose to interpret it that way, anyway.

Damn, did she hate meetings.

"Many agreed on three requirements going forward," Nadir continued. "The Scouthood must exercise no restraint with anything or anyone remotely unnatural. Assume any doubt or mercy shown to them will have consequences. And that those consequences will lead to the proliferation of zonbi, as we are seeing now. Second, data demonstrating the Scouthood's effectiveness. With this, we can make the adjustments needed to ensure your scouts are doing their jobs correctly. Third, a plan to locate and repatriate the new Saint here to Taisala by the end of the month." He spaced his sentences out to emphasize the importance of each.

"We al—"

"The new Saint not announcing themselves," Toiva cut in. She tapped her chair with the tips of her polished nails. Her eyes traced the room's ceiling. "Never heard of that before."

"We already have scoutmasters on each continent searching." Niesh didn't care for being interrupted and would have dragged Toiva under if she were one of her subordinates. "They're probably scared to come forward because Leonardo was assassinated. But we can only search so much for a person who doesn't want to be found."

Toiva continued eyeing the ceiling but stopped tapping the chair.

"Finding them is important but perhaps out of our control, somewhat," Kaima admitted. "No deadline then. The search will continue until they are found."

"But know that unnaturals will only become bolder as leadership weakens," Zenaida said. "And many leaders have lost a lot of faith in your people."

Niesh tucked a loose lock of her black hair back into her single braid. Her fingers flinched, and a chipped nail caught a few strands when one of her scoutmasters coughed.

Troll. She'd bury him in grunt work later.

Niesh pressed her hands back over the report, salvaging her control. "These complaints—with respect, these complaints are nothing new. Leaders of every level continually hounded the Saint, every cycle on every one of his tours, for results that we are already striving for. Always striving for. Over and over, they repeat the same demands. They've repeated the same demands to you."

Nadir didn't move.

Toiva hmphed and resumed tapping.

Zenaida broke in before Kaima could reply with a softer blow. "Then it's a good thing, scoutmaster,"—she rose from her seat, movement stiff—"that we are the ones making house calls. Because it seems your leader was as efficient as he is dead." The only force penetrating the air Zenaida choked with her words was Toiva's cackling. With a simple hand movement, Nadir synced a puff of air toward him, bringing the report back to him on the breeze. Niesh sensed that taking the file back meant the meeting—this talking-to, really— was approaching an end.

"The people have no spiritual leader to speak safety over them, and zonbi grow more invasive by the day," Zenaida said.

"Tributary has offered to help the Cathedral until the seat is filled again," Kaima said. "They seem eager."

"No." Absolutely not. Niesh would endure Zenaida's nonstop reprimands, but she refused to accept outside help, even if it was from the place she claimed as her homeland. The leadership people needed to see had to come from her and her alone, or Zenaida's proclamation would come true—people would completely lose faith in her ability to lead. That panic she needed to avoid above all. "The Cathedral is the Cathedral because it remains a separate entity from world governments."

"Yeah, see, we've already scheduled them to make a visit later this cycle," Toiva said. "Which I wouldn't have to clarify if Kaima wasn't Kaima."

Kaima just grinned. Niesh didn't know much about him other than he had multiple roots, like her. He was cordial to her, if not annoyingly patronizing.

"The Grand Scoutmaster comes third to the Saint in power." Kaima flexed his fingers before resting them back on the table, couching a fist into a palm. "So we trust you to do the job, and do it well."

Niesh knew someone rolled their eyes at his claim. Probably Toiva.

"The current training period is almost over," Kaima said, "and your scoutmasters will start screening for recruits soon."

Nadir slipped the report back under his kaftan, then pulled out a folded piece of paper. "We have made some recommendations to the onboarding process that will surely inform your recruits of what is expected, and needed, from them."

Niesh took the paper but didn't read it.

"We expect your scoutmasters to be stricter in their training and selection otherwise," Zenaida said, still standing.

"And I also recommend involving the medical branch in your endeavors," Nadir added. "They can provide additional support, especially with the increase in zonbi. Odomi has proven to be a brilliant medic and a reliable director."

Kaima started to say something as he lifted his head, but he faltered as his eyes locked onto the room's tall windows. Niesh followed his gaze—and watched shocks of gray slice the cloudy afternoon sky into strips. The wings advanced toward them with impatience, then, at a foot away from the windows, nosedived to the ground.

Niesh shot up and ran to the windows. Several scoutmasters pulled the windows open, then leaped out into the sky, forging weapons of ice, fire, and root in midair. The rest hung back at the ready in case some of the zonbi decided to infest the hall.

Niesh looked down and watched her scoutmasters incinerate and bisect the flying zonbi that got too close to the Cathedral's orphanage. Zonbi birds weren't the most serious threat, but she was relieved there wasn't a need to forge her ribbon blade, her weapon of choice for fighting zonbi. The Board would take her less seriously if it became necessary for her to enter a low-level fray.

"Zonbi this close to the Cathedral." Toiva got up and strolled toward the door, hands on hips. Her words put a not-so-subtle pressure on everyone in the room. "Never heard of that before either."

You. Your.

Everything on her shoulders. Lemana save her, these people knew how to peel back skin and apply a snake of a burn.

Niesh had always been a mostly silent attendee when the Board made their annual visits to the Cathedral. Their hard-boiled comments were not new to her, but Leonardo, the Saint now deceased, knew how to keep a charming and unbothered façade in the face of their criticisms. Niesh did not possess that same humor. She was a highly trained scout through and through.

The Board left the hall an hour ago, but Niesh remained because, admittedly, she wasn't finished sponging off the severity of their presence. She didn't know much about the four of them personally— they were all private, which she found odd—but Leonardo never took them as seriously as he should have.

And now look.

Now she was the one who had to signal the Natural Plane out of the fog. She was the one who had to respond to the growing rash of zonbi, the chimeric creatures without spirits who were attracted to strong emotions. And she had to do it all while running the Cathedral as its temporary head. All while running the Scouthood.

All while trying to find out why the assassin who ended Leonardo did what he did.

The Board's demands swam against the current of her mind. She crumpled the paper Nadir gave her—two recommendations she had to implement before the next group of recruits arrived in a few weeks.

She'd love to recommend a volcano for them to fall into. She'd love to—

"Master."

Niesh didn't turn to acknowledge the person who entered. Only one person continued to use the honorific reserved for scoutmasters with her.

"Stop calling me that, Ignacia," Niesh spat, pinching the space between her tired eyes. "I'm your commander. I'm not your damn teacher anymore."

Ignacia walked up next to her. She looked down through the window Niesh kept open for air. "Teachers never stop teaching," she said. She pulled her head in and leaned back against a closed window, her puffy brown hair providing a cushion. She was of average height compared to Niesh. Her own uniform was less faded, and she donned skort leggings instead of the pants scoutmasters typically wore. "So that wasn't too bad," she said.

"Are you joking?" Niesh hated how motherly Ignacia's voice was.

It made it hard to yell at her. She released her fingers from her face and moved closer to the window.

"The orphanage is safe," Ignacia said. "That child had an outburst again, but nothing got inside."

"Good."

A beat passed. The clouds began to part, letting some of the late afternoon sunlight breathe.

"You're recruiting this time, right?" Niesh asked.

"Yup. I leave in a few days. I guess we'll have to help you meet those recommendations before, though."

Ignacia was dependable, always understood what Niesh needed without her asking. One of the best scouts Niesh had trained in her time as a scoutmaster.

"Find me only the best, Ignacia. Make teacher happy and get me the best recruits you can find."

TWO

IGNACIA

Ignacia flashed her scouting identification card to the receptionist in Tributary's embassy. Clearing her for entrance, the receptionist balled a fist, then unclenched it into an open palm, the movement unlocking the root gate next to his station. She said her thanks and entered the building's lobby, tying her viridian scarf around her right forearm as she did.

She walked toward her designated meeting room with urgency, her still-damp brown hair done into a goddess braid. Ignacia would have resented the endless days of recruitment season travel if she had been assigned anywhere else but Tributary, the most prosperous continent on the Natural Plane, whose leaders held considerable influence over world affairs. Tributary's dramatic valleys and plains were always a sight to breathe in. It might have taken her a few extra minutes to reach the embassy that morning.

Following completion of a competitive application process, physical and mental exam, and test of combat ability, the interview was the last part of the screening process for recruits—or had been the last part until the Board made their recommendations. Some of the best scouts she and other scoutmasters had trained hailed from Tributary, which made the vetting process more challenging yet satisfying. Getting the cadets her former scoutmaster needed would be no problem.

But what Niesh and the Plane needed were human beings, not soulless soldiers trained solely to kill. Before Ignacia and the other recruiting scoutmasters departed, Niesh made it bitingly clear she had no use for baby adults who fueled their interest in scouting with romantic fantasies of saving the world. She wanted scouts to do their job, not fulfill a dream. Maybe it was because Ignacia hailed from Artemisa, a continent known for pushing the Natural's strict emotional boundaries, but she could never fully get on board with Niesh's vision of what a scout should be.

She knew better than to disagree aloud, but she kept her own list of the characteristics she looked for—compassion, understanding, devotion. Traits she demonstrated as a cadet and a scout—traits Niesh had made her mission to break Ignacia and her fellow cadets of. But Ignacia had managed to hang on to her convictions and knew she was a better scoutmaster for it. Her cadets, future and former, would be better for it too.

After all, a scout couldn't stand against zonbi while acting like one.

Approaching her meeting room, Ignacia pulled a stack of papers from her bag. She slipped the first one out from under a clip, her interview schedule for the day, and looked it over. Her first interviewee was a young woman, Rakiatu.

"HERE, MASTER!"

As Ignacia entered the room, the young woman shot up and walked toward her, excited but not so much that it overtook her composure. She wore an orange and blue geometric-print jumpsuit that looked like she had steamed it ten times over. Ignacia closed the door behind them. Not wanting the room's desk between them, Ignacia pulled the chair from behind it and set it in front of the interviewee's chair.

"Sorry, running a bit late this morning," Ignacia said. They shook hands and sat. She flipped through a folder and pulled out a paper containing her information. "Just give me a second to look over your file, Rakiatu."

"Yes, Master. And just Raki is fine," she said, crossing her legs at the ankle.

Ignacia glanced at her and smiled. Raki's dark brown skin, typical of the Plane's historic nomadic peoples, glowed like the ocean depths against the evening sun. Fine black braids sat on top of her head in a tight updo.

"Seventeen, top of your graduating class," Ignacia read, picking out the essential details. "Your mother was a scout, too."

"One of the best!" Raki said. Her gray eyes sparkled with pride, but she quickly added, "She had her time to serve the Plane. But now it's my turn to carry on her work and the work of all the scouts before her."

Ignacia wasn't sure if that comment was meant to save Raki from what she probably saw as using her mom as a prop, but it showed some self-awareness. A positive.

"Your academic resume is very impressive. Near-perfect marks, glowing character statements from your teachers. You can easily become a scholar with this record." Ignacia reached back to set the file on the desk. "So, Raki, why join the Scouthood with all its risks? Why not take the marked path and enroll at the university?"

Raki uncrossed her legs and ran her hands down her pants as if to smooth away wrinkles. But they were already as straight as truth. A negative. Interviewees got nervous, but Niesh would count it as a negative.

"Thank you, that's a great question. The reason why I want to be a scout is because..."

Restating the question *and* fluffing it up with filler words. Sounded like she wasn't sure. Definitely a negative.

"...well, scouting is a high calling. Scouts give so much of their lives and their safety to protect the rest of us from the unnatural. It's the next logical step for me. It's the best way to give back to my community, to all of the Plane."

And a rehearsed answer that didn't speak to *her* why. Absolutely a negative, on Lemana. Ignacia was wary of applicants who had been stars in the classroom. Academic achievement didn't always equal genuine dedication to the scout's mission. And Raki read as someone who cared more about looking good on paper. Her file *did* indicate she excelled on the combat test, but a cadet or scout showing confidence in their goals was an important factor in whether they pushed through or quit.

Ignacia chewed on Raki's response, preparing to spit it back out. Raki relaxed her body a bit. She must have picked up on the shift in Ignacia's demeanor.

"When I wasn't at school or with companions or family, I'd help out at our settlement's animal sanctuary. I didn't go every day or anything, but I loved being a companion for the animals who couldn't be with their own." Her gray eyes floated through a memory, then came back to Ignacia. "I guess...I think about the people who need someone to be there for them, to help them because not everyone can help themselves."

A sincere and personal understanding, even if caring for injured animals and felling zonbi were worlds apart. A positive. And one that just might save her interview.

"You have heart," the scoutmaster said, grateful that Raki had dug deeper. "I like that in my cadets."

HER NEXT INTERVIEWEE came from wealth and status, so she needed to question her harder. Ignacia didn't trust applicants from the higher end of society, regardless of how well they tested.

Yunai, a name Ignacia recognized as Artemisan, had roots in the nomadic peoples and Artemisa. She pretended to review her file as she watched the leggy young woman with light brown skin and curly, dark brown hair settle into the chair. Her blue glass bead necklace shifted on her neck as she sat down, and her hazel eyes, big and curious, took stock of the room's sparse furnishings.

"You focused on the loss of your arm in your personal statement. How long ago was the attack?"

"Five cycles," Yunai answered politely.

Ignacia glanced at her right arm, careful not to stare. Thick roots were shaped into an arm where flesh used to be. Within the arm, from what Ignacia understood about root limbs, was a network of root veins that connected to the natural veins at her shoulder, where her flesh began. Yunai's right hand was constructed from roots as well, her fingers an eerie counterpart to her flesh-and-bone left hand. Every aspect was shaped to perfection, like clay painstakingly molded by an artist. It was one of the best prosthetic jobs Ignacia had ever seen.

"I was young. I-it was a careless accident." Yunai did not go on. She didn't seem shy, but she lacked the energy Ignacia liked to see.

"I see you've had all your regular checkups since then," Ignacia stated, now reading her file in earnest. "You have a private medic and access to the best concoctions. You seem to be well taken care of."

Yunai gave her a weak smile. "I'm lucky I can get the care I need."

Lucky...or rich.

Yunai's arm didn't concern Ignacia—the Scouthood recruited cadets with root prosthetics all the time—but she needed to know how capable Yunai was of taking care of herself. She had to make sure her pampered upbringing would not influence how she carried herself through service.

"You mentioned you couldn't have recovered physically and emotionally without the support of your family. How involved are they in your daily life?"

"Oh, I don't need assistance with getting around or doing any tasks—"

"With your whole life, I mean. I gathered that your medic has your arm covered."

"Of course." Yunai pulled at her pencil skirt with her root hand, shifting the tight fabric down. "I still live with them, so we do spend some time together. Meals, events... We don't really—"

"What about when you were growing up?"

"Oh, ah, they were very involved, of course. I was homeschooled by my paternal grandfather and taught to fight by my older brother and his companions. Many of my days were scheduled, and I did everything my parents asked of me..."

Frustration nibbled at Ignacia. Her answers weren't really answering the question Ignacia was trying to ask. Time to be direct.

"Would you say being raised in wealth and privilege stripped you of the ability to manage your own responsibilities? We need scouts who are independent and who understand—"

"I won't apologize."

Ignacia was taken aback. She studied Yunai's face. Her soft features turned firm, her hazel eyes boring into Ignacia.

"Not for who gave birth to me and the expectations I had to meet as a child with no say."

Ignacia huffed out a chuckle. She wasn't expecting Yunai to cut her off, but it showed the determination of someone whose spirit hinged on proving something. If Ignacia had the ego of her fellow scoutmasters, she would have taken her tone personally.

"So what do you hope to prove, Yunai?"

The young woman's face did not break. "Myself right."

IGNACIA HAD NOTED that her last interviewee of the day was part of some diversion program, but the extra adult in the room still caught her off guard. Was she supposed to talk to the man standing to the side, who was chewing on a pen, or the...boy? She looked through Esera's file. Only sixteen? Was that why an adult accompanied him? Did whoever was in charge of this program think this minor would be chaperoned around Taisala? She couldn't decide between annoyance at the man or embarrassment for the boy.

She settled for concern when she noticed how bothered Esera looked. He sat rigid in the chair, arms tight across his chest, his dark brown eyes tuned to some object in space. The dark blue lavalava wrapped around his waist was pristine, in contrast to his bushy black hair, which looked like it hadn't seen anything but a bed all day.

"Ha, looks like no one informed you of anything at all," the man said, taking the pen out of his mouth. His presence seemed more mandatory than supportive.

Well, he wasn't wrong, but that didn't make Ignacia feel any better.

"Esera here is joining your scouts by order of Tributary's court. You don't need to interview him or anything. He's just here to confirm he is who he is. All the info should be in his file for you, signed and everything."

Ignacia saw that now. No blood parents, but he had been adopted into Raki's family, which explained why his lavalava was wrinkle-free. Attended the same school as her, but lacked her stellar record, didn't come anywhere near it. A rap sheet that grew exponentially with each cycle, and—

Her lungs iced over when she read the back of the page. She looked up at the boy, who now glared at her.

"Fifty percent of my life belonged to Tributary and the other fifty to Raki's parents." Esera let out a deep breath that he must have taken in while Ignacia read his information. "Guess I one hundred percent belong to you now. Can't promise I won't escape if someone leaves a window open."

The man, whom Ignacia surmised was this child's caseworker—because he wasn't going to introduce himself, apparently—squeezed Esera's cheeks with his wide hands. "And he's going to be on his best behavior for Niesh, 'cause otherwise his ass is homebound. Right? *Right?*"

"I'll behave if it means I won't have to put up with you anymore," Esera snapped, rubbing his cheeks after his caseworker let go of his face.

One of Niesh's requests based on the Board's recommendations. She had instructed the scoutmasters to actively recruit people who wanted more than the hopeless situations they were in. To position serving as a one-way ticket to a fulfilling life. A scoutmaster must have targeted Esera for recruitment during the application process. Being a ward of Tributary must have robbed him of some freedoms, but being funneled into the Scouthood...

"Esera's a bit underage and can't ear up worth a damn, but this one can throw down. Well, you see the evidence in his file. He should do fine in a more physical space."

Just how fine is fine?

Ignacia looked at Esera again. His brown skin had a ruddy tinge to it, a feature of some people with roots in the Fa'atasi archipelago. Anger sat under that skin and made a home in his blood. If this is what it took to meet the Board's recommendations...

"Look, lady—"

"Ignacia."

"—I may not be what you're hoping for, but I can fight. And I hate it here. I don't know about a dead Saint, but I know zonbi should be dead. Deader. Whatever."

And the Grand Scoutmaster had already signed off on him, so pushing back wouldn't change anything.

"You seem to understand what's expected of you." Ignacia closed his file. Her fingers refused to release their grip, not after reading that one piece of information in his history. She looked at his caseworker. "You'll want updates, I'm assuming?"

"Yup," his caseworker said. "Monthly."

Now it was Ignacia's turn to take a deep breath. Every training class had its challenges, but she knew, she just *knew*, that this would be her most...interesting...yet.

It was too late to ask for a raise, wasn't it?

"Okay then," she breathed out, releasing the file. "Congratulations, Esera. I guess you're my first recruit of the season."

THREE

ESERA

L ying on a piece of board someone was hilarious enough to call a bed, Esera tossed a small ball of fire up and down. He tossed it high enough to bother Raki but not so high that he'd start a fire in their musty cabin. Driving fleas into his adopted Sister's nerves always entertained him. Drying up what little air they had in this damn box wouldn't have.

"What kind of mother writes her only daughter a list instead of a letter?" Raki held the paper in front of her and watched as another part unfolded from the bottom. Then another. "What? How am I supposed to try every restaurant in Taisala while I'm training? Does this woman think I'm going on vacation?"

Esera continued playing with his fireball, his movement becoming mindless. "We have days off."

"Not the point, really. Oh. Papa wrote this. Of course he did." She rolled her gray eyes and folded the letter back. "Did you read the letter he wrote for you yet?"

"I would, but I don't need to read some tour guide."

"*I* get the tour guides. *You* get the heartwarming goodbyes."

Esera caught the ball, then tossed it back and forth between his hands. "When we're settled."

"Hm." Raki stuffed the goodbye letters their family and compan-

19

ions wrote for her back into her travel bag. She jumped onto her bed and made a face when she felt how hard the slab was. "We'll be in Taisala tomorrow, newly minted cadets."

Back and forth and back and forth. Esera kept tossing.

Raki turned on her side to face her younger Brother. "Are you okay enough to do this?"

"If I say no, you think the whales will turn the ship around?"

"Put the acid away. I'm just checking in."

Esera extinguished the fireball. He rested his head in his hands and stared at the ceiling of their dimly lit cabin. "Don't have much of a choice. You were at my last hearing."

Fight his way through school only to end up failing anyway, or enlist in the Scouthood, where his unacceptable behavior would be accepted, praised. Compensated. What did it matter if he was okay or not?

"I heard some recruits at dinner say things are going to be harder since the Saint is gone. I just want to make sure you're prepared."

"Are you?" Esera kept the venom or acid or whatever out of his voice. "Is anyone?"

"Just don't go beating up the other cadets, okay? Or mouthing off at the scoutmasters when they get in your face. I'm pretty sure that's part of their job."

"Raki, you've been an adult for all of seven months." Esera paused. He shot up and slipped into his sandals.

"Oh, come on, Esera," Raki teased, her mouth morphing into an impish smile. "I'm not being that overbearing."

"I don't need you pecking at me tonight." Esera walked to the cabin's door. He clenched a fist, then unclenched it. The web of roots that locked the cabin door retracted into the wall. He pushed it open.

"Fiiine." Raki sat up and worked her braids into a pineapple style. "Just don't wander too late. Or is that pecking too?"

The slam of the door was his answer. He locked the roots back and, very much, wandered down the dark walkway.

In the cycles Esera and Raki shared a bond, he never knew her to be anything less than his big Sister. Her arms calmed his outbursts in childhood, and her conscience advised him against too many fights in adolescence. Not all, but many. And when his blood family deterio-rated, when the people around him uprooted and abandoned him, she had convinced her parents to adopt him into their boisterous family. He would always be grateful for that, for her support. But Raki didn't need to pat his head anymore, not when he was months away from adulthood. Not when he needed to figure out what this accursed world wanted from him.

Esera walked out to the ship's gunwale, its surface still wet from the evening's burst of rain. Yawi Yema East, the part of the world ocean between Tributary and Taisala, was tranquil, a soothing interval for Esera's unsettled body. He watched the oblong shape of one of the steering whales under the waves. Its calm syncing, in rhythm with its partner's on the ship's opposite side, drove the waves that carried their vessel across the ocean and around the giant roots that shot up from the ocean floor.

Afato, Esera's good-natured caseworker, had advocated to get him into the Scouthood. It was a way for Esera to "pay back all the black eyes he had dished out," as Afato had put it. If he did well, the court would toss out his juvenile record, and he could start his adult life with a clean slate. If they kicked him out or if he quit, he'd be sent back home to finish school, and Esera didn't do well in school settings, academically or behaviorally. As a ward, his punishments were more severe when he got into trouble. And he usually did.

Neither quitting nor getting dismissed was an option. As far as he was concerned, school and juvenile detention's four walls were the same.

Whatever.

Esera usually jumped into the water to swim whenever he found himself on a boat, but the water seemed murkier than usual. The night made it hard to see, even with the silver of the moon unmasking the ocean, but it looked like the whale had a companion with him. Better to pass. No need to risk trouble before he even made it to shore.

Not as relaxed as he hoped the fresh air would make him, Esera made his way back to the cabin.

YUNAI

Bright skies. A savanna brought back from death. The struggle, long and challenging, that could have either remade or broken the world, at its end. Cheers from somewhere, a chorus in green. Fallen villains, the victims now freed, the first taste of liberation. A battle won by her hands.

A dream as carefully crafted as her daydreams...

...Yunai slumped from her side onto her back, her eyes peeling open. She had traveled across the ocean with her family a handful of times in the past, but her body could never accept traveling over a surface that wasn't the earth. She had woken up in the middle of the night every night since leaving Tributary, but...her cabin seemed darker than normal. Pitch black...

Yunai pushed herself up halfway, blinking rapidly to focus her eyes. A chill slid up her arms, a cold grin she felt in her veins.

Something was wet, dripping. Her blanket. Something had soaked the bottom half of her blanket. And that something dropped its head lower, *lower*, meeting Yunai at her head. She could light a torch to see what it was—but if she lit a torch, she *would see* what it was.

She swallowed a scream before it thickened into fear.

Act. Now.

Yunai turned to her utility belt on her bedside table. Using her flesh hand, she synced with the water from the water pouch on the belt and slapped the thing's...head? The thing, which could only be a zonbi, recoiled and slithered back into the dark, shaking the cabin. Then she synced the water over to her cabinmate, smacking him on the head. Her cabinmate shot up, prepared to smoke Yunai with complaints.

"In the room!" Yunai shouted. "Zonbi in the room!"

Her cabinmate struck one hand over the other, the friction creating a torch bright enough to illuminate their immediate area. He brought it to Yunai's side, revealing a tangle of dried-out tentacles stuck to one of the ceiling's corners. The large zonbi shifted its empty eyes at the flame, its head drooping like honey. It took the recruits a moment to realize the zonbi had wrapped its tentacles around the perimeter of the room. And that it had ripped off the tentacles of multiple octopi to lengthen its own. Then they saw it had not one head but two—three—four when the others pushed the first one up. It jerked, peeled two of its tentacles from the wall, then slammed them on the wooden floor, breaking up the old boards.

Yunai grabbed her utility belt, then she and her cabinmate leaped out of their beds. Yunai unlocked the roots with a shaky hand, then they bolted out of the cabin and onto the deck. She huffed, hands on unsteady knees. Other recruits filtered out of their cabins.

"How did a zonbi get in there?" her cabinmate asked. "The door was locked!"

"I don't know," Yunai responded. She synced with more water from her water pouch and froze it around her flesh arm, a ready weapon. "But we have to fight it." Her first battle on a semi-official basis. Fighting in nightwear had never been part of her fantasies.

They heard the zonbi lunge to the floor and the crash of more boards breaking under its weight. It squeezed through the door and charged into the open, its pale arms swinging against the walls like a starved child in anger.

Yunai pulled back her frozen arm, ready to strike, when a short young man with black, bushy hair brandished a pair of metal nifo'oti from behind him and ignited them. He surged forward, leaped into the air, and brought the toothed, hooked clubs down on one of the zonbi's tentacles at the same time her cabinmate drove a spear forged from metal into another.

Yunai looked at her arm, then back at the zonbi. The small amount of water in her possession wouldn't do much against the massive creature. And they needed to make a decisive blow before it sank the ship.

She suppressed the panic biting at her chest and assessed the situation. The zonbi raised itself on its tentacles. The thing was almost two stories in height. It ripped off its two pinned arms and whipped another around in retaliation. Her cabinmate threw up his arms in an X, creating a shield of air that cushioned some of the blow. The short man pulled his clubs out from the detached arm and raised them above his head. He hooked onto the arm the zonbi swung and latched on with his legs.

Yunai unfroze her water and aimed for two sets of eyes. She

synced the water at them in quick shots when she had an opening, freezing them on contact. She didn't know which of its eyes could see, but hopefully, that would give her—them—enough time.

"I'll be back!" Yunai shouted, not wanting her plan to be mistaken for a retreat. More recruits rushed out to help, including a young woman with black braids tied on top of her head who stopped Yunai by her shoulders. The woman's shocked face was questioning and understanding all at once. "I can stop it. Just need a minute."

"Alright." The woman let go and ran ahead.

Stepping over the wet floor and broken boards, Yunai ran into the closest bathroom and turned on a faucet in one of the shower stalls. She synced with the water coming out, freezing a thicker block of ice over her upper flesh arm. Its weight was burdensome, but she managed to hurry back out without falling over.

Hushed voices halted her steps.

"You see that thing? No way I'm fighting that."

"Turned around as soon as I saw it."

"Right? They can handle it."

"How did it even get on? They need to secure their ships better than this."

Yunai felt something uncomfortable bubble in her chest. It felt like the shame that creeps up as a person accepts failure in public. Were other recruits seriously hiding? They weren't scouts yet, but did they not have an obligation to fight? They weren't being escorted to Taisala by scoutmasters or soldiers, so who else was going to fight? Not to mention the workers on the ship needed to be protected...

No time.

Yunai fought off the emotions and rushed back. She skated on the slick floor with her bare feet to avoid falling. Fire singed and metal clanged as the recruits tried to subdue the irate zonbi. They had cut off a few more tentacles, but that hadn't stopped its rampage.

"Hold it down!" Yunai shouted.

"What does it look like we're doing?" someone shouted back.

Yunai ignored the prickle of that comment and looked for a way to get to higher ground so she could strike the zonbi from above.

What should have been an easy shot was made difficult by the zonbi's constant thrashing.

The woman who stopped her before punched back its swinging tentacles with earthen gauntlets encrusted with sharpened stones. "If you're going to do something, please do it before this thing prematurely ends our careers!"

Yunai looked at its four heads, at its arms, at the recruits, then up. She focused her eyes on the metal awning above the upper deck where the young man with the nifo'oti now fought.

"Hey!" Yunai called to him. "Can you give me a lift?"

He came down to the awning on the bottom floor and stretched out his hands, Yunai catching them with her own. He managed to pull her up despite their difference in height and the extra weight of the ice. They jumped over the guardrails and onto the upper deck.

"The hell?"

Without asking, Yunai climbed onto his shoulders. She synced her hands with the metal awning, then synced her feet with it, hanging upside down like a frog. Freeing her hands, Yunai unfroze her water and forged it into a spear twice her height, refreezing it after it took shape. She found a clean headshot from above. Drawing on all the blood coursing in her veins, she shot the ice spear straight into one of the zonbi's heads, steady syncing guiding her shot. It pierced the head like lightning through a tree—but zonbi never fell that easily.

Dropping down, Yunai clasped her hands together and slowly pulled them apart, the ice spear taking root through the zonbi. Ice bloomed through its heads, through its mouths. The recruits fell back as the zonbi's movements faltered. Its arm swinging weakened to soft jerks, and its heads became immobile, an iced monument dedicated to a distressing night.

"I didn't think we'd be completely safe," the young woman with braids said when Yunai and the short man came down. She kneeled and let out a breath. A few of the recruits cut the zonbi up and threw pieces of its body into the ocean.

Yunai turned to her new comrade. "Thank you, ah..."

"Esera," he replied, sheathing his nifo'oti into his back scabbard. "That's Raki."

A few more recruits appeared from the walkway. They took stock of the fallen zonbi before one of them said, "I knew I heard another fight."

"Another?" Raki forced herself to stand and shifted her weight to one side. "There was another of those things on here?"

"And I'm guessing it surprised y'all just as much as it did us," the recruit said, looking over the crowd. "Luckily, none of y'all got hurt, though."

Yunai rubbed her flesh arm with her root arm to give it some warmth. The ice had taken all feeling from her arm. They were certainly lucky, but two zonbi getting on the ship in the dead of night was no random occurrence.

NIESH

Niesh stood on a pier in Taisala's busy eastern harbor with an entourage of her scoutmasters. They watched as one of the recruit ships prepared to dock. The morning calmed her, with blue skies and easy winds. The ocean breeze sang through her loose black braid. Unfortunately, this was the last day for recruit arrivals. She'd miss these tranquil moments at the harbor.

Fortunately, it was the last day for recruit arrivals. She had quickly grown tired of stripping the attitude from arrogant children.

The recruits dragged their bags and bodies down the pier. They always arrived like this, human zonbi that collapsed on the trains to the base, their barely washed bodies their greeting to the island's citizens. They gathered in front of her and waited, eyes bloodshot, hair half-done, stomachs rumbling. None wore smiles, not that she cared.

"Your training as cadets typically starts in a few days," Niesh started. "But this season, it started as soon as you left home."

They looked at each other, then back at her.

"You had one final test, and it seems many of you failed. And we won't allow those who did to stay."

The protests, as usual, annoyed her. No one could ever accept what she said, could they?

"Some of my scoutmasters rode with you, disguised as cooks and cleaners. They captured and released zonbi onto your ship to test your ability and willingness to fight in unfavorable conditions—"

"*We could have been ripped apart!*" A wave slammed against the pier—an emotional reaction. A boy pushed forward. He met Niesh at her eyes, leaving less than a foot between them. "How the hell did you think trying to kill us was a good idea?!"

"Esera!"

Niesh gave the boy two seconds of attention before continuing. "A cadet who isn't ready to fight today will be dead tomorrow. And a scout who can't remain at zero isn't really a scout." She flicked her eyes at the girl who called out the boy's name. He held his ground longer than she had patience for. He eventually stepped back but remained at the front of the crowd, face scribbled with anger.

"My scoutmasters sent ahead the names of those who failed themselves and wasted our time. If you hid in your cabin, turned tail, or otherwise showed cowardice, you won't step any further onto the island under my direction. If you did your best to fight or defend, you stay."

A rose-red seagull, perched on one of the scoutmaster's shoulders, wore a chain with a metal tube hanging from it. With a flourish of a wing, it synced the tube open. The scoutmaster took a paper from the inside and unrolled it. He read through the list of names. The recruits who chose to forfeit their duty turned around and headed back on board the ship, about a third of the group.

"Consider your former comrades, if you dare call them that, a warning of what we will not tolerate. The Scouthood has no room for sloth or dead weight." Niesh turned and walked down the pier towards the train station, her scoutmasters and the recruits following. "Welcome to Taisala, cadets."

FOUR

BRAULIO

B raulio was fairly sure, *pretty certain* he had signed a contract to be a resident of general animal medicine before he began his medic training. No surgeries. No cutting into anything or dissecting zonbi for science.

Yet here the young Artemisan man of eighteen was, drawing upon all his strength to hold the frantic calf down on the operating table. His Taisalan companion, Siaka, who had also been roped into this tragedy, brought all his weight down on the animal's hind legs. The calf's teal color had saddened into a gray, and his innocent eyes were fading away. The poor thing had been brought in for his post-birth checkup—but this turned out to be the calf's last day as a creature with a spirit.

"Try to hold him down a bit more." Mirta, who also called Taisala home, and who did sign up to cut into animals, held a forged scalpel upright in one hand. Braulio's other companion watched for her chance to go for the chest. "Don't want us to catch any zonbi fluids when I open him up."

"Wouldn't have to catch anything if we were doing our actual jobs," Braulio said between grunts.

The calf let out one last cry, crushed with pain, before the color in his eyes vanished—the telltale sign of a fully fallen zonbi. Once zonbi caught a whiff of strong emotions, they didn't stop attacking until they satiated their hunger or someone felled them, so they needed to restrain it fast.

"Are you sure you can't do this the nice way?" Siaka asked. He diverted his one black eye away from the creature's eyes. Siaka's other socket was empty and covered with root stitches.

"Would love to, trust me," Mirta said, "but once an animal starts falling, there's no guarantee a concoction will do anything to put them to sleep. This is the kindest way I know."

Braulio and Siaka finally restrained the zonbi. With all the calm of a loving parent, Mirta inched up to the creature and brought the scalpel across its chest. A putrid smell and bodily sewage leaked from the opening. All three residents were clad in surgical attire, but both young men still backed up as much as possible without releasing the zonbi. Unable to look away, though, Braulio watched as Mirta synced roots down from the operating room's root chandelier. She formed her hand into a claw, the roots mimicking her movement. She directed the root claw into the zonbi's chest, moved it around until it located its heart, closed her fist in one quick motion—

Braulio looked away, blocking out the crying. He had signed up to work as a medic in the field one day, serving the neediest communities on the Plane, but that didn't mean he had the tolerance for death.

Siaka looked up at the operating room's theater. "Audience doesn't look too happy."

Braulio followed his gaze up. The medics—and scoutmasters—watching the routine shook their heads and exchanged words. They had agreed that the only way to fell a zonbi was to burn it. But their opinions combined weren't enough to change the directive of Odomi, the hospital's director, who sat in the middle of the theater. She believed that even creatures of the unnatural deserved mercy. A stance the trio thankfully agreed with.

What they didn't agree with, however, was the Scouthood's recent decision to establish a regular presence in the hospital. It was one thing to provide more protection against animals falling spontaneously in the middle of appointments. It was another to surveil every procedure they carried out.

"That's it," Mirta said. "You can let go."

Braulio returned his attention to the table. He let go when he realized there was no more reason to hang on. The zonbi lay immobile on the table.

Using a sterile knife, Mirta cut off the fluid-soaked roots and dumped them in the burn bin in the corner of the room. "We're done for today. Let's get cleaned up. I think Odomi wanted to check in with us."

The medics shuffled out of the theater. Odomi waited a few seconds more before making her exit. The scoutmasters made no move to leave.

Braulio gave what was once a beautiful calf one last look before he left the room to sanitize. The hospital's animal sanctuary felt less and less like one with each passing day.

THE COMPANIONS TOOK their unofficial seats in Odomi's office. Mirta sat upright in the middle, undoing the messy braid of her long, coily black hair. With roots in Artemisa, her brown skin normally resembled rich earth. But after many grueling days in the sanctuary, her skin had lost its hue. Siaka sat in a deep slouch to her left. He had the typical features of the old nomadic peoples, dark brown skin, full lips, and tightly coiled hair done in a mohawk of braids. And Braulio stood off to the side, arms crossed. He narrowed his brown eyes away from the glare of the late afternoon sun, which added a bronze tint to his light brown skin, typical of those with Artemisan roots.

Odomi sat with a smaller slouch in her chair. She shared the same roots and features as Siaka, with long, graying locs in a bun. She narrowed her gray eyes when Braulio rolled his own. "Refusing to sit in *my* chair will not change the situation."

Braulio hmphed. "Doesn't mean I can't hate it." He took his brown, shoulder-length hair out of its sweaty ponytail and scratched his scalp.

"So how long *are* we expected to handle this extra workload?" Siaka asked, scooching up his seat. He flopped the braids in his mohawk over the chair's head. "I can't keep pushing my appointments back. People complain more than animals do when they get inconvenienced."

"Don't assume that," Braulio retorted. "You've never had a fire-breathing crocodile in labor try to check you out of this life."

"Hey, I had to be the messenger in a who's-baby-is-this situation. I promise you it's much worse."

"Whenever you two want to be done." Mirta finished undoing her braid and also scratched her scalp, her hair spinning out like cotton candy. They had been in their surgical caps all day and were all in need of a good shower. "The load drops when the number of zonbi do. And the zonbi drop when the new Saint is found and people rein in their fear and anger. Until then, we all have to pull our weight."

"I can always rely on you to be responsible, Mirta." Odomi craned her head to the side and massaged her right temple. Her bun, tight this morning, was now loose to the side.

Watching his elder, as exhausted as she looked, took the irritation out of Braulio a bit. She had served as the director of the hospital for several cycles. The hospital sat outside the city of Lemana, on the base also serving as the home of the cadets. She had overseen many cycles of residents and the cadets who did their service hours here. In addition to running the hospital and liaising with the Cathedral, she also had her own patients she saw. Odomi could handle a lot.

Now she looked like she could barely stand for more than ten seconds. Since Leonardo's death, animals were falling in the hospital at a high rate, putting everyone at risk. They had attacked staff, visitors, and even patients, resulting in more than a few lawsuits and prompting the Grand Scoutmaster to station scoutmasters throughout the hospital. Braulio knew the lawsuits burdened Odomi on the administrative side of things. But she also seemed more...anxious. Unsettled. As if she carried something heavy deep inside her heart. Braulio considered Odomi a mentor, but it wasn't his place to ask about her personal life. Her stress eased some of his frustration, but he was still too angry to take a seat.

"I'm relying on you three to set an example for the rest of the residents," Odomi continued, fixing her neck upright. "I can't be on the floor as much as I used to be, and I may be out of the hospital on some days. You're the best students I have, and I know you won't let these scouts run this place amok. I know you three don't care for the Scouthood much—"

"Neither do you, Mom," Siaka interjected.

"*But* with the increase in zonbi, we can't assume we'll be safe. That calf could have done a lot more damage if it were an adult, or if one of you lost your grip. We need Niesh's help to handle these attacks if we're to do our jobs."

"Whatever," Siaka said. "As long as they don't get aggressive."

"And stay in their lane." With the sun below the horizon, Braulio turned to the office window, seeking respite from their ten-hour day in the glow of the evening sky. Relying on the help of scoutmasters who couldn't even protect the Saint—it sounded like the joke it was. The four didn't care for the Scouthood, the Saint, the Cathedral, and the harsh policies of all three—and Braulio had more personal reasons for denouncing them all. Their wildly unpopular opinions bonded them, but they took care not to broadcast their thoughts outside their little circle.

"Keep each other close and stay on your toes," Odomi said. Braulio heard Odomi shuffle books and papers around, signaling the end of their day. "Things are going to be difficult for a while."

ODOMI

Difficult for the hospital and difficult for her plans.

Odomi kicked off her sneakers. Inside her lake house, she commanded the roots along the entrance floor to straighten her and Siaka's shoes. She secured the root locks on the door and collapsed back against it.

Cycles of working as a medic through disease, danger, and death had taught Odomi the need to leave work at the last hour of her day. But with the Scouthood invading every inch of the hospital, she now had to bring work into the night—and away from their prying eyes.

Odomi loved Braulio and Mirta as her own. And she knew Siaka, her adopted Son, would always support her, even if he griped while doing so. With their leadership and discerning eyes, Odomi knew the residents would be in reliable hands, and the medics could hold their own. Leaving her the time and space she needed to dedicate to her plans.

For the Revival, her full attention was required, or her people, deemed unnatural by word of the Cathedral, would never know freedom.

The last of Odomi's thoughts dissipated when she noticed a drum beat overlaid with a rap pumping from upstairs. Siaka was home then. Had he been blasting his radio all this time? During the week, he usually stayed at the base's resident apartments with Braulio, his roommate. But he occasionally snuck back to their home in the city when he wanted the comfort and safety of his own room. Their quiet lake house in Lemana's eighth parish afforded him the privacy to play music the Scouthood would label provocative.

Odomi walked into the kitchen and, with a finger snap of electric charge on a conductive root on the wall, struck on the root lights that ran along the ceiling. She set her bag on the spotless dining table. The entire kitchen had been cleaned from counter to floor. Siaka never came home without a helpful welcome.

Odomi made sure the windows were shut and pulled the curtains closed with deft gusts of wind. She sat at the table and pulled a violet journal from her bag, its pages thickened from the passage of time. Thin chains bound the book closed, secured by a lock requiring complex synchronization to open. Anyone could simply break the trick chains, but making that move would give the sneak a poisonous surprise—one that a hospital visit wouldn't cure.

Odomi had read the contents of the journal several times over, but she especially needed to read its words again to give her the confidence she needed to execute her next steps. She traced the lock with two fingers, working out the intricate mechanism with muscle memory. When she finished the physical part, she moved her hand back.

A thousand times she had opened the journal, but each time she reached this last part, her anxiety bubbled up. Anyone who followed the Natural—the philosophy that condemned the beauty of true emotions—would think the lock open as soon as she removed her hand. But those like her—inspired by deeper emotions deemed unnatural—would know through a subtle glow of her gray eyes that the lock opened with a small pour of emotion. They would think nothing of this security feature.

The Natural would have tried, convicted, and executed her on the spot.

Odomi set the chains aside and opened the journal to the dog-eared page. She read the page, rereading to absorb the parts her heart needed the most. Its writings were raw, as unapologetic as its author —something else the Natural would have condemned. Odomi didn't have the full support of her comrades in the movement, but she could always rely on the journal to reassure her that her plan was worth the effort.

The journal was the seed from which Revival would overgrow, that had given Odomi the courage to bring the Saint down. She and her comrade pulled off Leonardo's fall perfectly. Her comrade paid the ultimate price, one Odomi would never forget. And now it was time to move on to the next stage.

With the Saint removed and a populace in fear, it was time to find the burning spirit she needed.

FIVE

RAKI

E ven with the induction ceremony and welcome dinner canceled, two casualties of the Saint's untimely death—not that they compared at all, of course—Raki still didn't get enough sleep in her assigned cabin. The unwelcome sun stung her eyes as she pushed herself up from her bed. The other nine cadets she shared the cabin with moved through varying stages of hygiene, eating, and preparedness.

Esera, who slept on the opposite side of the austere cabin, was out of the room. Raki was overjoyed she'd get to train alongside her Brother for the next six months. And her bed neighbor, who was also out, was the tall young woman who felled the zonbi on the ship over. Two friendly faces were as good a start as any cadet could have.

"I thought I was going to drown when the zonbi knocked me overboard. Can you believe they sprung that on us? I'm not a diver!" Raki looked over to where Obi, a young man from Artemisa and a name with roots in the nomadic peoples, put on his boots. Raki thought she had heard about a near-death incident.

"Hey, you tried, and that's what counts," Estefania said, furiously shaking out her bedsheets. She had also arrived from Artemisa, and her name sounded like it originated from there as well. "My cabinmate heard the commotion on our ship and decided to just sleep through it. Embarrassing."

"How do people like that even make it to interviews?" Raki jumped in, more awake. She reached under her bed and opened its drawer, pulled out her uniform and the utility belt her mother gifted her, and sat back up. "Can't imagine any of these scoutmasters putting up with cadets like that."

"I think we lucked out," Sega stated. She was a Fa'atasi woman, by roots and residency, with striking red hair in a buzz cut. "Some of the other cadets said Ignacia is, like, the most lenient scoutmaster here."

"As long as she doesn't throw me off any moving surfaces," Obi said, unenthused.

Raki wanted to get to know her new comrades more, but she didn't want to be the last cadet ready on their first day, no matter what Ignacia was like. She grabbed her boots, got out of bed, and entered the bathroom next to their quarters. She snapped the root lights on with an electric charge and looked at the papers pinned to the toilet stalls. Each one had a list with their names and a chore next to them. She saw the papers in the kitchen yesterday when they arrived, but was too frazzled to pay them any attention.

"Rakiatu..." She traced a finger across the paper, then scrunched her face. "Wash dishes?" That could wait? Surely getting ready to start training was the priority, right?

Raki entered a stall and changed into the sandy brown shirt, navy blue bottoms—she had chosen a skort—and brown combat boots that made up the cadet's uniform. After securing the utility belt around her waist, she stretched a palm out, synced her fingers with the air, and used slick streams to pull her braids into a ponytail, securing it with a band. She left the stall and looked herself over in the mirror, sighing. If she stood still in these dull "colors," someone would mistake her for a list of chores and pin her to a door.

"Position!"

Raki raced back on Ignacia's command. Their scoutmaster waited in the middle of their quarters, weight on one leg, hand on a hip—and the other holding a dirty frying pan? Raki positioned herself next to Yoel, a Taisalan cadet with Artemisan roots whose straight stance she tried to outdo. Esera walked in seconds later, dusting crumbs from his uniform. He stood next to Raki casually, as if their scoutmaster never gave a command, and eased himself into position.

He was going to make this as difficult for himself as possible, wasn't he?

"Salute!"

The cadets gave the salute. Right arm straight across the stomach, signifying the scout's dedication to defending the foundation of society. And left arm diagonal across the heart, a promise to give their lives to protect the people. Raki had practiced on the ship until she had it down. According to the corner of her eye, some of the others hadn't.

"Guard." The cadets relaxed, moving their arms to their sides. Ignacia's brown eyes scrutinized them. The frying pan started to seem like a threat. "When you enter a new environment, it's normal for someone familiar with your new surroundings to give you the guidance you need to adapt. No better way to learn, right?"

"Yes, Master!" That over-eager affirmation sounded like Umaru, a cadet from Faʻatasi poised to be the cabin's mascot. By appearance and name, he, like Raki, had roots in the old nomadic peoples.

"The citizens of Lemana will help you get to know her streets. When you're assigned to your future posts, your Master in Command will guide you in your scouting. And I will serve as your teacher for your six months of basic training."

Raki watched Ignacia twist the pan around and wondered if it was too late to switch scoutmasters.

"But what you have to learn to deal with are the unique encounters, people, and circumstances you'll find yourselves in, on and off duty." Ignacia held the pan with both hands now and paced back and forth before the cadets. "Navigating uncharted territory takes a mind willing to stretch itself in ways it never has before. It takes a courage that may reflect itself as doubt or discomfort in the eyes of your comrades and companions. But a willingness to develop both traits is what will solidify your success as scouts and as citizens of the Natural Plane."

"Absolutely, Master!" Umaru again. Raki twisted her mouth, then quickly fixed it as Ignacia approached her end.

"Initiative is what you need. This necessary skill will serve as the foundation for your career." Ignacia stopped pacing and held the pan up. Her eyes scanned the quarters before returning to center. "We'll meet in the courtyard in twenty minutes to begin physical tests."

Raki shoved down a jump when Ignacia focused on her. She tossed the pan at Raki—*This woman's lost her damn mind!*—and she synced with it at the last second before it smacked her face. Ignacia exited their quarters with all the assuredness of a river not caring what it carried away in its current. The cadets exchanged questioning looks.

Esera flicked off a few more crumbs. "I already made breakfast, so I'm out. Later." He followed Ignacia out.

Sega and some of the others tidied up their bed areas. Yunai scampered out of their quarters and headed to the bathroom. Raki tightened her grip on the pan and hoped whatever dishes she had to do could be done in under twenty minutes.

WHEN SHE DECIDED to follow in her footsteps and become a scout, Raki mined her ex-scoutmaster mother for information. Everything her mother told her supported one conclusion—all thoughts, opinions, and decisions influenced by emotion were a liability. While a cadet, the word of her scoutmaster mattered above all. Raki's mother trained several cadet classes in her time before retiring. If the way she raised Raki was any indication, she had been a no-nonsense scoutmaster, and Raki knew that was the norm.

But Ignacia appeared to be the opposite at first impression, the whole pan thing notwithstanding. Initiative was a nice word to toss into a first-day speech, but how far did she expect them to stretch their minds before their thoughts turned unnatural? It seemed irresponsible. Raki's goal was to become a scoutmaster, to be someone important whose actions affected people. She wasn't sure how true Sega's info was, but it was best to keep her mother's advice closer if she wanted to succeed.

Raki came out of her toe stretch and stood straight, pressing her lower back in with her hands. Her cabin had gathered across large roots that jutted out of the base's lakefront, located in front of the cabins. The other cadet groups were spread out across the lake as well.

"If I'd known we'd be getting paid to take physicals all day, I would have complained less." Esera crouched next to Raki, fanning his sweaty shirt. The tropical sun and physicals had drained all the fluid from their bodies.

"Then you must be thrilled for this next part." Shielding her eyes from the sun, Raki watched as two cadets much further away traded wind, water, and metal on a floating sparring circle. The earthen circle crumbled with each blow, their fellow cadets' cheers electrifying the match. "Nothing better than doing what you love for a living."

"I won't even get mad at that. Better than being talked at."

"We'll begin the next part of your assessment." Ignacia looked up from her clipboard from where she stood barefoot on the lakefront. Another scoutmaster had joined them to assist Ignacia for this part. "Which I'm sure you've figured out. Distance running, weight lifting, and stretching tell me what your body can do and where it needs more work. But sparring will tell me what *you* can do and where you need improvement."

Ignacia dropped her clipboard to the ground with synced air. Starting with their backs to each other, she and the other scoutmaster each walked in a wide half circle, stopping when they met each other. That part of the ground was now synced with their blood. Slamming their hands down on the circle's edge, they pulled a large disk of earth up and, using all their strength, levitated it out over the lake about six feet above the water.

"Sparring on earth that can break apart under you will test your thinking and fighting ability. The match will end when a person is down for more than five seconds, on the earth or under the water. And that includes diving by choice. No time limit, so do your best to take your opponent out. But do it fast because we won't be breaking for any reason."

A couple of stomachs grumbled as if appealing to any kindness she may spare them. Raki grabbed her stomach. Washing dishes took all twenty minutes, and she only ate an apple before the day started.

"Anything goes. Forging, syncing, weapons, blood enhancements. If you choose to forge, make sure your weapon is blunted." Ignacia looked among the tired cadets for a second. "Yunai. Raki. You're first."

Raki glanced at Yunai, who enjoyed a brief celebrity after taking out their ship's zonbi. She massaged her root arm and took a deep breath before using the root she sat on as a spring to jump onto the earth. Raki boosted herself onto the platform with a blast of air from her hands. Yunai flashed a shy smile. Raki returned the gesture.

Seconds to profile her—good with ice and excellent aim. Would be a challenge.

Arm yourself first.

"Two. One. Begin!"

Raki drove her fists into the earth, stopping when a hail of icicles pierced the ground in front of her, cutting her off from forging her gauntlets. She didn't see Yunai sync with water from the lake beforehand, so she must have taken it from her utility belt's water pouch. Something Raki also forgot to fill this morning.

No problem.

Raki recovered her stance—then jumped back when Yunai whipped a root at her legs, the same root she synced with to jump onto the earth. Raki landed on the earth's edge, blasted herself forward to avoid falling into the lake, and threw a punch at Yunai—stopping her fist right before her, the momentum blasting wind at her opponent. Yunai deflected the heavy blast as much as possible with raised arms, her upper body bending backward. But her legs didn't budge. With a sharp glance down, Raki saw she had frozen her feet in place.

This woman was damn smart.

"Good thinking."

"She's good!"

"This'll take forever."

Okay then. If Raki couldn't land a blow from above, she'd go below. Blocking out her cabinmates' commentary, she jumped back from Yunai, all the way off the circle. She grabbed the edge and swung her legs up until her feet jammed into the rough underside. Syncing her hands with the earth, Raki crawled underneath. She sensed Yunai moving around. When she thought her feet were close, Raki punched up through the circle, sending a gust of gravel up. She listened for her movements again and kept punching holes until she heard Yunai fall.

Got her.

Raki let go of the earth and, before she fell into the water, blasted through the earth, stopping in midair several feet above, ready to throw Yunai out. She soared down, stuck an arm out to grab her root arm—then switched and went for her flesh arm. Which gave Yunai enough of an opening to whip the root she had used around Raki's wrist. With a full-body tug, she slung Raki into the water. Raki was not a strong swimmer or great with water, so she lost her five seconds of recovery.

"Match!"

Clapping, comments, and cheers resounded from the cadets. Raki swam to under the earth's edge when Yunai extended the root toward her. Hair from her loose braid plastered her face and neck, but through it, she gave Raki another friendly smile. Raki, soaked, again returned the gesture as she grabbed the root for a lift. "Thank you."

"It's okay," Yunai said as she pulled Raki up, her voice breathy. "I mean, you didn't have to switch."

"I agree." It was then that they realized Ignacia and the scout-master were moving the platform back to the ground. Raki and Yunai jumped back onto the lakefront's roots before the scoutmasters returned the platform to the space where they had pulled it up. "Cadets, when you see an opening, I suggest you take it, no matter how you feel about a situation." She set her hard brown eyes on Raki. "The match could have gone the other way."

Raki felt her lips do something funny, and she suppressed whatever they wanted to say. "Yes, Master."

"Give your comrades a hand."

As the cadets clapped, Raki glanced at Yunai and saw that her face wanted to do something funny too.

"Octo-zonbi and nagging Sisters," Esera jested. "You're pretty good."

Raki froze a drop of water from her body and flicked it at his forehead.

Esera flinched. "Petty."

"Thanks." Yunai chuckled. "But both were close matches."

The scoutmasters filled in the holes Raki created with more earth. Ignacia didn't say anything *wrong*, but something about her statement made her brain itch. Maybe she should have gone for Yunai's root arm, but in a sparring match? Why risk damaging her limb?

After repairing the platform, the scoutmasters returned it to the lake. It had to take a great deal of strength and skill for them to levitate the platform while people fought on it.

"Matagi. Moraima."

Matagi, a solitary young man from Fa'atasi with brown skin and thick black-brown hair similar to Esera's, casually walked on the water with bare feet. Raki noticed part of the tattoo adorned by some men with roots in Fa'atasi above the back of his knees. He jumped up to the earth's edge and pulled himself up. And that's when Raki also noticed his left hand had a root thumb and middle finger and root stitches on his pinkie finger.

Moraima, a sweetheart of a cadet with Artemisan roots, fawn skin, a sandy brown pixie cut, and soft facial features, synced with one of the lake roots. She was one of the few to tackle her chores without prompting. She attached the root to the platform and walked across it, returning the root to its original position when she made it on.

"Begin!"

Moraima threw her arms out. Veins of slim roots emerged from her sleeves and surged toward Matagi. Matagi opened his mouth. He inhaled a deep breath, a guttural twister forming, and sucked her roots into his mouth.

Raki winced. Natural skills were as diverse as the people who wielded them, but she had never seen anything quite like that.

"I don't think I've ever washed these." Moraima tried syncing her roots back—and stopped when Matagi started chewing. He ripped off a few inches, chewed for a few more seconds while everyone watched, then spat the roots out. They didn't come out marinated in slobber—he had ripped them to pieces, clear tears in the roots. How...

Raki caught a glint of light from Matagi's teeth—both rows were made of metal.

Disgusted but determined, Moraima synced off the chewed ends and unleashed her roots like tentacles, two arms and two legs, and Matagi fell backward into the lake.

"Good choice!" Raki turned to Umaru, who sat with his legs crossed and his fingers on his chin. "Attacking her head-on is risky, and Matagi is an excellent swimmer."

Before his five seconds were up, Matagi jetted out of the lake from the other side. He stuck his fingers in his mouth, then took them out, brandishing a full set of forged claws. Landing, he went after Moraima. She tried buffering his assault with her roots, but he had caught her off guard. He shredded the roots as much as the one he had chewed.

Moraima jumped back. She tore off several thinner threads from one of her more intact roots and sicced them on Matagi. Their smaller size made them harder to counter, giving her more of an advantage. Moraima managed to land a few threads on his fingers—then she yanked.

Collective gasps shuddered through the cadets.

Moraima clearly meant to pull his claws off, but she accidentally ripped off his root thumb. "Oh! I'm so sorry!" She retracted her roots into her clothing. "I didn't mean for that to happen. Here, let me—"

The top of Moraima's shirt hung from its neckline by a thread before everyone realized Matagi had slashed it. The roots synced with her torso had also been cut, and they fell to the earth. Matagi lifted a leg and kicked Moraima in the chest, sending her into the lake. Five seconds passed.

"Match!"

"Seriously?" Esera shot up, nearly dumping himself into the lake.

"She gets knocked out for trying to help him?" Sega questioned.

"She got knocked out for dropping her defense," Ignacia stated.

After Matagi recovered his thumb, Ignacia and the scoutmaster brought the platform back. Moraima chose to swim back to the roots.

Raki felt heat rise in her chest. Moraima was honorable to stop, but her match with Yunai had set the example.

"Matagi listened. And took initiative. He saw an opening and went for it. In the field, a zonbi or an opponent won't give you a second for any reason. You shouldn't give anyone the same courtesy, too."

Sega helped Moraima back onto the root. The cadet hung her head down. Raki couldn't see her face, but she was probably fighting back tears.

"Moraima, your willingness to help will be a boon when it's your fellow scouts in danger. But an adversary will strike you down if you're not more mindful. Matagi, head to the base hospital and ask for help. Tell them I sent you..."

Raki followed Ignacia's lost voice to a figure further down the lake. No matter how far away she stood, Raki would always recognize the imposing figure of the Grand Scoutmaster. The Scouthood's commander finished speaking to another scoutmaster and walked down the lake toward their group. Raki wondered how long she had been observing.

"Before the next match," Ignacia said, her voice leaping from composed to authoritative, "let me reiterate the single most important expectation a cadet must meet—your emotions *must stay down to zero*. Leaning heavily into emotion will not only get you in trouble, but it will endanger your comrades and our already fragile world. Understood?"

"Understood," the cadets replied quickly.

"Understood, Moraima?"

"U-understood, Master." Moraima lifted her head a bit to answer but immediately lowered it back.

Raki looked between Ignacia and Niesh. Ignacia was amiable and seemed to care for their well-being. But Niesh set the tone before they even made it to Taisala. And one wore a scarf darker in green than the other. So it wasn't hard for Raki to decide which scoutmaster's words would guarantee success.

44

SIX

YUNAI

Yunai lowered her book when the voices in her head defeated her concentration.

Foolish. Running off to die when she could do more for our people here.

She'll change her mind in a month, don't worry.

She shut the book. She needed the silence of the cabin after a week of intense training. Instead, it reminded her of all the words—and people—she wanted to forget.

Yunai looked around the cabin's communal area. Everyone was out exploring the city of Lemana on their first day off, and Ignacia left a note on her office-bedroom door stating she spent her off days with her partner who lived in the city. Raki and Esera, whom Yunai claimed as companions, had asked her to go out with them, but Yunai had declined. She liked the Siblings a lot and wanted to get to know them. But after a week of learning to live with nine people with different ideas of when a toilet should be flushed, she needed her space. She also visited Lemana often with her family, so she wasn't itching to go out.

But now the solitude was turning into loneliness, and the voices were only getting stronger. Yunai needed more than fictional characters to fill the empty hours. A mid-afternoon stroll through Lemana wouldn't kill her.

She changed out of her nightwear and put her dark brown hair into two loose braids. She put on shorts and threw on her favorite top, a shirt with a geometric lightning design she wore when she didn't want to feel weak. After signing herself out in the cabin's record book, she exited the cabin, locking the roots behind her. Sixteen cabins formed a circle around the courtyard, each cabin housing ten cadets. The absence of their noise left the courtyard as forlorn as the cloudy sky above. Only a clowder of golden-brown cats hung out in the stone courtyard.

Yunai signed out of the base with the scoutmaster on duty. After he unlocked the gate's roots, she walked out to one of the hills surrounding the base. Beyond a sea of hills and a sprawling system of giant roots was Lemana, the city named after the first Saint. Her colors never faded, even against a dreary backdrop. And in Lemana's center was the Cathedral, a beacon with no guiding light. It made Yunai uneasy that the new Saint hadn't come forward yet. The people who lived on the island probably felt more unsafe than ever before.

THE CLAMOR of voices young and old and the movement of goods back and forth settled Yunai's mind. She loved visiting Lemana's trading posts, tasting food and drink foreign to her. Their swirling aromas were a testament to the city's reputation as an international meeting ground.

Stalls of fruit from the Plane over, passionfruit, guavas, mangoes, more than she could name, lined the street to her right. Yunai gave a few coins to an elderly vendor wearing a bright yellow headwrap and grabbed a bag of guavas. Tourists bargained with a shop owner over the price for a length of wax prints, and a girl with an intricately braided updo air-braided her mother's graying hair next to a table of dry goods. A herd of pale pink goats struck their hooves on the ground, shooting small pillars of earth up and down. A small group of giggly children tried to dodge the pillars, sitting out when they got hit.

The streets painted a picture of daily city life. What Yunai wasn't prepared for, though, was the number of scoutmasters patrolling the streets.

She caught their viridian scarves as they left buildings, sat in restaurants, walked up and down the streets. She noticed a couple listening in on conversations. Then another talking in a stern voice to a boy, the boy's face aching with worry. Yunai's eyes lingered on them, but she kept moving. Hopefully, it wasn't serious.

She couldn't recall a time when the city had been this heavily patrolled. The Saint's death warranted the security increase, but it still made her nervous. A silly feeling for a cadet to have.

Chewing on a guava, Yunai looked up at the homes and offices she passed. Lemana was known for its colorful architecture, but what piqued Yunai's curiosity were the violet candles sitting in several of the windows. Some were lit, some not. A man opened his window and lit one with a finger snap. Saint Leonardo had been killed over half a cycle ago, and the mourning period would not stop until his successor came forward.

Yunai tossed the guava skin into a bush and turned onto a smaller street hidden from view. A group of elders chatted on a porch, and a couple of people synced paint onto a side wall. No scoutmasters in sight.

Yunai paused to observe the painters. She wasn't well-versed in art, so their design was unknown to her. They filled in a wheel with eight spokes, each section a different color. Pink in the top left section, red in the next, then orange—a rainbow. The colors spilled out of the lines' boundaries and into each other, and Yunai found no discernible pattern in how little or how much they painted out of bounds.

As they worked on the yellow part, Yunai moved closer to them. "Excuse me. Sorry. What are you painting?"

One of the painters, a woman with tawny skin and thick black hair, paused and turned to Yunai. She smiled, then turned back to the wall. "You tell us. What do you see?"

Yunai raised one eyebrow. She saw a messy color wheel? She

wasn't sure how they wanted her to answer. "Err...a color wheel?" What else was she supposed to say?

The woman's companion, a man with similar features, tched as he finished the yellow section.

"Right," the woman said, syncing with green paint. "But what do *you* see? What do you personally get from it?"

Yunai took a minute but came up with nothing. She could think longer, but her answer wouldn't change, and she wanted to continue her day. Guess it couldn't hurt to humor them. "I guess—"

"What's going on here?"

Yunai jerked. She backed up fast when a scoutmaster stormed down the narrow street.

"What's this?"

The woman turned, dropping the pail of green paint. "We're just—"

The scoutmaster didn't give her a chance to finish. She ignited a torch in one hand, rapidly grew the flame, and doused the painting in fire. The elders got up and rushed inside.

"This kind of work is not permitted anywhere in the city. The law is clear."

"It's just a wheel!" the woman protested. "We weren't—"

"Are you involved with this?"

"N-no!" Yunai pushed out the word when she realized the scoutmaster was talking to her. She almost mentioned she was a cadet to protect herself, but decided against it. Not a good look for a cadet to show interest in this kind of art.

The scoutmaster turned back to the couple. "You'll need to come with me now."

The couple exchanged sick looks as they walked away from the wall, the scoutmaster following close behind.

Yunai regained the feeling in her feet after she zeroed her heart rate down. She got off that street as fast as she could. She felt foolish for indulging the couple. As a cadet, she should have known their work was unnatural. She wouldn't make that mistake again.

But...

...there was a small part of Yunai that failed to see the blasphemy in the painting. To her, the wheel was as meaningful as a child's drawing.

...SHE COULD DO MORE for our people here.
   She'll change her mind in a month...

Most recruits left home with heartfelt letters. Yunai left with an eviction notice.

Her home was free of the constant fighting many families dealt with. But her family didn't move through the gray areas of conflict and misunderstanding that communication could work out. They acted in black and white—obey or take the consequences. Yunai joined the Scouthood against the counsel of her parents—they may never welcome her home. So she was determined to prove that she wasn't making a mistake by giving up her sensible life as the daughter of a Headman to protect the Plane.

Which meant she couldn't repeat that painting incident.

Yunai shook off that scene and passed into a busy plaza deeper in the city. She walked in a haze, her thoughts robbing her of her attention, so she didn't notice when she ended up at a statue in the center of the plaza.

She looked up. An effigy of Leonardo, about twenty feet tall and cast in gold. His confident eyes held an eternal lock on the space before him, and the replica of his ceremonial cape hung from his shoulders. Clay vessels, shells, flowers, personal effects, and dozens of violet candles lay at his feet, and roots curled up to his knees.

"Bold move to add the blood."

Yunai turned to the man standing next to her, then turned back to the statue. She searched for splotches of red up and down. No blood. Did she miss something?

When the man walked away, Yunai walked around to the statue's back—but she found nothing. No hint of red anywhere. A joke? But who would openly joke about the Saint's death, or make something up?

Stop. He had the same strange energy as the couple. She should have reprimanded the man. The Saint's death meant more unnatural activity. She needed to be more on guard.

Yunai walked back around. Now someone stood at the statue's feet, a man who looked a bit older than her. He slapped a hand on Leonardo's left leg and pulled it down slowly. This was a day for questionable characters.

"Lemana seems fine with the skull you're holding," the man said to himself. "Maybe people are finally ready to admit what you truly are—a criminal."

Now there were skulls? Was this part of a show? Was someone directing this from a hidden spot? She knew she had to do something, but Yunai searched the immediate space for reassurance first. But so many people came up to the statue to pay their respects. One man muttering nonsense to himself wouldn't catch any civilian's attention.

"My Partner would still be with me if not for you." His voice grew louder, angrier.

Yunai looked around again. There had to be a scoutmaster nearby. They monitored restaurants and backstreets, but not the Saint's memorial?

"You're no Saint of mine. *And you deserve the death you got.*"

As if his ranting were a summons, fiendish barking descended upon the plaza. People fled, scrambling on top of each other as four-legged zonbi homed in on the memorial. They were a freakish sight, with the bodies of decomposing foxes, fish fins sticking out of their bodies like spikes, and feathers jammed around their muzzles. Yunai touched her waist instinctively—then cursed. Zonbi rarely appeared in Lemana, so she didn't think bringing her utility belt was necessary.

Searching the area quickly, Yunai spotted a puddle left from the early morning rain. She synced her hands with the water, forged a spear of ice in one, and slapped back one of the zonbi with water in the other hand before it ripped off her face. On impact, pale feathers shot out from the creature's swollen lower lip. It scratched its nose, the water nothing more than a nuisance.

"Help me!" The man tried scrambling up the statue. The zonbi rushed at his wild emotions, ignoring the panicked crowd. He would attract more if he didn't zero down.

Yunai forged the other hand of water into a spear and fought off the zonbi with both weapons until her first spear broke. She hopped onto the statue and synced with the gold. She struggled to climb up —the gold must have been mixed with something synthetic—but she made it high enough. She broke her spear into shards and fired them at the pack, piercing eye, fin, and leg. The rest of the spears broke on the ground.

"Hurry up and stop them!" the man shouted.

Trying not to let his desperation affect her, Yunai synced the broken shards at the zonbi, but they were too melted to do any damage. She was losing her grip on the sync.

Water evaporated and ice melted when bullets of fire smoked the dead flesh of the zonbi, charred skin revealing ashen bones. A dark-skinned man wearing a viridian scarf around his neck strolled up to the memorial with a finger cocked. He fired more shots, striking skin and exposed organs. Lifting his other hand, he unleashed another barrage of fire bullets. They bored holes and incinerated decay until smoke swallowed all senses. Yunai blew the smoke from her airspace and dropped down. The scoutmaster condensed the smoke into a funnel and directed it into the sky.

"Are you a cadet?" he asked without taking his eyes off his task.

"Uh, y-yes," Yunai said.

"Report."

"Of course..." Yunai turned back to the man who hugged the statue as he slid down. "This man here. He—the zonbi attacked him. I don't know where they came from. I did my best to fight back, but they were fast."

"For what reason did they attack?"

"He was angry. H-he said the statue was holding a skull, that he lost his Partner..." Something held her back from mentioning his comments about the Saint. Would the scoutmasters take him away like the couple?

"Freeze him!" the scoutmaster commanded.

Yunai snapped around. The man was running. She threw the water still synced with her blood at his feet, freezing him in place, bits of zonbi freezing with it. He fell to his knees.

The scoutmaster finished funneling the smoke, and the crowd

trickled back into the plaza. "I'll handle him. Report this to your scoutmaster when you return to base. And I suggest you return now."

"Yes, Master."

He walked over to the man, broke the ice with a kick, and hauled him to his feet. The man held back sobs while trying not to choke on them. "I'll send someone to clean up here. Good work, cadet."

Yunai saluted. Should she have done that first?

The crowd swelled into the plaza when the scoutmaster left. A few clapped. Some complained about the scoutmaster getting there late. Several flocked to the statue as if they were needed to inspect the damage.

Not knowing what else to do with herself, Yunai heeded the scoutmaster's orders and headed back to the base. The fight had run her ragged, and she needed to process all she had seen today.

ODOMI

The rooftop juice bar was a favorite of hers, so it was the perfect spot for Odomi to observe from. She watched the scoutmaster walk the man away from the plaza, and it took all her common sense to stop from intervening. Knowing what punishment awaited anyone the Natural deemed unnatural made her stomach curdle. She was taking a huge risk with her plan, knowing the danger. And she wasn't sure she had the resources to save the man without risking her own life. It pained her deeply, but she had to do what needed to be done—even if it violated the oath she took as a medic to do no harm.

Her attempt, nonetheless, was more successful than she expected. The only issue now—avoiding the omnipresent eyes of the Cathedral and the public on her next try. No sense in continuing to lure potential subjects out only to serve them up to the Scouthood. Odomi had put her search for the spirit she needed on hold after taking down the Saint. Security was high and tight in the weeks after, so it wasn't wise to take any chances. But it appeared the Scouthood would not let up, and Odomi couldn't wait any longer.

"You haven't ordered yet, Odomi. Everything good?"

Odomi turned to the waiter. She had no appetite, but best to act as if the poor widowed man hadn't been dragged away. "Sorry," she said with a smile. "I'll take a guava juice."

SEVEN

NIESH

"All I'm saying, since this *is* a meeting for general business, is that the quality of the food has gone down in the last month. Might be time to let go of certain staff."

"And all *I'm* saying, dearest Celia, is that being bored with a position created for optics doesn't give you the right to create problems to inflate your importance."

"And all I'm doing, *Ibrahim*, is raising a legit concern that's worth looking into. Isn't that the point of these meetings? What do you think, Niesh?"

Niesh looked up from her stack of reports, stared at both fools with bloodshot eyes, then looked back down. The official meeting needed to start and end fast before she let go of them both. Off a cliff. Thankfully, these monthly meetings with the Saint's Circle, the leaders of the six departments of the Cathedral, were less painful than the meetings with the Board. They were annoying but painless.

The Minister of Foreign Affairs was off-island meeting with world leaders, and the Assistant to the Saint was dead, so that just left...

"Where *is* the poor woman?" Celia, the Cathedral's Liaison for Animal Affairs, asked. With roots in Artemisa, the woman tended to overestimate the urgency of...just about everything. "I know things have been hard, but... Oh, look at me making predictions."

Niesh looked up again when the meeting room's door peeked open. A woman skirted in, a tired wind trailing her. Also with Artemisan roots, her brown hair hung in clumps, and Niesh recognized the black dress she wore—the woman had already worn it twice this week. Her normally soft brown skin was leeched of color, as were her normally black eyes. Niesh made it a point to never complain about her stress around Paloma, the Cathedral's Director of Youth Services—and a widow of Leonardo. Paloma brought herself down into a chair and waited.

"Paloma..." Celia started. And no one liked it when chirpy Celia started. "Why don't you—"

"Let's start the actual meeting." Niesh slammed her hands on her reports and blinked her eyes wide open. "Celia. Anything to report?"

Celia opened her notebook and uncapped her pen. "Well—"

"The Cathedral's menu doesn't count."

Celia, who was always trying to overcompensate for the decoration that was her position, closed her notebook and capped her pen. "Then I have nothing to report."

One down. Animal affairs were easy. They managed their business without much trouble and generally moved on when one of their own died. Unless they went zonbi. Then their affairs fell under her dominion. Of course.

"Perfect." Niesh placed a hand on top of her Sister's bony hands. "Paloma...if you can." Even though she got the position through her late Partner, Niesh couldn't think of anyone more suited to the role that oversaw the Cathedral's orphanage. The gravity of grief weighed her spirit down, but she possessed the rare skill of keeping calm in the face of stress.

"Yes..." Paloma squeezed Niesh's hand, then released it. "I apologize for my absence lately...but the orphanage is fine. My staff has been running it well during my time off. I understand there was a zonbi attack on it a few weeks ago."

"My scoutmasters handled it swiftly," Niesh said. "Are the children growing afraid? I know Leonardo spent a lot of time with them when he could."

Paloma perked up as if Niesh's train of thought coupled with a thought of hers. "One of our girls has been causing more trouble than usual lately. Having outbursts and fits. She's having a hard time keeping zero. It may be because of the Saint's absence."

Niesh twisted her lips. Children were...she didn't hate them, but she didn't love them either. Probably more accurate to say she didn't know what to do with them. Cadets were no different to her either.

"Zonbi are drawn to uncontrollable emotions, so if she doesn't stop..." Niesh pondered aloud. The solution was obvious to her, but she'd let Paloma make that call when the time came. In any case, she couldn't let zonbi attack a place as sacred as the Cathedral. She couldn't have it. The Board would *not* have it.

"The cadets will be starting community service soon," Paloma said. Or asked. Niesh couldn't tell. "Maybe it would help to assign a specific cadet to her. Someone who can mentor her and guide her."

"Not a bad idea." *More ethical than mine.* "I'll keep that in mind when I meet with my scoutmasters next time."

Paloma smiled as much as her broken spirit allowed her. She sat back.

"Ibrahim?"

The older man, who served as the Chief of Medicine, crossed his arms and leaned back in his seat. With roots in the nomadic peoples, he had warm brown skin, tired black eyes, and a shaved head. "My medics are strained. Obviously. And under pressure. From both the increase in zonbi and patients and the presence of your lackies."

"No need to spit at me, Ibrahim." Niesh rolled her eyes. "It's not exactly irresponsible to provide more protection for people in constant danger."

"It is when having extra people watching over your shoulder *clearly* adds more stress to an already high-pressure environment."

"*Clearly. Obviously.* I dare you to add one more synonym to whatever you say next."

"Oh, zero down, woman. Or do you need to be babysat by a cadet, too?" Ibrahim, always ready to trade barbs with Niesh, said before she had a chance to punch back. "I know the Board makes you nervous—they don't sit right with me either—but just because they suggested doubling down on our efforts doesn't mean it's a good idea. The increase is an issue with society embracing unnatural thinking, and it will only grow worse without a Saint. If you want to protect your people, you must start with them."

Niesh laughed, almost hysterically. "You want to tell them that? Be my guest. I have enough dead bodies to worry about."

"I'm not suggesting we push back. Our opinions mean nothing —*needless to say.*" Ibrahim grinned. Niesh grimaced. "But I suggest we turn our attention to a more pressing matter. One we've overlooked in all the chaos."

Niesh narrowed her eyes.

"We may never know how Leo was killed exactly, but we have reason to believe the perpetrator didn't act alone."

"And who is 'we'?" questioned Niesh.

Celia shuffled around in her seat, and Paloma hugged her tense body tight.

"Security is always tighter when a Saint speaks in public," Celia said. "We all keep saying he acted alone, but how can one man, no matter how dangerous or clever, enter the Cathedral without anyone noticing?"

"We don't know the full extent of what the unnatural can do," Ibrahim continued, "but to navigate the Cathedral's hidden passages and make it to the balcony for a clean shot? I strongly doubt it was a one-person job."

Niesh leaned back in her seat, rubbed her temples, and gave herself pause. Unnatural persons did tend to act alone, at least on Taisala, where it was harder for them to organize due to the Scouthood's heavier presence. But Niesh was well-versed in the behaviors they demonstrated on other continents. If the assassin was working with a comrade or in a group, one person striking out on their own prevented the others from being exposed if the person got caught. "So he had an accomplice."

"Not just an accomplice," Ibrahim said. "Someone with inside knowledge of how the Cathedral operates. Someone *we* would trust to be in these walls."

Niesh considered the possibility before but had no leads and had been too busy. Instead of normal stairs and doors throughout the building's lower levels, the Cathedral contained hidden passageways that required specific patterns of synchronization to open. And only select people knew the patterns—the Circle and a handful of the senior scoutmasters and medics. Not even the Board had that access. Anyone who came in on business had to be guided by someone with clearance. Natural or unnatural, there was no way to sneak in without aid. That's what they thought, at least.

Paloma took a steadying breath. "Few people in history have attacked a Saint so brazenly. And no one has managed to successfully kill one until…"

"So there's no way he could have done it alone," Niesh said, finishing her Sister's thought.

"I suggest you form a hunter force," Ibrahim said. "Scoutmasters dedicated to investigating any leads. I understand your people are stretched thin, but this is an issue that demands our full attention. We can't let unnaturals spread their reach any further."

"You're making decisions now?" Niesh was too tired to remind him who was in charge, but it wasn't like she disagreed with him. "Fine. Done. We'll assemble a force. But no scoutmasters. They're required to wear their scarves when on duty, and that would immediately alert anyone suspicious."

"So who do we use?" Celia asked. Niesh almost forgot she was there.

"Cadets. No scarves and they can be molded more easily into what I need."

"Excellent." Ibrahim smiled, satisfied. He gave Niesh an expectant look. "Niesh?"

Niesh tched. "Leave me alone, man. I'd report, but you took up my time. And I have other things to do."

Celia and Ibrahim stood up and gathered their things. Niesh synced part of her armband off and forged it into a massaging tool, rubbing it across the back of her stiff neck.

Paloma remained seated, coming to life when the next thought appeared in her head. "Niesh…I would love to have dinner tonight. It's been so long. I know you have a lot to do…"

"I can. But it'll be late. Someone made a bold move at Leonardo's memorial today, and I have to follow up."

BRAULIO

Braulio signed into the hospital with the scoutmaster on duty. He wiped the moisture from his forehead as he entered. He had lived on Taisala for over a cycle now but could never get used to her balmy nights.

Before leaving for the day, he forgot to grab a few medicinal plants for a concoction he wanted to make for a patient's rare condition. *Well*, that was the story he'd tell if someone caught him taking more supplies than allowed in a week and for non-work reasons. His companion from his hometown in Artemisa was moving to Lemana in a few weeks, and they were someone who needed constant support. A few concoctions for stress reduction and sleep would help them stay leveled. No one would miss a few plants. Or maybe someone would. He didn't care either way.

Braulio walked through the near-empty halls of the hospital's front admin building. A handful of scoutmasters patrolled the halls, some alert, some visibly tired. He ignored their eyes and kept straight.

Reaching the end of the admin building, Braulio took the left of the two doors that led to the sanctuary where animal patients were seen. Braulio had never been in the hospital after hours. Nighttime settled the normally tense place into a serene building. He wondered if the moon unmasked the day's secrets. Malpractice or a love affair, perhaps? With his blood-enhanced hearing, he would hear it all.

Braulio slowed his gait. Above, there was not much to hear— footsteps, pen on paper, words here and there. The rhythm of sleeping animals' heavy breathing in the aquatic and forest rehabilitation areas brushed his ears. And below was the basement, where they stored extra furniture and equipment. Rarely anyone went down there.

Disappointing, but what was he expecting? Maybe his stale personal life made him a bit too thirsty for excitement.

Braulio opened the back door leading to the pharmacy at the sanctuary's far end. The night technician sat in the window, his hand cradling his head. Residents didn't have access to the pharmacy, but Odomi had given him, Siaka, and Mirta clearance since they were taking on a semi-leadership role.

"Braulio…" The tech yawned. "You here to meet up with Siaka?"

"Siaka?" His companion wasn't at their apartment when Braulio left. He assumed he was home with Odomi.

"Yeah, he's out in the greenhouse. Harvesting some plants we don't have in stock." The tech rubbed his eyes.

"Didn't realize he was here. Guess I'll head back when I'm done here."

The tech synced the pharmacy's complex metal lock open from his side. "Take your time."

Braulio went in, opening the bag he brought with him. The pharmacy was lined with clear cabinets stocked with a plethora of plants harvested from the greenhouse or imported from across the Plane. He grabbed some tau suni, which was native to Fa'atasi. It eased headaches, and his companion *was* a headache. Avasa would be good too. Chauko from Artemisa for their harder days…

Braulio paused. He heard two voices coming from behind the hospital where the greenhouse was. One belonged to Siaka, and the other…it was too faint. And it didn't sound human.

Braulio finished his business, waved goodbye to the tech who was nearly knocked out, then left the sanctuary at the rear exit. The greenhouse was a short walk away from the hospital, down a marble pathway. As he got closer, he could make out words.

"…so I would settle down…" Then a sound, like plants creeping around a tree trunk.

The greenhouse's root lights were off, so Braulio lit a small torch before opening the tall glass door. "Siaka?"

…

Braulio moved deeper into the greenhouse. The sounds stopped, and he didn't hear the crackling of another lit torch. Surely he wasn't desperate enough for juicy secrets that his brain was making up sounds.

"Siaka?"

He was being ridiculous. Should have just—

"Braulio?"

He jerked. Siaka emerged from the darkness—torch lit. The greenhouse was big, but Braulio would have heard a torch hissing in the quiet of the night, no matter the size.

60

"What are you doing here?" Siaka asked.

"Hoarding plants." No need to lie. Siaka especially didn't care about following regulations. "Who are you with?"

"It's just me. Hoarding too." He held a potted plant in his other hand—passionflower. Medics used the ghostly lavender blooms to strengthen sedatives.

"Thought I heard you talking to someone." Braulio tapped an ear.

"Nope. Just I. Your special ears heard me talking to myself and messing with plants." Siaka adjusted his hold on the pot. "Mom's stress is almost unbearable, so just getting her something to help."

Help her what? Sleep forever? "Oh...same actually. For my companion."

"Guess we're both playing caretaker."

"Looks like." Braulio understood the strain of taking care of a loved one. But his ears rarely lied to him.

"Tomorrow?"

"Yeah."

Siaka gave Braulio a rascal's smile and headed for the door. Braulio returned the gesture and followed him out. Siaka could be funny and was defiant when it mattered—they had that in common —but he knew when to shirk frivolous orders and when to follow necessary protocols.

So why didn't Braulio see Siaka's name on the sign-in sheet when he came in?

EIGHT

YUNAI

Standing at guard before her scoutmaster, the scoutmaster from the plaza, and the Grand Scoutmaster was like standing before her elders. Yunai was careful to measure her language, both verbal and physical.

"I didn't see a skull anywhere near the memorial," Yunai said to her seniors at the cabin's front steps. "I don't think anyone in the crowd did either. No one said anything or pointed anything out. He was very angry, and that likely warped his sense of reality."

"A sensible theory," Niesh said. "Strong emotions are disruptive and destructive."

"I don't think he intended to harm anyone—"

"If he willingly went to the memorial to let out his anger," the scoutmaster interjected, "then he intended to attract zonbi and cause harm."

Yunai nodded. She thought no words were best here.

"Was there anything else?" Niesh asked.

Yunai returned to Niesh's center of gravity. Yunai was tall for her age, but Niesh was towering. She couldn't put off telling her what the man said much longer.

"There was someone else who said they saw blood on the statue. I checked but didn't see any, and he left before I could take action."

Stop delaying. Just say it. Just say *it.* "But the man who was arrested, he...he said—" Hesitation. Doubt. "He-said-the-Saint-deserved-the-death-he-got." It came out in one exhale.

The scoutmaster crossed his arms. "You didn't mention that to me."

"I'm sorry." Yunai's guard nearly broke. "There was so much happening, and I wasn't completely focused...I'm sorry."

Ignacia finally jumped in. "Yunai, you did good. You took initiative in the situation even when you had hesitations." Yunai was grateful for the ease Ignacia's presence brought. Her scoutmaster felt like the elder who always made sure her grandchildren were okay. "Just be sure when you make reports to keep an even mind and report everything that happens. It's important your team and your superiors have all the details to help keep people safe."

"Yes, Master," Yunai said. "That's all I have to report."

"Thank you, cadet." Niesh turned to her subordinates. "Continue to report directly to me when incidents like this happen."

Ignacia and the scoutmaster saluted, then the scoutmaster left. Yunai quickly saluted as well, then, before Niesh left, asked, "So... what will happen to the man?" She didn't think asking that was out of line.

Niesh set her eyes on her. The look on her face was reassuring. "The Cathedral will bring him the justice he deserves."

ESERA

Someone should have told Esera the Scouthood was just school all over again. Sitting at the cabin's kitchen table, he synced his fruit cereal into his mouth as he watched his comrades in their morning flow. He was getting to know the other cadets, their personalities and their backgrounds. Their physical features, names, mannerisms, and cultural markers revealed where their roots originated.

Raki and Yoel, his roots in Artemisa, with his light brown skin and gray eyes, were both on cooking duty for the week. Raki tried convincing Yoel that paprika was the best seasoning to add to corn-meal porridge. Which was hilarious to watch because Raki was a shit-ass cook. Raki was an overbearing parent, and Yoel was a no-nonsense adult, so neither would concede anytime soon.

Moraima, who both resided and had roots in Artemisa, was usually quiet but came to life around the right people. And Sega was the right people. Their interactions were cute, almost intimate. No one else in the cabin appeared to be fraternizing yet, so it fell on them to fulfill the romantic arc of the cadets' training period. Residing in and with roots in Fa'atasi, Sega lifted the compost bag from its bin. And Moraima rushed over to help her take the neither-heavy-nor-full bag to the compost heap the residents used for the hospital's greenhouse.

Umaru. Oh, *Umaru*. What could Esera say about Umaru? His biological need to respond to everything Ignacia said pissed off half the cabin. It probably irritated their scoutmaster, too, but he didn't seem to care. Or he was oblivious. Either way, Esera had no issues with Umaru, who resided in Fa'atasi but had roots in the old nomadic peoples, like Raki. He washed dishes right in between Paprika and No Paprika, popping in and out to set dishes on the drying rack. The scene was damn comedic. Esera cackled between bites of fruit.

He almost choked when Matagi entered the kitchen. Matagi... They both shared Fa'atasi roots, but Esera didn't like him. He was cold. Indifferent. He treated his training partners like gym equipment, not as people training alongside him.

Esera spat him out along with the seeds in his mouth, turning his attention to Estefania. Like Moraima, Estefania resided in and had roots in Artemisa, with long black hair in a tight bun, brown eyes, and tawny skin. She used synced air to float a soiled towel to the washroom. She twisted her nose and mouth in a disgust that wanted to let everyone know of its existence. Who else was going to set the standard for cleanliness in their cabin but Estefania and her visible disapproval? There was always one. And poor Obi, carrying the whole basket of cleaning supplies behind her. Esera couldn't tell if he was being a good cadet or a good boy. The young man was from Artemisa and had multiple roots, with hazel eyes, sandy skin, and sporting a buzzed mohawk.

And lastly...

"Yunai!" The cabin closed in on her when she entered from the front door. She got up early to meet with Ignacia, another scout-master—and the Grand Scoutmaster.

"What happened?"

"They kicking you out?"

"What did they say?"

"Let her breathe, sheesh!" Raki chided.

Esera noticed the tension in Yunai's shoulders.

"I fought zonbi at Leonardo's memorial last week," Yunai said. "Ignacia told me to keep it to myself until I met with Niesh."

"Are you okay?" Moraima asked.

"A scoutmaster came, so I was fine. There was a man there too... he said some horrible things about the Saint, so the scoutmaster took him..."

"Took him?" Sega asked when Yunai didn't go on.

"Took him out, she means," Yoel said. "They're dragging him under if he criticized the Saint."

Esera watched shadows gather in Yunai's hazel eyes. Yoel was probably right. Esera heard enough stories about scoutmasters "removing" people for speaking out against the Cathedral. But no one ever knew what the punishments entailed.

"Is that worth a man's life?" Estefania asked, washing her hands. "Just lock him up."

"Anyone against the Saint is against the Natural," Umaru declared. "That makes them unnatural. And to speak ill of the dead... reprehensible!"

"And scouts are literally supposed to take care of unnatural threats." Raki walked up to Yunai and rested a hand on her shoulder.

Esera continued watching Yunai. He saw the extra words stuck in her throat.

The cadets stepped back when Ignacia came in. "Ten minutes, then we gather in the courtyard with the other cabins. Remember to meet with your assigned scoutmaster." She ran to her office-bedroom, and the cadets dispersed to finish their morning chores.

Esera set his bowl in the sink and returned to his companions. "Now that those extras are gone, you can tell us the rest."

"Esera—"

"It's okay." Raki removed her hand before Yunai continued, her voice lowered. "I also saw a couple get taken away for painting something on the side of a building. It was a circle of rainbow colors, but it didn't look offensive to me."

"But it could be to people in Lemana," Raki stated. "Esera and I saw a few incidents ourselves when we were out. If a scoutmaster intervened, then it couldn't have been anything good."

"What do you think it meant?" Esera asked.

"I don't know. I don't think it had any significance personally." Yunai relaxed her shoulders and pushed her hair back with both hands. "I'm sorry, guys. A lot happened yesterday. I think I'm just overthinking things."

"If the scoutmasters handled everything, I don't think you have anything to worry about," Raki said. "But we should get ready before *we* have something to worry about."

"Agreed."

Yunai grabbed what breakfast was left, and Raki helped Yoel put the food away after Yunai made her plate. Esera studied her from behind. He didn't know where her mind was, but there was more to her words than simply "overthinking things."

"The zonbi on land and in the air are fearsome predators. But the zonbi of the ocean are far more deadly than anything above the water."

Humberto, a scoutmaster with unforgiving scars slashed across his face, lectured his group of cadets. Esera, Moraima, Matagi, Umaru, and several other cadets with strong diving abilities had gathered on one of Taisala's beaches to start their diving training. Other diving groups were scattered across parts of the beach and on the other beaches along Taisala's coasts. Those who couldn't dive tested their ability to fight on top of water on the island's lakes and rivers.

"Water's everywhere," Humberto continued. "No matter where you're assigned, you'll be expected to dive and fight underwater. And fighting underwater, where the physics are different, is a whole other style of combat."

Esera let his mind off its leash. The sun, inviting breeze, and delicious waves made him want to strip down and float away from all this talking. Coast on a wave and catch some rays...

"...so you'll be put on teams of three for the first exercise. You three." Humberto pointed three fingers at Esera, Umaru—and Matagi.

Great. This won't end well.

Humberto continued assigning teams as Umaru and Matagi circled up with Esera.

"Excellent!" Umaru declared. "Our familiarity with each other will make this task go smoothly."

Doubt it. "You're absolutely right, Umaru!"

Matagi remained silent.

"Matagi, do you agree?" Umaru asked.

More silence. Then, "Just stay focused."

"Of course! Focus is what every scout needs."

Yeah. Umaru was oblivious.

"In the field, you won't always get the chance to change into your diving suit on base. So you'll be changing out here." Humberto turned to a wooden box next to him. He synced the box open and used air to toss the diving suits to each cadet. The cadets caught their suits, sharing nervous looks. "You're adults now. And cadets. Figure it out in five minutes, then we dive."

Moraima maneuvered into her suit while still covering her body with her uniform. Some cadets whipped up towers of sand to hide their bodies. Some exchanged suits with others when they realized they had put on the wrong size. Humberto expected them to figure that out, too.

Umaru and Matagi went for it and stripped down.

Esera walked down to the water. He was underage and didn't want to start any awkward conversations, so he changed away from the group. He synced a wall of water up from the ocean and froze it, changing before it melted. He strapped his utility belt around the suit, strapped on his nifoʻoti, then returned to his comrades, where he dropped his uniform and boots. The group followed Humberto out to the middle of the ocean.

"Twenty minutes for the first task," Humberto said, positioning himself to float. "Begin!"

The cadets plotted with their teams or submerged.

Okay, all they had to do was... *Shit. Wasn't listening. Shouldn't have sucked on air like that.*

"I suggest not instigating anything with the other teams," Umaru said.

"Unless they instigate first." Matagi went under.

"Oh, he's difficult. Esera?" Umaru followed Matagi.

"Yup." Esera dived. Best to hang back. He'd follow their lead and figure out what to do.

The cadets dived through the clear waters. Some teams swam further away from the others. Matagi propelled down, his body straight and focused. Umaru mentioned after his fight with Moraima that Matagi possessed enhanced speed. Umaru kicked his feet, and Esera, with enhanced swimming skills, undulated down.

Matagi boosted forward as they neared the ocean floor. Schools of fish scattered when he reached the bottom. Matagi and Umaru searched the immediate area. Esera searched too, but he didn't know what he was searching for. Matagi faced Umaru, and Umaru pointed further down the floor. They swam in that direction, Esera following.

The other teams were out of sight now. The floor grew greener and rugged as they went on until they approached a coral reef. Umaru swam ahead and scoped out the reef from above. Matagi stopped and waited, and Esera followed suit, sinking to the floor. Umaru swam away when a team of cadets shot up. One wielded a forged spear and another a forged machete. The third between them held a small orange flag.

Matagi rocketed after the team, the force throwing Esera off. Umaru waved at Esera, then pointed to Matagi and the other team. He swam after them. Esera trailed behind. Matagi gained on the team. He shoved his arms forward, the resulting force sending strong turbulence upwards. The team separated in time to avoid it—giving Matagi an opening. He puffed up his chest and shot a sharpened tooth at the flag-bearer, syncing his tooth with the water to give it speed. The cadet with the machete used her weapon to block the tooth and swam backward to keep an eye on their advance. Matagi caught the tooth on his way up, then, sticking his hand in his mouth, forged his claws.

Capture the flag. Easy. Esera overtook Umaru and gained on Matagi. He unsheathed his nifoʻoti and swam straight for the flag. But before he made a move, Matagi lunged for it. He slashed the flag-bearer's hands. Blood billowed out, red ink stark against the water.

Again? Seriously?

Matagi snatched the flag, tucked it into his suit, and swam for the surface. Sucking on unfettered anger, Esera whipped up to him with scary speed. The water twisted and turned behind him. He hooked his weapons around Matagi's ankles and dragged him back.

Esera's wild eyes invited Matagi to fight.

Matagi surged at him and swung his claws at Esera. Esera deflected with his weapons. The water made things too damn slow, and Esera wasn't looking to stage a show. He grabbed Matagi and hooked his arms around his torso. Drawing on the store of electricity in his body, another of his enhancements, he squeezed, stunning Matagi. Matagi floated there, the fight still in his eyes. The adrenaline rush left Esera drained as well.

Next thing Esera knew, someone pulled him and Matagi to the surface. Umaru and the other team watched the scene unfold. Humberto dragged the two to the shore and threw their worn bodies on the hot sand. The other cadets scrambled onto the beach.

"I wasn't sure what was happening, so I went for the scoutmaster," Umaru said to them.

"Umaru, is it? Sounds like you have the only ears in this trio," Humberto said, his voice a mountain overlooking a valley. "Want to explain to your team what my instructions were?"

"Y-yes, Master. Each team was to find a flag and bring it back to you. If a team without a flag encountered a team with one, we could fight for it using whatever skills we have."

"Which is what I did," Matagi countered, his senses coming back. "Until that one over there lost his mind."

"*I lost my mind?*" A crater formed in the sand where Esera stood. "You—"

"Both you idiots took shots at this cadet." Humberto directed a hand at the cadet Matagi cut. One of his teammates wrapped a strip of cloth around his hand. His head bobbed back and forth as if he had just been tossed around. "One sliced him open, and the other was so out of control, he sent him spinning in a damn current. 'Whatever skills we have' doesn't mean making me write an incident report."

Esera's gaze froze on the cadet. He forced himself to look away when the reality of his reaction sank in. The water reacted to his anger more than he realized.

"Aren't your scoutmasters teaching you to control yourselves?"

"I followed your orders," Matagi stated. "'Whatever skills.'"

"More like 'whatever kills,'" Esera said. "How did you even—"

"Shut up, both of you. Like tiny, little cacti." Humberto hocked a loogie on the sand and rubbed his nose. "Cadet, you're out for the day. Haul yourself back to base and get yourself looked at. Claws, you're root sewing for the next two tasks. Something calm and sweet for you. Humberto wants a pretty coaster by the time we're done." He pulled a ball of root thread from his pocket and threw it at Matagi. It landed at his feet.

"Fine." Matagi snatched the ball and unwound it.

"And Mr. Feelings, you get to take your anger out on the cliffside for the rest of the day."

Esera turned to the towering rockface further down the beach. "We're punching that thing until your knuckles bruise into a reminder of why you need to keep zero."

"He *purposely* draws blood, and *I* have to punch walls all day?!" The crater grew bigger.

Humberto grinned a grin that let everyone know he was ready to stop talking. "Everyone enjoy the show? Let this be a reminder of what happens when you let your emotions be your judgment. Back in the water!"

Esera balled his hands tight as the cadets returned to the ocean. He looked at Matagi tying roots together, then faced the cliffside. The threat of being sent back home was the only reason he moved his feet away from him.

NINE

IGNACIA

"**M**y cadets are handling themselves well, for the most part. I have a couple who need to learn that doing your duty doesn't always mean being nice, but otherwise, no issues to report." Ignacia sat back down as the scoutmaster next to her stood up to deliver his report. She didn't mind meetings, but she hated these meetings in particular. Scoutmaster meetings were nothing more than a contest to see who taught the best—or, lately, tortured the worst.

Niesh leaned back in her chair at the head of the conference room's table. Ignacia couldn't tell if her old teacher genuinely listened to these empty reports. When the scoutmaster next to her sat down, she braced herself for the stream of bile Humberto was about to spew. They shared Artemisan roots, but she had no respect for this obstinate man, on Lemana.

"Had a couple of cadets be knuckleheads in diving," Humberto said. He pulled a coaster from his pocket and fiddled with it. "Made one sew this for me. Had the other punch rocks the whole day."

It took everything in Ignacia not to set fire to his chair. Esera returned that day with bloody hands and a temper teetering on edge. He had ignored all attempts she made to talk to him.

"Those are yours, right, Ignacia? They'll make pretty good scouts once you clean them up a bit."

Ignacia kept zero, but it wouldn't be long before she started counting. "Not if you think punching walls is a good way to instill control."

"They can tolerate a little extra pain."

"Doesn't mean they should," another scoutmaster said.

A low rumble from the stone floor commanded them to stop. Niesh sat forward, moving for the first time since the meeting started. "Let's segue into that. Tell me about these boys, Ignacia."

Humberto sat back down, and Ignacia stood back up. "Matagi is extremely focused. A good fighter who doesn't hold back. Esera is too, though he does struggle with restraint."

"Esera?" Niesh thought for a second. "One of the cadets with a juvenile record?"

"Yes. So you know what he's capable of."

Humberto put on a self-congratulatory smirk. "And they can both dive, which is perfect. Never know when you need someone to crush a fool's lungs."

Ignacia kept her mouth closed and sat back down.

"I'm looking for cadets with natural fighting ability to help me out with an investigation." Niesh rose and paced around the table. "The details of that are the business of the Circle. I want everyone in this room to start vetting your cadets for potential. Community service starts soon, and the ones you pick will be of the greatest service to the community."

Did Ignacia just serve her cadets to Niesh on a platter Humberto set out? She was familiar with Niesh's teaching style—and it worried her. Especially with her high stress levels. Niesh didn't always make the most rational decisions when she worked beyond her limits.

During her recruiting interviews, Ignacia rejected applicants who came across as aggressive. They tended to become the corrupt scouts that gave the Scouthood its growing negative reputation, especially under the training of the wrong scoutmaster. She would have rejected Matagi if she had interviewed him, and she didn't have a choice with Esera.

"I'm also looking for more mature cadets to serve at the orphanage. The children don't have a Saint to visit them anymore, so Paloma needs cadets who will set an example for them. Vet your cadets for this position as well." Niesh continued pacing. "And the cadets serving at the base hospital this cycle will do more than assist staff. They will be expected to provide the same level of protection the scoutmasters are currently giving."

"Commander, if I may," a scoutmaster began, standing up, "why have untrained cadets serve as guards? They're a liability. The scoutmasters should suffice."

"I agree," Ignacia said. "Hospitals are vulnerable places. That much emotional potential can prove to be a risk."

"You're right. They are vulnerable, which is why I need them to step up this cycle, and I never gave you permission to opine," Niesh snapped at the scoutmaster.

They sat right back down. Ignacia gave the scoutmaster a look of support—and saw Humberto open his mouth from the corner of her eye.

"Think Ignacia needs to learn that doing your duty doesn't always mean being nice."

"Listen, you oaf, I—"

Niesh stopped pacing. "Do you two need to brawl out whatever you have for each other, or can I continue?"

"My money's on Ignacia!" a scoutmaster called out. A few jeered and started calling out numbers.

"No," Ignacia said. Humberto waved a hand and turned away from Niesh.

"Good. Then let's keep going."

Ignacia kept quiet the rest of the evening. These meetings, she *especially* hated these meetings.

TEN

RAKI

Raki watched officials trickle up and down the steps of the fourth parish's council hall. Today was field trip day for all the cadets, their unofficial introduction to the city of Lemana and her people. She stood with her cabin on the hall's grounds, listening to Ignacia speak while taking in her surroundings.

"What can you tell me about Lemana?" Ignacia asked. "What do you know about the island's only city?"

"I know!" Raki raised her hand. "Lemana has twelve parishes, each governed by a representative."

"Yes—"

"It's home to the Plane's only university, Maogatai University, and has the highest level of refugee resettlement. Oh! And the island is the only continent without a military to maintain neutrality."

A second to soak it all in.

"Raki, good job," Ignacia finally said. "Your academic reputation precedes you."

"You were the popular girl more popular girls forgot about, weren't you?" Yoel asked dryly.

Raki glared at the little rat. "I didn't spend my time in school just to—"

"Don't forget who's still speaking here," Ignacia chided.

Raki and Yoel peeled off each other. Esera snickered.

"All good facts," Ignacia continued. "Lemana is an impressive city with a rich history and diverse population. The Scouthood, Cathedral, and the representatives that make up the council do their best to protect her and the whole Plane. But while you're immersed in your training to protect the Natural..." Ignacia walked down the steps, through her cadets, then stood in front of the busy street. "... we can't forget *who* we protect."

The cadets looked out into the plaza before them, at the people. Raki spotted children eating lunch during their school break. Further down, a couple sat on a bench, their body language intimate. Workers and parents and students rushed from one location to the next. And scoutmasters patrolled the streets, their presence a reminder of societal expectations.

"Now, who can tell me what they know about the *people* of Lemana? No facts or stats this time."

Raki pursed her lips and coyly took her eyes elsewhere. An uncomfortable silence hung over the cadets.

"They're dealing with the current climate in their own ways," Yunai said. Raki turned to Yunai, who rubbed her shoulder with her root arm. "The Saint's death, the rise in zonbi... They're reacting because they're scared or angry."

Ignacia nodded. "Anyone else? No? Right. So that's why every cadet is out in the city today. When you become scouts and are sent to your stations, you'll likely live in a location you've never been before. It's important to get to know the people you'll be protecting and their stories.

"We're going to meet some people in the community who have been affected by recent events. I'm sure you all know people from your homelands who have been affected too. So I encourage you to use your experiences to connect with the people you'll meet today."

Raki felt a shift. Ignacia exuded a gentleness her teachers or elders rarely emanated. She was still wary of her scoutmaster, and she didn't think that would change.

"Community service will start soon as part of your training. You'll work directly with people in various capacities based on your background and personality. You'll be assigned to sanctuaries, schools, the Cathedral's orphanage, and more. It won't be as heroic or glamorous as felling zonbi, but it will be to the people you help."

∾

AFTER A TEN-MINUTE WALK from the council hall, the cabin made it to a well-manicured, domed building. The surrounding area was eerily quiet, devoid of the traffic of animals and people. Raki admired the tall hibiscus bushes framing the gate. Their elegantly synced red and white flowers flowed down like loosely braided hair.

"This is the Fourth Parish Hospital, but it's known to the community as 'Aute's House," Ignacia said. She walked up to the gate and flashed her scouting identification card at the guard in the security booth. The guard synced the lock open and opened the gate. "The House serves as a hospital and a rehabilitation center. There are several of these institutions across Lemana. This one was founded by a wealthy couple who wanted to keep their community safe and healthy. They retired back to Fa'atasi many cycles ago, and their Children continue to manage the House to this day."

The cabin walked through the gate and followed Ignacia down the walkway. A few other cabins walked ahead of them, entering the hospital.

Raki noticed the perfect circles of the walkway, the fastidiously cut bushes, the even grass of the lawn. She expected someone to emerge from the bushes and cuss her out if she dared sync a leaf out of place. "You ever see a place this...lined?"

"Rich people love maintaining things," Esera said as he walked beside her.

Ignacia led them into the hospital, which was built more like a home than a medical facility. Coconut leaf mats of varying sizes and quality hung on the pillars of the entryway. Underneath each mat was a name. Works of landscape art hung next to the mats—but better to just call them art. The work that went into them was very little. Names were under them as well.

They passed through a set of doors and into an area that did resemble a hospital floor. Scoutmasters were posted at stations throughout. Raki felt a little embarrassed for her cabin as they passed medics rushing to save their patients. There were crises behind doors and scoutmasters on standby, and the cabin...passed through.

"Many of the patients here are victims of zonbi attacks," Ignacia said as they continued. "You may know zonbi rarely appear in Lemana, thanks in part to the Saint's presence. Now hospitals around the island, including the one on base, are dealing with an influx of people and animals recovering from their injuries."

Ignacia stopped at an open wing with multiple human patients, curtains separating each one. Some were awake, some asleep, and Raki wasn't sure about the state of a couple.

"The patients are no different from you all," Ignacia said. "They had plans for the day, jobs to go to. And these are the lucky ones— many don't make it to a bed."

Raki's eyes met those of an elder who appeared to share her roots. The woman smiled and looked like she wanted Raki to come over. Raki smiled back but didn't move.

"Everyone is here because someone couldn't keep zero. Or someone wasn't doing their job. Or they came to believe something that led them to be hurt. Every action you take as a cadet or scout determines whether someone gets to end their day peacefully—or not at all."

The cabin moved on when Ignacia finished, and Raki was taken aback when they weren't given the chance to meet with the patients personally. The stop felt more like a museum tour than connecting with people in the community. She gave one last look to the elder as they left the room.

A SCOUTMASTER LED the cabin to a detached building behind the hospital. She directed them to an amphitheater where more of the same art hung. Basic furnishings. No touch of the personal. For a place built by rich people to serve the community, 'Aute's House felt pretty empty. Raki shook off her unease and followed the scoutmaster's directives.

Two other cabins waited in the amphitheater, sitting on rows of wooden bleachers. Their scoutmasters stood behind the bleachers, arms crossed and eyes sharp. Before the cadets sat a group of people in a row of chairs. An elderly man with black hair in a fussy top knot and wearing a necklace with a single glass bead sat off to the side.

"Have a seat." The scoutmaster gestured for them to sit. Ignacia joined the scoutmasters behind the bleachers.

"Welcome." The elderly man wasted no time starting when the cabin finished seating. "This is the rehabilitation center at 'Aute's House, a facility dedicated to the healing of troubled adults in the parish. My name is Luafata. We have some of our wards speak to cadets every new training season so you may learn from their mistakes and apply them to your practice."

Something about Luafata's choice of words, his congenial but no-frills affect, made Raki sit up as straight as possible. And she wasn't the only one—others fixed their postures too. Including the wards. Their expressions...they matched the décor of the House, generic faces that revealed no story.

"To maintain privacy, we don't give out any names." Luafata turned to the ward closest to him, a man with light-brown skin and an unshaven face. "Our first ward is a father of two children with a devoted Partner. A spear-throwing coach at a local school. Until he let a bad start to his morning dictate his actions one day."

The man roused himself. "I got into a fight with my Partner that morning. She wanted our family to move away from Lemana because she didn't think it was safe anymore. And I wanted to stay because my family is here... When I practiced with the children later that day, some of them kept bickering about the others who were not as good or losing them points. At one point, I lost it. All I remember were flames. Children screaming..." He didn't continue.

"He became a danger to his family and his students," Luafata said. "Thankfully, his own children did not bear the brunt of his inability to control himself."

After a few seconds, the man continued. "I'm here because I don't want to get mad or frustrated like that again. My loved ones can't see me until I get better."

Raki jerked her body on purpose when she caught herself stiff. Her parents got into arguments all the time, but she had never seen them go off like that, at least not when she was around.

Luafata moved on. "Our next ward failed to act when she needed to the most. And it almost cost a life." If the first ward was fire with no restraint, the woman next to him was water afraid to fall. She looked like she didn't know how to sleep. Her wiry hair, graying early at the roots, hung over her face. "She was training to become an animal surgeon, much like you all are training to become scouts. You can probably imagine where her story goes."

"I-I." Silence. Silence enough to make everyone in the room feel ashamed for her. "I thought... I believed I could be a surgeon...then I had to cut for the first time. It went zonbi and I-I got scared...th-the roots, they..." She just sat there. Her mind retreated to a place only she knew.

"Her fellow residents did not react quickly enough to avoid her emotional reaction. Her fear made sure the roots were hard to pull out from them. They are alive but not well, and they must live with her mistake for the rest of their lives."

The cadets collectively tensed up. A chill in the air passed.

"That's why I chose the Scouthood and not medicine," Raki heard Sega say.

"One slip can cost too much," Umaru said to Sega.

"These people are freaky," Raki whispered to herself. "What kind of person blows up like the first guy?" She felt Esera shrink into himself next to her. When she made the connection, her heart sank. "You know I didn't mean—"

He shook his head. He knew what she implied—and it went beyond aggressive cadets and bullish scoutmasters. Raki slipped her hand into his. Esera squeezed it as much as he could without exacerbating the pain in his bandaged hand. Raki knew he did his best to hide his anger, but she knew how much pain he had to be in.

"Scouts are the examples of zeroing," Luafata continued. "They show us how to behave so that ordinary citizens know how to act to protect their fellow people and the Natural world. When you show control, you encourage others to do the same, keeping everyone safe."

"And if control doesn't keep others safe?" Esera asked under his breath.

Raki knew better than to open her mouth again and rile his

emotions, especially after being reminded of the high cost. Hoping to allay her Brother's painful memories, she placed her other hand on his as Luafata introduced the next ward.

~

RAKI LEFT THE AMPHITHEATER, glad to be out of that uncomfortable space. The wards' stories left a hole in her, and she needed a touch of the Natural to recover.

She scanned the House's lawn. Luafata gave the cadets permission to speak with the wards in private, and Raki wanted to talk with the woman who had been in surgeon training. She spotted her at a hibiscus bush. Raki walked over, almost feeling guilty for stepping on the manicured grass, and tapped the woman's shoulder.

"Ah!" The woman jumped.

"Oh! I'm sorry," Raki said. "I should have said something. I'm sorry."

The woman turned back to the flowers. Raki stood there, feeling awkward for a beat. "Uh, are you braiding flowers?" The woman synced a couple of white hibiscus petals to close and gently twisted their stems together. She didn't respond. Raki kneeled beside her, minding the space between them. "Is that calming?"

No response again. Better to leave her be. Raki got up.

"...it's easy."

Raki stopped, then came back down. She waited for her to continue.

"Flowers can't do anything." When she finished twisting, she synced the blooms back open with the control of a child trying to sync for the first time.

Raki had questions, but where to start? How do you even ask someone who failed in their duties how not to fail in hers?

"The people you protect come before you...always," the woman said through heavy breaths.

Raki watched as she proceeded to braid three hibiscus stems together. She probably already knew why Raki had approached her.

"Nothing else matters."

YUNAI

Yunai strolled through the center, weaving in and out of cadets and wards. She didn't feel the need to talk to any of the wards. Their stories had left her shaken, and that was lesson enough.

She found herself in an art room on the second floor. Several easels were set up, but only two people used them.

"Come in," someone called from behind an easel. "Don't be shy."

Yunai wished she hadn't heard that, but she didn't want to be rude. She entered the room and walked up to the person behind the easel—

"Oh!"

—the woman who had been taken along with her companion for painting that wheel in the city. Yunai expected to see the man from the memorial here and thought the couple would have been let go.

And that made her nervous.

"So you're a cadet," the woman said. She synced a mixture of blue and white paint onto her canvas. "Probably shouldn't have asked your opinion."

"No, it's—" *Okay? You didn't know?* Not becoming words for a cadet to say. Yunai had an example to set. "It wasn't right to do. Or for me to answer."

Yunai examined her painting, and this one she understood. A horizon on the ocean was coming together, a far cry from the abstract wheel on the wall. The painting looked like the ones hanging throughout the House.

"We're not having class till later, so feel free to observe."

Yunai didn't feel comfortable asking her what happened after the scoutmaster took her away, but she wondered if her companion took these classes as well. "Does your partner paint too? Or make the leaf mats?"

The length of time it took the woman to respond made Yunai even more nervous. "No." She focused on a wave's foam, fixating on the spot for longer than Yunai thought necessary.

Move on. "What kinds of things do you draw in class?"

"Luafata tells us. Drawing natural scenes reminds us what's important, and they teach us control." Working the white into the foam had become her singular purpose until she decided she was finished with the spot.

Luafata walked in. He observed the other person and made comments before walking over to the woman's easel. He remained silent. His proximity making her feel weird, Yunai inched away, giving herself more space.

"Be sure to control the waves more next time." He pointed to one that was half an inch higher than the rest. "Softer crests. Less white."

The woman nodded and moved on to the clear blue sky.

"She was one of the few who came here of her own accord. Usually, people are referred to us by the courts." Luafata moved to the other side of the easel, his hands clasped behind his back. "Her punishment would have been much more severe if she hadn't communicated to the Scouthood that her companion was the one to persuade her into unnatural art."

Luafata answered the question Yunai couldn't bring herself to ask about her companion. And she wished he hadn't.

"Always commit to bettering yourself, especially for the sake of others and your community." The woman synced blue paint across the upper half of the easel. "I'm sure it'll make you a better scout."

ESERA

What kind of person blows up—blows up—blows up—

"Damnit." Esera knew his Sister meant no harm, but that didn't stop him from cursing the air the louder the words got. He sat outside the facility, next to the gate. There was *no way* he'd talk to any of those people. What would a bunch of worm brains know about losing control? Know about—

Air.

Esera forced a deep, deep breath into his lungs. *One, two...* He exhaled as the words grew quieter. Afato had taught him to take deep breaths whenever his thoughts ran faster than he could catch them. He admittedly wasn't doing it as often as he should have. It wasn't the same as submerging into a watery abyss, his preferred method of regulating his emotions. He didn't know how he was going to make it through this scouting thing without being threatened with dismissal.

Air, Esera, air.

In and out again. The street before him returned to his senses. He hoped Ignacia wouldn't keep their cabin here for long. He needed a change of scenery.

A cadet walked through the gate and then stopped. Esera looked up.

Matagi.

They locked eyes for a second. Then Matagi turned away and walked to the opposite side of the gate. He leaned against the wall, the tall bushes hiding his face. Esera couldn't imagine someone like him wanting to talk to anyone either.

ELEVEN

IGNACIA

Judging by their stale flesh, Ignacia knew today had worn her cadets down. It was her least favorite part of basic training, the field trip to "connect with the community" and to "remind cadets why they gave their lives to protect others."

It made her feel dirty. Using real people with real pain as props to drive the Scouthood's agenda. Truly understanding those who had been harmed took more than a day tour and a bunch of prepared speeches.

Nevertheless, Ignacia guided her cabin through the memorial field, a field filled with the persistent love of candles, flowers, jewelry, notes, food, and personal items with their own stories to tell. The ones who never made it to a hospital bed and had fallen since the Saint's death. Those whose life stories were more than the tool of a Scouthood Ignacia wasn't sure she believed in anymore.

YUNAI

Yunai walked in tandem with Raki and Esera through the memorial field, the silver of the moon guiding their path. The pressure she felt was immense. One wrong move, one bad judgment call, and the memorial would expand. That guilt would be hers to shoulder for the rest of her life.

"Can you imagine ending up in a place like that?" Raki asked. None of them had said a word since leaving 'Aute's House hours ago. "Going to rehab because you got into a disagreement with your spouse."

Esera, hands in pockets, just shrugged his shoulders. Yunai shook her head, saying nothing. Better the House than under the ground.

"Guess we're too shaken to speak," Raki said when neither responded.

"I mean, we are walking through a mass grave," Esera said, irritation in his voice. He removed his hands from his pockets, then massaged his bandaged hand. Yunai was getting to know Esera as someone who hated taking orders, so she couldn't imagine him punching at rock without some resistance.

"I told you not to mouth off, Esera." Raki looked at his hand. "Anyway, that can never be me. It can't be any of us."

Yunai, still short on words, kneeled before one of the burial mounds. It held only a picture of a family in a frame, two parents and presumably their three children. They were smiling, sitting in a restaurant.

Raki sat next to Yunai on the ground, hugging her knees with her arms. "My mom was a scoutmaster. She used to tell me one simple choice equaled the weight of someone's whole life. The Scouthood is harsh, but I get why."

"It's just like home for me," Yunai finally said, still kneeling before the frame. "Your superiors tell you to do something, and you do it. No questions asked."

"Sounds about right," Esera said. "We're here to take orders and feel nothing and get punished."

"But it's more than that," Raki said defensively. "If we're not strict with ourselves, then, well, we've been getting examples of the consequences all day."

Yunai got up. She didn't want to linger on the picture any longer. Her mind ran through scenarios of what could have happened to the people who had returned to their final resting place.

"Are you okay?" Raki asked. "You've been pretty quiet all day."

Yunai replied with a weak smile. "I'm just reflecting, I guess. I don't want to be the one who fails someone's life. My parents would never let me forget it. Not that it matters anymore."

"It's okay. I get it," Raki said. "You have a brother too, right?"

"Yes, older and the favorite. If he wasn't supportive of me, I'd be bitter about it."

"Raki supports me, and I'm still bitter about her," Esera jested.

"He says that, but we love each other." Raki playfully snuggled against his legs. Esera tched and yanked his leg away. She rolled her eyes. "Bonds are everything in our family. I don't know what I'd do without their support."

"Support or no support, this whole thing is just something to get through." Esera pocketed his hands back and walked on.

After several seconds, Raki got up, sighing, and followed him. She motioned for Yunai to come with. Their conversation made her feel better, but 'Aute's House and the memorial still left Yunai stricken with fear.

But what gave her hope, what gave her the courage to believe in her decision to join the Scouthood, was the statue of the vibrant woman at the end of the field. Imagined from the earth, with roots and fresh flowers covering her body like a dress, and ornamented with elaborate shells was the first Saint who continued to watch over returned spirits—Lemana. The woman who had given everything to save the Plane.

If she could be even a fraction of the woman Lemana was, Yunai could be the scout the Plane needed.

ODOMI

How long since her last pilgrimage? So long that counting was inconsequential. Odomi came here often for her mission under the guise of conducting medical research. But to open her spirit, to release the agony inflicted upon her by a world so repressed, rarely had she descended upon this most sacred of sites—Vaiola.

Vaiola was an enigma, a wonder neither science nor synchronization could explain. The ancient swamp, with its infinite pathways and titanic roots, swallowed the two islets west of Lemana. Once a pilgrimage site open to the whole Plane, the Cathedral had restricted its access generations ago, damning it as unnatural because of their inability to explain its behavior. They couldn't eliminate it like everything else they condemned, so now only cadets in field training and persons with clearance were allowed. A travesty.

Vaiola reminded Odomi how connected she was to those bonded with her, alive and returned. Her importance in their lives in all seasons.

"Oh, my son, why..." Odomi looked to the quiet of the silver moon for comfort. She needed its light to help her walk with words that never became easier to hear, no matter how much time had passed...

"You can't expect me to just sit here! Not when our people, who have a right to be here, are being slaughtered in front of our eyes!"

"I'm not telling you to do nothing. I'm telling you to consider the danger! They'll slaughter you, too, and then what? What will you have achieved?"

"Then you sit there. Sit there and ask for your destruction so you don't have to wait patiently for it. I will take mine to them."

...those last words she heard from her son, she gave them to the moon.

On the anniversary of her son's death, Odomi sat before Vaiola, invisible to all. She pulled her mini recorder from her bag and hooked it to roots that could take a charge. She snapped the device on and turned it to a gumbe drum beat, one her son played and recorded for her a long time ago. The music, rooted in the culture of the nomadic peoples, was lively in tempo and high in spirit.

Odomi shuffled her feet as the drum set out. She stepped through memory, bending to scenes and sounds that flashed through her mind. The drumming intensified. Her limbs remembered their rhythm—and her son appeared before her, banging on his drum, his face so happy.

The grass beneath her swayed, and the wind around her kicked up. The roots bent back with her agony, stretched as far as her longing, and swelled to meet the size of her love. She forgot this sometimes, the ability of the Natural to dance with the heart.

Instead of the weapon the Cathedral and the Scouthood forged it into. They had turned the Natural into a tool of the mundane, a weapon of control and something to be controlled. Stripped of all its sexuality, its inspiration. The Plane was leaving its humanity behind, and life would soon fall with it too.

Her son faded away. Odomi collapsed to the ground as the drumming continued, her tears flowing. Today, on the anniversary of a murder she blamed herself for every day, Odomi vowed on her son's spirit that she would bring Revival to the Plane.

PALOMA

Paloma entered the Cathedral's mausoleum as she did every night. With support from her Sister, Niesh, and Ibrahim's cocktail of concoctions, she had finally achieved some semblance of peace. She was ready to make this the last visit to her dearly departed Leonardo.

She approached the coffin in the middle of the mausoleum designated for recently deceased Saints. Roots curled around the coffin's base, and dried flowers sat on top. Paloma lit a small torch on one finger and lit the violet candles on stands that encircled the coffin. The widow spoke her final words to her Partner in the loneliness of the mausoleum. Now, one last look.

Lacking the skill to sync the heavy cover off, Paloma pulled the heavy slab forward using all the strength of her body, careful not to throw the flowers off. She walked up to the coffin's head, waiting a second as she always did before peering into the coffin.

Nothing could prepare her.

Her screams tore through the Cathedral and ripped into the night as she looked into the face of a man who was not her Partner.

PART 11

8th Month of the 801st Cycle, ES

TWELVE

RIZA

J ust a little longer. Just a bit more. Then they could take a break from performing this façade.

Riza leaned against the rail of the passenger ship. They had been staring at Taisala's horizon since the island faded into view and had no intention of looking away until the ship docked. Lemana made no promises for their future, but Artemisa was a graveyard of a life they no longer wanted.

"Riza."

They didn't notice that their personal guard had walked up behind them. They continued looking outward. "Yes."

"I'm only asking because I've cared for you since before you were born." Their guard rested a hand on Riza's back. "Are you absolutely sure you want to stay? Your mother will not let anyone come back for you."

"Absolutely." Just a little bit more, and they could start over. Whatever that meant. "I have no reason to return."

"Alright then," their guard said, removing his hand. "I'll gather your things. Should be landing soon." He walked off.

Riza kept their gaze fixed ahead of them.

BRAULIO

Braulio finished wrapping a clean bandage around the sky-blue rabbit's burned leg. As calm as its coloring, the rabbit looked into the eyes of its companion, who stood by the examination table. A resident shadowing Braulio stood to the side, observing.

"Thank you so much!" the girl cried. "The other rabbit just started breathing fire. This one couldn't get away in time."

Braulio had seen all kinds of animals do all sorts of things, but fire-breathing rabbits would never not surprise him. He was glad he was able to squeeze them in before another zonbi-related incident threw off his schedule. "Just make sure to change the bandage every day, and your rabbit should heal up fine."

Braulio set the rabbit in the girl's cushioned basket. She waved to him and left the exam room with a sprinkle in her step. He smiled. Healing animals was his main source of joy on this Plane.

"Don't think children can't handle seeing injuries, no matter how ugly," Braulio said to the resident as he washed his hands. "Some are stronger than you think—and some have seen worse than most adults."

The resident nodded and helped Braulio clean up.

"Uh, mister?"

Braulio turned to the doorway, the girl's back to him. She looked straight up. He and the resident stepped out onto the walkway of the sanctuary's second floor—but he didn't need to look up to see the zonbi infestation smeared against the outside of the glass ceiling. They made no noise or movement—and that disturbed Braulio more than the sheer number of them.

"Take her into the room and make sure she keeps calm," he told the resident. "This is one thing she doesn't need to see. Make sure rabbit doesn't see either." Braulio couldn't handle putting down another innocent animal if it somehow managed to fall.

The resident ushered the girl into the room, then closed the door. Medics and residents stared up at the mass. They were so stuck together, Braulio couldn't tell what animal, or animals, they were made from. And why weren't they moving? Zonbi never stood still.

Then Braulio wondered how long the zonbi had been there. Where were these damn scoutmasters? They swarmed every corner of the hospital, but Braulio saw none as he scanned the first and second floors. Most hospital workers had little to no fighting ability, and if the infestation decided to move...

He heard heavy footsteps coming from the sanctuary entrance. He looked over to see Niesh, the Grand Scoutmaster, make her way to the middle of the main hall. Ibrahim, the Chief of Medicine, followed behind her in his easy manner of walking.

"What's the point of flooding the hospital with your people if they disappear when they're needed?" a medic asked from below.

"Niesh is trying to see something," Ibrahim said. He looked around. "I hope everyone standing around here doesn't have patients."

Those who did scrambled back to their duties, while some stayed. Braulio stayed too. He also wanted to see something.

"See what?" the medic demanded. "What on the Plane would you risk our safety to look for?"

Niesh didn't respond, just kept looking up.

"Oh, settle down. She has scoutmasters in position on the roof." Ibrahim turned in a circle as he looked up. "This pack of feline things is peculiar. We saw them charge all the way here from the city, from every alley and sewer. Then they scramble onto the roof and...stop." He looked back down at the medic. "Wouldn't you be curious?"

The medic shrugged her shoulders and threw up her hands. "You're the chief."

"What is she doing now?"

Braulio turned to Siaka, who walked up to him. Siaka hadn't slept in their apartment much since their run-in at the greenhouse. Odomi probably needed more support than Braulio realized.

"That's an answer we're all waiting for," Braulio said. He turned back to the floor but studied Siaka from the corner of his eye. He still wanted to know why Siaka had snuck into the hospital that night. "Where's your Mom? Maybe she can knock some sense into Niesh."

"She's—watch out!"

The zonbi pressed against the glass with their paws, and Braulio saw now that they were cats, or cat-like. The force of their weight on the glass alone would break it, forget about them attacking. What were they waiting for? The cat things pressed harder, harder until web-like cracks formed in the glass. Then, on the stroke of an invisible maestro, the cats *screamed—screamed—screamed*. Braulio and Siaka slapped their hands over their ears. The sound of fury invaded their bodies.

Niesh didn't move.

A pane of glass shattered. The zonbi poured into the sanctuary with haste. A festering disease, each cat body leaked onto, under, through other parts of the whole. They melted into one morass, claws dripping onto the floor like melted snow. Debris accumulated from the street crumbled from its flesh. *Screaming. Screaming.* The feline at the tip stretched its only leg out, reaching in desperation for Niesh.

Niesh took five steps back. Ibrahim and everyone on the floor got out of the zonbi's way. The mealy glob vomited onto the floor. *Screaming. Screaming.* Braulio watched as it spread across the floor. Niesh said something. She continued to back up as the zonbi continued spreading.

Braulio didn't give a shit if they were curious. He cared that they felled the zonbi now.

The medic became exasperated. She launched words at Niesh, who continued to act as if replying to anyone was beneath her. Ibrahim replied for her, and the medic lashed back, arms flying everywhere—understandable but not smart in the presence of zonbi.

The medic met a melted casserole of feline limbs and organs. And the mass would have engulfed her if not for Niesh's quick reflexes. With a spiked metal glove forged onto a hand, Niesh grabbed and crushed the arm of the zonbi that pushed out of the mass to attack the medic. She ripped the limb off and slammed it on the floor. The zonbi's screams intensified, then broke into a cacophony, screams falling on top of one another. It jerked and seized. Braulio and Siaka dropped their hands, Braulio's ears still ringing. The medic fell to her knees.

"It wouldn't have gone wild if you had kept yourself in check," Braulio heard Niesh say loudly. "Clean this up."

Braulio watched as scoutmasters pulled out cracked windowpanes and dropped down from above, their bodies secured with roots. They surrounded the zonbi, then ran around it with the roots, squeezing it. It struggled against the pressure, its dying screams a cry for release. The scoutmasters tightened the roots until the crying stopped. The roots sagged, then slumped to the side.

Niesh burned the part she ripped off and synced the smoke through the opening in the ceiling.

Braulio wondered what the point of it all was. "They really just barged in here to watch that thing scream. And now we have no ceiling." Braulio looked at Siaka, who was fixated on the scene below. "I don't think I've ever seen you *not* say something smart when called for."

Siaka brought his attention back to Braulio. His companion gave him an easy smile. "I gotta tell Mom about this. She needs to hear about it before she sees it."

"Right..."

Siaka took off as quickly as he had come. Braulio almost started after him until his resident called for him from the room. He forgot about him and the girl in all the madness. Braulio gestured for them to come out.

Upon seeing the damage, the girl gasped. The rabbit burrowed deeper into the basket. "Are we safe?"

Braulio gave her a long look before turning back to the scene. He didn't know what answer to give her.

"So they've gone from unnerving the medics to letting us be threatened." Mirta sat next to Siaka and across from Braulio in the city train. Flashes of color passed by as they rode through the parishes. "If I wasn't in surgery, my machete would have spoken sooner than Niesh's fist."

Braulio smirked. Mirta wore sleeves of metal on her arms that she forged into machetes when needed. Not only was she a gifted surgeon, but she was also one of the few medics who could hold her own in a fight. "You against the GS? I'd love to see that."

Braulio looked over at Siaka, who gazed through the window. Mirta followed Braulio's line of sight to him. She clasped Siaka's hand and squeezed, the touch bringing him back to his companions.

"Is Odomi okay?" Mirta asked. "I feel like I haven't seen much of her lately."

"You know how she gets around this time," Siaka said, stroking her hand in response. "Her son's anniversary never gets easier."

Braulio completely forgot. Odomi had a son who died cycles ago. She never spoke about him at length. Braulio didn't know how he died, but this time of the cycle was always hard for her, which explained the passionflower. He guessed Siaka didn't announce himself to the scoutmaster that night at the greenhouse out of respect for her privacy.

"She tends to drift away, so Son number two has to keep her grounded."

"And a busy hospital has to be overwhelming," Mirta said.

"Then I hope chewing Niesh and Ibrahim out will lift her spirits." Braulio grabbed his bag when the train slowed to a stop at the station.

"Sure you don't want to do dinner with us?" Mirta asked. "We're getting pumpkin salad delight. You can bring your companion!"

"I'm good. They're not exactly a people person." Braulio stood up. "You two have fun doing whatever it is you do when I'm not around."

Mirta snatched her hand away from Siaka's. "You'll take any chance, won't you?"

Siaka shifted in his seat, doing this and that.

Braulio winked at them and disembarked onto the platform. He waded into the late afternoon crowd and navigated to the street leading to his companion's house. Thinking on it now, he probably should have invited Riza out. Siaka, with his brand of charming stoicism, and Mirta, with a pleasantness that could hold the sharpest of thorns, could make them feel some sense of ease. Because Braulio wasn't sure he could.

He walked the quiet residential streets until he spotted the old white house. It looked more picturesque in the childhood pictures Riza showed him once. Seeing it in person, it looked like it had been unloved for ages, with patches of brown where grass once lived, and roots struggling to hold themselves up.

Braulio walked up to the door, green mice scuttling out of the way. He almost knocked but tried the doorknob first. Unsurprisingly, the roots were unlocked. Braulio entered and followed a woman's voice into the living room. He entered the room, coughing when the dust hit him. The woman, dressed in a gray skirt suit, acknowledged his presence. Riza turned his way, barely meeting his eyes, before turning back to the table where they sat with the woman. Sheets of paper were strewn across the table, and Riza studied the one in front of them. Braulio took a seat on a couch in the corner of the room—then bolted right back up when something inside it moved. Standing it was.

"This last document acknowledges that the university handed your father's house to you and that they can't take it back for any reason," the woman said. Braulio recognized her as Riza's parents' lawyer. "Once signed, it's yours."

Riza pricked a finger with a needle. Drops of blood dripped onto the paper. They pressed their thumb on the blood, officially signing the document.

"Great! I'll get these to the council hall." The lawyer stood up and gathered the papers, careful not to smudge the blood signature. "Congratulations, Riza! The house is now yours."

"The family's," Riza said flatly. They pushed themself up.

"Right. But since you're seventeen, it's yours to do as you wish." She waited a second before going in for a bear hug. Riza didn't reciprocate. "Again, I'm so sorry for your loss. Your father was a great man." She let go, straightened out her skirt, threw Braulio a smile, and left.

Braulio eyed Riza. Poor woman probably struggled to carry the conversation. "She's gotta be cringing all the way back to the ship," Braulio said, stepping forward. "Returning a hug couldn't—"

Riza turned to face him. And Braulio saw what his companion, who shared his Artemisan roots, had been holding in for months. For cycles. Tears flooded their black amber eyes. Grief and fear had washed out their skin, its hue once goldenrod, and it looked like they let the water fall on their short, dark brown hair whenever they showered.

Braulio opened his arms. Riza had to push themself to come to him. They embraced, Riza crying silently. Braulio held them close, his childhood adventure buddy, his lifelong companion whom he hoped would forgive him for leaving them alone.

AFTER A JOURNEY from Artemisa and a release of bottled-up emotions, Riza had passed out on the couch. The only zonbi their emotions attracted were the mice in the couch, which Braulio easily dispatched. Braulio left Riza to rest while he tidied up the house. He wiped away most of the dust and opened the windows to sync fresh air inside. Thankfully, Riza's father had been neat and owned few possessions.

Braulio entered the small kitchen and peeked into the thawed-out fridge. A few near-empty containers of spoiled food and a jug of foul-smelling juice. Riza, with an enhanced tolerance for expired food, could stomach the rot, but he'd rather not let his companion eat moldy food. Braulio threw it all out and put his concoctions in the fridge—then he had a hunch.

He went back to the living room, where Riza's unpacked bags were. He shook them all, careful not to wake Riza, until he heard liquid sloshing around. It sounded like a bottle had been wrapped with a thick layer of cloth to prevent anyone from hearing it, but Braulio's hearing was too strong. He unzipped the bag and dug for the bottle. He found not one but four medium-sized bottles containing a clear liquid. He wasn't surprised.

Braulio returned to the kitchen and drained the bottles down the sink. He got to the third when he heard Riza shuffle on the couch.

"I was going to empty them," Riza said when they entered the kitchen.

"Down which hatch?" Braulio set the empty bottle on the counter and opened the last one. His nose twitched at the smell of hard alcohol. He'd never understand the appeal of this stuff. "Taisala's prohibition laws aren't as lax as Artemisa's. You know that."

"Nothing's lax about this place." Riza opened the cupboards.

"Then you know you can't have this here." Braulio chased the alcohol with the cleaning mixture he used to clean the surfaces, then ran the tap for a few seconds. He turned it off and faced Riza.

Riza stopped with the cabinets and shook an invisible force off their shoulders. They gripped their hands on the counter. "I feel him everywhere," they said, taking deep breaths. "There's anger all over the house."

Braulio knew Riza was different. The Natural would label them unnatural. He didn't understand how or why they could do the things they did or feel the things they felt—Riza didn't either—but he knew he had to protect his Sibling from a world that would damn their emotions and curse their life.

"We should get rid of everything, then," Braulio said. "Get new furniture. It's all nasty, anyway."

"And the walls? The floor?" Riza took their hands off the counter, shook them, and crossed their arms.

Braulio needed to say something, but what? What was there to say to a companion he hadn't seen or spoken to in over a cycle? He could ask what their family planned to do now that their father was gone. But "family" was a word that would lead to specific thoughts. Thoughts that would lead to memories. Memories that would bring up feelings of anger and regret. Neither needed that this soon.

So Braulio would support Riza in the way they needed now. The hard conversations would come when they were ready to come. All Braulio knew was that Riza needed to understand why their father, a former teacher at Maogatai University and a well-respected man, would take his own life.

THIRTEEN

IGNACIA

"Your surroundings can work to your advantage or disadvantage. Use them as your cover as you would your offense."

Near a river, Ignacia watched Raki, Estefania, Yoel, and Moraima maneuver through dense bush, roots, and murky waters. She pitted Raki and Estefania against each other and Yoel against Moraima. The double one-on-one brawl would test their ability to stay focused, take stock of their surroundings, and adapt. Ignacia and the rest of the cadets observed from the other side of the river.

"Combat is unpredictable," Ignacia said. "You have to contend with other opponents, your comrades, distractions, and a landscape that can change at any second."

Estefania took a fighting stance on an elevated root. Blunted macana in hand, she slashed her forged metal blade upward at the coconut tree in front of her, small daggers shooting out from her weapon. Raki, who punched gusts of wind at Estefania from the treetops, jumped up using synced air to dodge the daggers. But they only managed to cut down the coconuts.

With a sleight of her hands, Ignacia synced the root Estefania stood on further up and moved another root on the river's edge closer to the bank. Estefania took notice instinctively and kneeled to gain balance. Now at eye level, Raki continued punching gusts at her, Estefania moving her body to avoid the blows.

Ignacia kept an eye on Raki. Estefania moved with enhanced dexterity, was a versatile forger, and could fight hand-to-hand, so she was tough to fight head-on. Raki knew this and had decided to take her on from a distance. Ignacia was curious to see how she handled Estefania's level of skill.

A few yards away, Yoel and Moraima engaged in close combat on top of the river, close to the bank. Yoel was a more capable fighter than Moraima, but Moraima had the advantage of being a skilled diver. Yet Moraima had done very little diving during their match. A strike of roots from underwater would have incapacitated Yoel quickly. Instead, Moraima only dove to escape Yoel's iced jabs. Esera, Matagi, or Umaru would not have hesitated to take the opportunity.

"Few minutes left. Make them count!"

Estefania jumped down from the root and dashed for the coconuts. Raki started to punch air down—then instead bombed down to the ground, earth gauntlets first. Estefania jumped back before Raki cratered her. Raki crashed into the ground with a powerful impact, recovering her stance swiftly.

Good, Ignacia thought. *Estefania was vulnerable from above, and she took the opening.*

"Can't be up to any good with these coconuts," Raki said. Ignacia took a closer look and saw that Raki had shattered the shells on impact.

Estefania replied with a one-shoulder shrug and a smirk. She forged her macana into two longer daggers. The moment she went in for Raki, Yoel sent Moraima flying back to the ground using her own roots as a sling. Raki got out of the way before Moraima hit the tree, and Estefania scraped it with a dagger, missing Raki and nearly striking Moraima.

Ignacia raised her hands. Time to test their wits.

Raki raised her fists in a fighting stance—then looked up and down her body when she felt coconut water stuck to her skin.

"Not what I planned," Estefania said, syncing her weapons back into metal bracelets, "but Ignacia will love it." She synced the water over Raki's body like bugs looking for a bite of blood. Poor Raki slapped at her arms and torso.

Moraima got back up, rubbing her head, and Yoel charged at her from the riverbank. Ignacia synced the roots out of the ground, swinging their bodies in every direction. Moraima gained more time to recover with the protection the roots provided her. Yoel navigated the new obstacles with some difficulty. When he reached Moraima, they resumed their fight, Moraima striking at him through openings in the moving roots. She had an advantage again, and Ignacia concluded this advantage was fairer to Moraima than the one she had on the water.

A root shadowed Estefania, breaking her concentration when she looked behind her. Raki, not one to forget a lesson, moved in. One hand grabbed Estefania's shoulder, and the other wrapped around the back of her bent knee. Drawing on enhanced strength, she lifted her opponent over her head and threw her toward the river—and Estefania would have hit the water instead if not for the root Ignacia synced in the way. Not on purpose, of course.

Estefania *smacked* into the root. The cadets made a low "*ooooh.*"

"Time!"

Raki cupped her hands over her mouth. When the shock passed, she raced to Estefania to help her comrade up. Yoel walked across the river, and Moraima decided to swim over, a winner undecided between the two.

"Master, was that not—"

Ignacia raised a hand to Umaru, already anticipating that he would question Estefania's knockout. "That was not."

The cadets laughed or sighed.

She continued when the four made it over, wrapping a caring arm around Estefania's head. "You're all progressing well. And I'm happy to see you're learning from your past matches. As our training continues, you'll start to learn essential skills in addition to sharpening your combat skills. Remember, you need to demonstrate proficiency in six of the nine competencies to be sworn in as a scout—cooking, shelter making, diving, root work, first aid, proficient syncing, camouflage, night navigation, and one style of martial art. Some of these you've started unofficially. Official skills training will start soon, but today—"

"Community service assignments!" Sega couldn't contain her anticipation, and her excitement gave way to side chatter. The cadets stopped when Ignacia raised her hand again.

"You'll carry out your service twice a week—"

"Six hours each day, under supervision, until field training..." Her cadets echoing the information she gave them days before was almost annoying, but at least they were paying attention. Did she ever have a training class this squirrely before?

"C'mon, we know," Obi said. "Just tell us!"

Ignacia rolled her eyes, then went on. "Yunai and Umaru, you two will be working with the residents at the hospital's sanctuary. They need extra protection, and you two are the cabin's best strategic fighters."

Yunai nodded and smiled, her eyes drifting off somewhere. Umaru, surprisingly, nodded solemnly without a word.

"Moraima, Obi, and Yoel, you will be placed at primary schools across the city. And Sega, you will help out at Maogatai University."

They whispered among each other, facial expressions in differing levels of acceptance. School placements were the least liked. Nothing bummed a cadet out more than going right back to school.

"Estefania." Ignacia smiled at her combat princess when Estefania looked lovingly at her, her brown eyes sparkling. "You'll be back at 'Aute's House with Luafata."

The love turned to hate. Estefania broke away from her embrace. "*That* creepy place? Why can't I—"

She stopped when Ignacia's expression swapped humor for sternness.

"Yes, Master."

"Raki..." Her little overachiever came to life as if she didn't just throw Estefania face-first into a root. Niesh and Paloma needed someone special for this placement. Ignacia hoped Raki's interview spiel about being there for others who couldn't be there for themselves was true compassion and not an emotional grab. "You have the honor of working in the Cathedral's orphanage. You're one of my more responsible cadets, so I believe you'll be perfect for this role."

Everyone oohed and aahed, and Yoel said something smart, but Raki didn't hear him. Ignacia couldn't tell if she was stunned or disappointed.

"Lastly, Esera and Matagi...you'll also be helping out in the Cathedral." The oohs and aahs hit a fever pitch. Matagi brushed off the attention, but Esera brimmed with excitement.

"Looks like you're stuck with me for life," Esera said, shaking an absent Raki by her shoulders. His Sister didn't realize he was talking to her.

"With the Saint's assistant gone, they'll need support with clerical tasks of all kinds." The lie was necessary but uncomfortable to speak. Even as her former cadet, Ignacia couldn't imagine what kind of training awaited them under the Grand Scoutmaster.

Esera thought for a second. "Whatever, I'll take it!"

"You'll report to your supervisors on your first day. We'll talk more over dinner."

The cadets chatted incessantly on their trek back to base. Ignacia followed them from behind, her children she was getting to know and understand. She hoped, on Lemana, that those with harder placements would be resilient enough to make it through the rest of basic training.

NIESH

"What do you make of that scene in the sanctuary?" Sitting on the window ledge, Niesh looked out at Taisala's hills. They reminded her of Tributary's ancient hills, powerful and all-knowing.

"Your scoutmasters inspected every room and said they found no evidence of emotional mismanagement. Except for that medic, anyway." Ibrahim sipped his tea from the conference room table. "Shame I had to let her go. She was a good worker."

Niesh let the night air calm her troubled mind before she responded. "I want to keep tabs on that hospital. That was no anomaly."

"Of course, dear." Ibrahim set his cup on the table. "Executions, hunter training, grave robberies... Will you ever get any sleep?"

Niesh synced off her armband and forged oblong shapes with the metal. The movement helped settle a mind racked with suspicion and anger—and fear. "I don't know who did it or why they did it. But the Saint's missing corpse won't stay missing for very long. And we're going to make an example of every unnatural threat that dares undermine the Cathedral."

FOURTEEN

RAKI

Breaking up fights Esera got into. Getting her first and only behavioral report from school. Her first breakup. Nothing in her life would be as awful an experience as this.

Raki stepped into the Cathedral's courtyard, an expansive lawn that filled her with primal dread. The air weighed on her like an omen, like the very act of stepping onto the sacred ground was a crime punishable by death. Save for the scoutmasters on duty, the area was empty, silent. She remembered seeing this place in newspapers after the Saint's death—crowds rocked with fear, a dead body on the ground...

No trains stopped anywhere near the Cathedral grounds, so Raki had to take a long walk through the plain to reach the building. No other vegetation, not even animals, were permitted on the lawn. A scoutmaster served as her escort from the time she disembarked from the train in the city and had dispensed that trivia. If he meant to break the ice and calm her nerves, he had failed.

"The orphanage is behind the Cathedral," the scoutmaster said. "It's the only place you'll have access to while you're serving. You'll need clearance for anywhere else, and I wouldn't worry about getting that."

"Okay..." That one word and "thanks" were the only words Raki had managed to say since arriving.

"Did you know Saint Leonardo was the founder of the orphanage? People assume it's always been here."

"Yeah." Three words now.

"I think you're the last cadet to arrive. The other orphanage cadets are in orientation, and the ones doing the assistant's work had to get here before the sun."

After what felt like the entire morning, they made it to the Cathedral's entrance. A pair of scoutmasters guarded a looming metal door, locked by tangled roots. The scoutmaster flashed his identification card to his comrades. Acknowledging it, they untangled the roots, their movements in perfect sync. After a pause, the door burrowed into the earth, and the two scoutmasters on the other side of the door stepped aside. Raki noticed the scoutmasters working on the Cathedral grounds wore scarves embossed with gold, as opposed to the plain viridian scoutmasters typically wore.

The contrast between the lawn and the inside shocked Raki's senses. The inner courtyard cradled a garden, a rainbow of flowers and butterflies. A statue of Lemana sat in the middle of a pond. Lost in eternal dreams, she gazed lovingly into the still water.

"Paloma, the Saint's widow and the orphanage's supervisor, enjoys sitting out here," the scoutmaster said.

Raki nodded and followed her escort through another door and into the main hall. Devoid of any furniture, it reminded her of 'Aute's House. Portraits hung in niches on either side, violet candles illuminating them. Raki recognized them as the past Saints, people from all backgrounds, all connected to the sacred power only Lemana, and those she chose, wielded.

Raki noticed they passed no doors or stairs, but her mind was too saturated with new sights to wonder why. They exited through the end of the hall's gate and passed through another garden, this one less lush. A brick wall encircled the area, and roots formed a tight dome above.

"Here we are." They entered a modest building that was about a third of the Cathedral's size.

The uproar of voices startled her. The scoutmaster ran ahead and

Raki trailed him. They ended up in a bedroom that reminded Raki of the cabin's quarters. Crafts and drawings hung on the walls, and the room's beds were bunked instead of single. Some children sat on their beds, while others huddled in a corner. The ones in the corner taunted a girl hanging upside down from the ceiling, her bare feet synced with the stone.

"Where's Paloma?" the scoutmaster asked.

"Out there," another girl answered.

Raki looked around but couldn't figure out what "out there" meant. She saw no other doorway apart from the one they entered through.

"Wait here. I'll be back." The scoutmaster took off before Raki had a chance to protest. He did *not* just leave her here alone with this scene.

"She has to get down before Miss Paloma gets back, auntie." Yet another girl, similar in skin tone to Raki, tugged her hand.

Raki looked down at the girl, then back at the ceiling.

Nothing, absolutely *nothing* in her life would be as awful an experience as this. Children were...she didn't hate them, but she didn't love them either. More accurate to say she didn't know what to do with them.

"He should have stayed, and you should have gone." The girl on the ceiling looked directly at Raki with eyes of coal. It took Raki a second to understand what she meant. The scoutmaster would have been better equipped to handle...whatever this was.

"Why are you up there?" Raki asked, moving into the middle of the huddle.

"Because she stole extra grapes for breakfast, and she knows it!" a boy cried.

"She has to act special," the first girl added. "It's because she's bloodless."

"Bloodless?" Raki gave the girl an odd look. "What does that mean?"

"It means they think they're allowed to beat me up," the girl on the ceiling said.

"It means she's a freak," a child called from behind.

"It means she's gonna stay here forever!" another shouted. "No one will ever take her home."

"Okay! Children. Why don't you go back to whatever you were doing and let me talk to her." Raki waved them back. She waved harder when they didn't obey the first time. They finally moved away, some with eyes still glued to the girl. "Why don't you come down now?"

"Go away, you cadet."

A sensation shivered through Raki. The spirit of her father over-took her, who gave her tongue lashes whenever she gave him attitude. This child was not going to talk to her like that. Suppressing the urge to give this girl her own tongue lashing, she said, "Look. I'm trying to help you, okay?"

"So you can help yourself."

Raki didn't know what she meant, but she was already tired of this. "You're not the only one who can climb walls." She started climbing when the girl suddenly dropped to the floor.

"Toya, please don't aggravate your new mentor."

Raki turned to see a woman, the scoutmaster, and a couple of other people rush in. She slid down the wall. The girl, Toya, hung her head down, her brunette, chin-length hair draping over her face. The other two people tended to the children, while the woman and the scoutmaster walked up to Toya.

"Why were you on the ceiling again?" the woman asked, kneeling in front of Toya. She placed a hand on her shoulder and moved her hair from her face, revealing dry skin. "Didn't I say to come get me if this happened again?"

"Why?" Toya spat, moving her head away. "So they can bully me for being a crybaby, too?"

The woman sighed and turned to the other two adults. She gave them a command with her eyes. Raki heard them reprimand the children.

"I'm sorry," the woman said. She stood up and faced Raki. "You must be Rakiatu. I was out back doing a little orientation with the other cadets. I'm Paloma. I'll get you caught up soon, but it seems you already met your mentee."

"It's okay..." Raki said. Ignacia had mentioned that while cadets generally worked with groups of children, Raki was specifically assigned to mentor one of the girls. She examined Toya. She looked older than the other children, with her severe eyes and developing figure. Healing wounds pocked her brown skin. Raki had seen Esera with skin like that many times, and that gave her some idea of what to expect.

"Uh, one of the kids said she's—the word bloodless," Raki continued.

Paloma glanced at Toya, who stood frozen in silence since they started talking, then back at Raki. Raki didn't like the way Paloma's eyes shifted from corner to corner. "People who can't sync because of blood disorders are sometimes called bloodless as a slur, but that's not what the children mean. It's not that Toya can't sync. She just chooses not to. And that's one of many things she needs help with."

YUNAI

Yunai, Umaru, and the other cadets assigned to the sanctuary gathered in its lobby. They tried paying attention to Odomi, the Hospital Director, who briefed them on their placement, but the workers repairing the glass roof distracted them. The cadets weren't on base that day, but they had heard the news of the bizarre zonbi attack.

"I know the damage is glaring, but try to pay attention, please," Odomi said.

The cadets returned their full attention to her. Yunai couldn't help but notice how exhausted she looked. The medic life had to be tough.

"The safety of our patients is our highest priority, so even as you serve as their bodyguards, you'll be under the strict supervision of our residents. I would also take this time to get to know them. When your field training starts, they'll be the ones making sure you don't die when you decide to eat the wrong plant."

Yunai couldn't tell if she was being sincere or sarcastic.

"You have your pairings and assignments. Direct any further questions to your resident. Have a good first day." She left the group on their own.

Yunai's partner was Farid, a cadet from two cabins over. He

scanned the document Odomi gave them at the start of their briefing. "Resident's name is Braulio. His room's on the second floor."

"Great! I'm excited to—"

Farid walked off. Maybe he didn't hear her? Yunai shook it off and followed him.

Farid knocked on a door on the second floor. He opened it when they heard a loud "come in!" The pair walked in on a resident wrestling a burned orange goat on the ground. Yunai shot forward.

"Stay back!" the resident, Braulio, shouted. "And close the door!"

She stopped in her tracks, and Farid shut the door. "You'll get hurt!" Yunai cried, her anxiety rising.

Braulio tried restraining the goat with roots, but it kept syncing them off. It kicked the desk with its hooves, knocking down tools, and kicked a cart across the room.

He would certainly get hurt. Yunai needed to take action. She synced with water from her water pouch, froze it into two spears, and launched them at the animal.

"Don't!"

The goat kicked Braulio off in his distraction. In one moment, the goat's orange soured into a rotten fruit peel. Thick fluid leaked from its mouth, and its black eyes went blank. The goat was falling.

Yunai and Farid leaped out of the way when it charged for the door, leaving a trail of mucus. It rammed the door open with a headbutt and then threw itself over the railing, plummeting to the first floor. Yunai heard bones crack. The three rushed outside to see the zonbi race on three legs to the end of the sanctuary, a scoutmaster chasing after it. The zonbi slammed its head on the rear exit door—slammed its head on the door—slammed its head on the door until matter oozed out. Slammed its head on the door until the movement became mechanical. Until it stopped. The scoutmaster inspected the mess when she made it to the door.

Shock gripped Yunai by her throat. She had never seen a zonbi go out in such a gruesome manner.

"I said not to attack!" Braulio slapped his hands on his face and huffed out an angry breath.

"But it—"

"Attacking it makes it angrier! And that helps it go zonbi faster, putting everyone in danger." Braulio took a few steps away from her, visibly frustrated. After a few tense seconds, he turned back to her. "I'm trying to see if we can stop animals from falling if we zero them down. But an untrained cadet bringing her desperation into the mix will screw that up."

Yunai ignored the sting in her eyes. Weakness was the last thing she needed to show on her first day. Part of her wished Farid would say something in her defense, but he was bound to Braulio's directions.

"I'm sorry." *I thought he would get hurt. I took action. That's what we're assigned to do. There's nothing wrong with making a decision I thought right.* Over and over Yunai repeated those sentences to herself.

Braulio sighed. "Let's just go back in. The scoutmaster will handle...that."

Yunai followed the young men back inside the room. She tried desperately to cool feelings of shame, but the rising temperature around her body revealed otherwise.

ESERA

They weren't here to do clerical work.

Esera stood in a semi-circle of about twenty cadets, including Matagi. Those who could heated their bodies in the chill of the vault. Root lights barely lit the dark underground, and torches uncovered what roots did not.

Niesh stood before them, her face a painting of shadows. Esera didn't forget their near-death experience on the ship to Taisala. Seeing this woman made him tremble with rage, but even he knew this wasn't the time to let his emotions boil over.

"About eight months ago, our Saint was murdered in broad daylight," Niesh said. "Brutally, by an unnatural. That man was arrested and put to death. Since then, the deterioration of the Natural has sped up significantly with zonbi invading our sacred island.

"Now more people, thinking they can embolden themselves on the spilled blood of a Saint, are acting out. They are in our streets.

Worse, they wear the mask of teacher, of banker, of librarian, of business owner. They lurk among the normal of daily life."

Feet shuffled from further down the vault. From the darkness emerged five bodies in a line, a scoutmaster in front, then two men and a woman. A second scoutmaster brought up the rear. Niesh stepped aside as the scoutmasters lined the people up side-by-side. They were clad in dirt, clothes ragged, hair disheveled, their faces haunted. One sobbed uncontrollably. Esera didn't see any restraints on them. Were they prisoners?

"The man who killed the Saint is not alone," Niesh continued. "There is a movement to destroy the Natural, to upend everything our ancestors worked hard to establish and protect. That's where you all come in."

As if rehearsed, the wall behind the cadets broke apart. A man opened the vault the same way Niesh had when they came in, by syncing parts of the stone walls apart to make a stairway down. The Cathedral's main hall was devoid of doors, and Niesh had warned them that trying to sync the walls open was inadvisable for unauthorized personnel.

"Niesh, you know I hate morning procedures," the man said, walking up to her. He synced a ball of coffee above a hand and held a coil of roots in the other. Wearing a belt of medical tools and with access to this level of the Cathedral, Esera deduced that this was Ibrahim, the Cathedral's head of medicine. "Some of us like to enjoy our mornings."

Niesh paid him no attention as he synced coffee into his mouth. Esera didn't like where this was going. Both wielded the calm of distant storm clouds.

"You have been recommended to become hunters, cadets who specialize in more discreet matters. We need people with your skills to quietly smoke out and deal with this menace."

Ibrahim synced the last of his coffee down his throat. He unwound the roots.

"If you don't believe hunting is for you, don't come back after today. You will forfeit the assignment—and your cadet training. But if you choose to stay, you get to brag to your cabinmates about all the fancy pens and paper you get to use—and nothing more."

The cadets showed their understanding with obedient silence.

"We've interrogated these three for information already. They say they know nothing, but that doesn't mean they get to walk free. They spread unnatural propaganda, and there is no returning from your word once it has been uttered. One of them even had the audacity to desecrate the Saint's memorial."

...the Saint's memorial. Where Yunai had encountered people seeing things that weren't there. Esera took a look at one of the men and felt ill.

Ibrahim synced the root ends in the man's skin as if to deliver multiple shots. Esera knew what this was. They all did. How many parents warned their children about throwing tantrums by telling them stories of blood-sucking monsters who would come after them if they couldn't calm down?

Air, Esera. Air.

Esera knew what the term bloodletting meant. But he never, ever needed to know what it looked like to understand it.

FIFTEEN

ODOMI

Zonbi emerged in the hospital at a constant pace now. Not one more incident could happen again.

Using the light from the silver of the moon to see, Odomi clenched her fist tighter and pulled her elbow back more. The roots tunneled deeper into the skin, bulging into an extra set of veins. The root chandelier hanging from the middle of the greenhouse's roof shifted back and forth, but Odomi saw no sign she was getting the power she needed. The roots should have moved on their own, and they should have emanated light. Ten minutes had passed, and neither was happening.

Odomi pulled the roots out of the skin, synced off the contaminated ends, and tossed them into the burn pile. She didn't understand what she had gotten wrong. Her research was thorough, and she had fact-checked her process with some of the most well-known experts in "unnatural" medicine.

"...looks like you...need a stronger arm."

Odomi moved to the worktable away from the statue of the Artemisan hero Raíz erected in the center of the greenhouse. "And it looks like you need a stronger dose." She pulled a sack from her bag and loosened its strings, pulling blooms of passionflower out. She dropped them in a mortar filled with water and other plants, then synced the stone pestle up and down in hard movements. She could have easily taken the flower right off its shelf herself, but Siaka had insisted on putting his name on the checkout form to avoid suspicion. Her Son was overprotective, but she appreciated it.

"That's my fault. Even with a damaged heart, you still have a lot of strength left." Odomi pounded until she pulverized the plants into a gray-green mixture. Then she loaded the concoction into a needle. With the addition of the passionflower, this concoction would knock him out for longer than her previous doses.

Odomi turned from the table—and faced Saint Leonardo. The beloved spiritual leader of the Natural Plane was now a body of ash. He stank of sweat and shit, a wretch of the man he once was. But he held his head up, a miracle of a spirit refusing to break. The only thing connecting the man of today and yesterday was those eyes, those burning violet eyes, a legacy of Lemana's power—her vibrancy.

Vibrancy was life. It gave color to the world and gave the roots their power. And that power that continually evaded Odomi's grasp since making the Saint her captive in the greenhouse.

Odomi moved closer to where she bound Leonardo to the statue with trick restraints. With the needle in one hand, she raised her other, the roots surrounding the statue's base prepared to strike if he somehow found the energy to retaliate. He could no longer sync with his heart damaged, but it would be foolish to underestimate the Saint.

"You wouldn't have to suffer if you would just hand over your power." Odomi stood to his side and placed her free hand over his bony shoulder. She stuck the needle in and pushed. "We would make much better use of it than you drawing zonbi to the hospital every time you have a fit." She pulled the needle out.

Leonardo creaked his head toward her. His lips, blistered and peeling, twitched. "...why..." He coughed, his body rattling. He rarely had the energy to speak. "Then...why keep me alive...if I'm...a threat..."

Odomi returned to the table and set the needle in her hazardous waste bin. She synced with water from her water pouch and rinsed her hands, depositing the used water into the bin as well.

"We have every reason to end you right now. *Every* reason.

Putting you to rest would certainly protect my patients from the consequences of your emotions. But I don't make these decisions by myself." She paused, giving her own emotions space to settle. "My son, our people, deserve full measures. Your power will give us the strength we need to topple the Cathedral. So we won't put you down without good reason."

"...this is...worse...to deprive a man...of the sun..." His body shook to the sound of his dry heaving.

Odomi needed this concoction to hurry and knock him out. Her anger was rising, and she wouldn't be able to keep them hidden from sight if she lost control. She returned to the table and set her hands on her bag. She breathed in the waves of emotion emanating from the violet journal inside. "I won't give up on claiming your power, not until I'm sure my other plan is successful without it." She released her hands from the bag when her agitation subsided. "The people deserve to know who you are. And they deserve someone who will lead them to a better life."

"...you're too smart...to divulge your evil plans, Odomi... A true unnatural...would have killed..." The concoction took the rest of his words.

"Now why does it matter?" Sensing him drift away, Odomi put her mortar and pestle and hazardous bin in her bag, preparing to leave for the night. "Like you said. You're as good as dead."

SIXTEEN

ESERA

Esera watched Raki rifle through her bag for her money as Yunai hopped onto the train station's platform. The crowded train ride overloaded his senses, and he didn't want to stand in any more crowds. They needed to get moving.

"Thanks for coming out with me," Yunai said. "I don't want to be alone tonight."

"Of course," Raki replied. "We don't have a curfew, so might as well take advantage."

Esera couldn't stay still. He started walking.

"Wait for us!" Raki called.

He kept walking. He heard them catch up.

"Fleas in your pits?" Raki asked.

"Just want to get there."

Raki didn't push him, and he was grateful for it. She knew when to nag and, mostly, when to back off.

"Anyway, don't worry about that guy," Raki said, falling behind to match Yunai's pace. "He sounds like a cactus. I hear the residents are pretty snooty."

"Thanks," Yunai replied. "What about you? Do you know what to do with your mentee?"

Esera anchored onto their conversation. He needed to stay afloat. Deep breathing was not enough.

"I don't even want to think about it. The children don't need to be bullying her, but...how can a person not want to sync? Have you heard of that? What do you even do with that? It's unnatural."

"I haven't, but how old did you say she was? Maybe she hasn't started puberty yet."

"I'm not allowed to give identifying info about the kids, but she has. And the director said she could sync."

Their conversation wasn't helping. The two discussing their service assignments forced Esera to think about his. And he did *not* want to think about his.

"How much longer?" Esera blurted out, stopping.

"The venue is only a few blocks away." Yunai jogged up and put her hands on one of his shoulders. She smiled. "You haven't said much about your placement."

Raki linked her fingers with his. "Working in the main office has to be better than working in the daycare."

"It's boring," Esera said quickly. "We get nice pens."

"Okay..." Raki released his hand.

They walked the rest of the way in silence, darting past bodies as the crowds grew bigger. Smooth beats invited them to their destination, a stage in the middle of a plaza. Yunai wanted to see The Return, a jazz group whose sound was rooted in Fa'atasi, who was performing tonight. Esera enjoyed the music of his people but didn't care too much for this group. Either way, hearing them perform would distract him from the images looping through his mind.

The trio moved to a relatively empty space in the crowd. The group finished a cheesy love song, "See U(s) Soon." It was the anthem of weird kids who tried to woo their crushes with overly romantic gestures that were really just creepy. Esera had laughed at enough rejected school dance invitations to know. After a round of applause and cheers, they started "One," a song the music stations overplayed in the months after the Saint's death. They wrote it in tribute to him, a sappy song Esera found overstated in its lyricism.

He rolled his shoulders back. Being in his skin felt a little better. Silently judging The Return's set would keep the thoughts at bay.

"I can't move to this," Yunai said, bummed. She settled for swaying her body, as most of the crowd did.

Raki wrapped her arms around Esera's shoulders and pecked his cheek. He swayed along with her, grateful for his Sister's presence.

About a minute into the song, he heard a curious sound. After hearing "One" a million times, he knew he wasn't picking up on an instrument he hadn't heard before.

And then he saw it.

Roots coiling up the stage, snaking up the singers' legs. Digging into their skin.

Blood running...

Life draining...

Esera's body stopped. Raki unwound her arms. She turned him around to face her. "Okay. That's all the space I can give. What's wrong?"

Esera spun back, closed his eyes hard, then reopened them. But he wasn't seeing things—the roots were still there.

Bodies struggling...

Words suffocated...

He couldn't move.

A shout from the front of the crowd, followed by the clash and clang of instruments and equipment being shoved down. Someone threw themselves on stage and started fighting with the group. Two scoutmasters jumped on stage and apprehended the person swiftly. One handcuffed them in chains, while the other instructed the crowd to calm down.

Esera blinked. The roots disappeared.

"What was that about?" Raki asked.

Esera didn't like this. He didn't know what he just saw, and he didn't care. He wanted to go. But his legs wouldn't move.

"Yunai?"

Esera forced his head around. Yunai was searching the crowd.

"Why are you both acting so weird?" Raki shot her head back and forth between them. "Can one of you say something? You're starting to scare me."

Esera didn't respond and neither did Yunai, but Yunai moved toward the back of the crowd.

"Where are you going?" Raki called after her.

Esera's feet managed to move when Raki pulled him away. They pushed through the crowd, following Yunai until they reached an open space.

"Yunai!" Raki cried, doing her best to hide her frustration. Esera pulled his hand away from her.

"I saw someone suspicious head this way," Yunai finally said. She scanned the immediate area.

"Suspicious how?"

"This is like that day at the memorial. People were seeing things and acting strange. I can't let this one get away!"

"What? But how is someone running off suspicious?"

"I heard them say something about seeing zonbi, but—there!"

Raki followed her gaze up, and Esera shook his trance off and looked up. A person scaled a wall between two buildings, syncing bricks out and using them to climb. They synced the bricks back in haphazardly as they went up.

Yunai took off after them. Raki threw up her hands and ran after her, and Esera injected what sense he could into his feet to bring up the rear. The person broke open a window and disappeared inside.

Yunai synced with the brick wall, but she lost the sync when she tried to ascend. "The wall's too impure," she said.

Raki searched their surroundings and pointed at a big root protruding from the ground. "Use that. I'm going before they get away!" More skilled at syncing with natural objects with impurities, Raki scaled the wall.

Yunai and Esera used all their might to sync the thick root from the ground, then ran it up the side of the building. Yunai went up first, and Esera felt for his nifo'oti before going up.

Was this person unnatural? Was *he* unnatural for seeing those roots that others didn't? Was it on his shoulders to deal with them? To turn himself in? Was he helping Yunai hand over another person to Niesh? Where they would—

He banished the pointless questions. He didn't turn down the hunter assignment. Which meant bringing this person to justice was on his shoulders. But he would not tell anyone what he saw—or he would suffer the same fate as the prisoners in the vault.

Esera entered after Yunai into a dark room. A torch Raki lit provided the only source of light, and she had forged a brick gauntlet onto her other hand.

"Are they still on the floor?" Yunai whispered.

"I don't hear anything," Raki whispered back. She made her torch bigger. "Remind me why we're chasing this guy again?"

"Because it's our job," Esera said dryly. He moved around steadily, nifo'oti in each hand.

"You know what I—"

A hail of wooden stakes hurtled toward Esera. He swiped a club at them, hissing when one broke skin. The person, a woman dressed ready for combat, her hair cut short, flew out from the darkness, root whip at the ready. She slung it around Yunai's leg and yanked it, bringing her down hard. Raki synced the torch at the whip, missing when the woman retracted it. Raki went in and threw a punch of gust at the woman, distracting her with the blast before popping her in the face with the brick gauntlet. The woman stumbled back as Esera slid in and hooked his nifo'oti around her ankles, tripping her when he pulled them in. Recovered, Yunai came in with forged spears, prepared to strike. The woman synced more stakes around her body, their splintered ends a protective shell. A bloody gash appeared where Raki struck her, but the woman wasn't fazed.

"Cadets?" the woman said, struggling to breathe. "Why on Lemana's Plane would cadets be here when the threat is out there?"

"I heard you say you saw a rash of zonbi, but there weren't any," Yunai said.

"Don't be this stupid." The woman eyed them as if they were missing something glaringly obvious. "A whole bunch of people going zonbi, and none of you cadets saw it? Niesh would blow a vessel."

"There were no zonbi," Raki stated incredulously. "We were in the middle of the crowd. We would have seen people running away."

"You're a scoutmaster," Esera said. She looked younger than the ones on base, but her reflexes were more refined than theirs for her to be anything less. She likely knew they had been tracking her, too, and hid at first to avoid a surprise attack, and to spring one on them.

"Scout. Until I was sent to die in a conflict-stricken wasteland the Saint created with a stroke of a pen."

"How did you see zonbi when the crowd and the scoutmasters saw nothing?" Yunai demanded.

Esera noticed water dripping from her spears, saw the hot air wafting from her. Something was eating her, and she needed to reel it in fast.

"Yunai."

But the woman cut in before he warned her. "The question is, how did you not?"

Sensing Yunai's break, the woman drove her stakes at her. Raki punched gust at them before they turned Yunai into a bloody corkboard. Yunai collapsed, shaken. The woman slapped her whip on Raki's arm and synced it, along with her, at Esera. Raki went flying and fell on top of him. From the floor, Esera watched the woman race to a window facing the crowd, bringing her stakes with her. She set one stake in front of her and refined its aim.

"No!"

She brought an arm back and pushed it forward, shooting the stake into the crowd. Screams and gasps. Someone had fallen.

Esera pushed Raki off and darted for the woman. She fired another stake before Esera clamped on her from behind, rapidly heating his hands on her body. The agony forced itself up her lungs, pushing out a painful howl.

Then Esera felt a sting on the side of his neck. He slapped it—but felt himself losing his sight before he could figure out what stung him. He fell backward, hitting the floor, the room leaving him alone...

~

"ESERA! ESERA, WAKE UP!"

The room slowly returned to Esera's sight. Consciousness slammed in when he realized someone was shaking him. He pushed himself up, wiping the drool from his cheek. His body felt heavy as Raki helped him to a seated position.

"What happened?" he asked, massaging his pounding head. "I fell."

"We all got knocked out with something. I don't see any darts, but..."

Esera turned to the window. The woman was gone, and Yunai stood in her place, looking outside. The uproar of voices filled his ears as his senses returned to him.

"She's gone," Raki said, "but...she killed two people. The scout-masters are trying to disperse the crowd."

Esera got up with Raki's assistance and walked to the window. Yunai had cooled down but was still visibly upset.

"I don't know how long we were out, but we should report to the scoutmasters," Raki said. "Ignacia should know about this, too."

Raki led Yunai away. Esera lingered at the window before following his companions. Niesh would soon hear about this too, and that made him anxious—and not just for himself.

ODOMI

"You know who I am?" The two stopped in a poorly lit street blocks away from the chaos of the plaza. Her home was nearby, but she wanted the full cooperation of the woman before inviting her in.

"Odomi. What scout worth their Word doesn't know you?"

"Good." Odomi continued walking. The woman followed.

"Which means you can do something about these burns."

"As long as you agree to help me. Yes."

"I'm down for anything that involves taking the Cathedral down a notch."

"Then I believe we can help each other out."

This woman had just the right kind of fuel. Her spirit felt like the one.

SEVENTEEN

RIZA

Riza walked up the steps of Maogatai University's faculty building. They blocked out the scholars chatting and studying around them, but couldn't help but notice the strong presence of scoutmasters on campus. They did read something about a couple of homicides last night. Nothing gave Riza's unnatural status away, but they kept walking with the sole purpose of going straight to their father's office from the house.

Riza entered the building and located his office down the hall. Its door was the only one without root locks. They stopped in front of the door and stared at the decorative plate hanging on it.

Efraim
Professor of Ancient Literature
768 – 801
May his spirit return in safe hands

How long had the plate been up? Had they not hired anyone to replace him? Several months had passed since his death.

Riza reached for the door. They stole glances to their right and left to make sure no one was too close, then pushed the door. It creaked open—but Riza didn't go in. Dust swallowed the room, and no light penetrated the space. It looked exactly as it felt.

Without sticking their head in, they felt the wall for the root light source and tried snapping it on. Nothing. The room was also as dead as it felt. They'd have to open the blinds on the other side of the room—which meant going into the room—which they were not prepared to do. And not because it meant acknowledging the space of their loss.

But didn't it? One touch of the desk, an inhale of dust, and their grief would break the emotional dam. They couldn't allow anyone to see that, especially the scoutmasters. But they had to go in at some point. People gave them long looks as they passed by.

Riza took measured steps into the office. They pulled the blinds open with a steady hand, shielding their eyes when the morning sun blinded them. They pushed the window open, letting birdsong in. Using the fresh air, they synced the dust out through the window. A good start. Opening the room up to the Natural was calming. For insurance, they took a small bottle from their bag and sipped some of its green contents. Braulio's concoctions worked well to reduce their stress.

Their father's room was as simple as the house. A desk, a bookshelf, a couple of chairs. The only things that stood out were the posters of Artemisan action shows. They had spent many nights watching the overacted shows together. His diplomas hung next to the posters. They'd take those home with them, but Riza was interested in searching the desk first.

They pushed the chair out of the way using their foot, not wanting to sit with any of its latent emotions. There was nothing on top of the desk, so they pulled the top drawer open, feeling a brush of anxiety as they did. Riza clenched their hand and shut their eyes, waiting for the feeling to disappear. When it passed, they opened their eyes and looked at the drawer's contents—standard office supplies, neatly arranged as if he had never used them.

Riza wasn't exactly sure what they were looking for. But they wanted to find something, *anything* that would make their father's death make sense. They refused to call it a suicide. They refused to accept that he had taken his own life.

Riza's father was far from jolly, but he was a man who had pursued his goals with unwavering dedication. He lived for teaching, for research, for breaking down and examining the written word and sharing that knowledge with those who wanted to listen.

Yes, he had separated from his Partner a cycle before his death, moving to Taisala permanently for a peace his homeland no longer gave him. And leaving Riza in a home that no longer felt like a home. But Riza had a hard time believing his failed partnership contributed to his last moments. The partnership between him and the woman he married had never been a true bond, one based on love for each other. Nothing proved that more than the woman barely sparing his body a glimpse when Lemana repatriated it to Artemisa.

Stop.

Riza had to stop. Their thoughts were running wild, which meant their emotions would let loose soon after.

They sipped more of Braulio's concoction, then used air to close the drawer. They moved to the bookshelf, the only thing not perfectly arranged. Four rows of books were jammed together, textbooks, novels, and poetry, titles from cultures the Plane over. Riza wouldn't find anything there. They kneeled to the bottom shelf. His personal notebooks were crammed on the bottom, papers peeking out everywhere. The lack of organization piqued their interest more than anything.

"Hello?"

Riza swung their head toward the door they forgot to close. A man with a left root ear stood at the entrance, an awkward smile on his face.

"Are you a new scholar here?" he asked. "I've been meaning to clean this room."

Meaning to? For over half a cycle? Riza got up. "No. I'm Efraim's child."

"Oh!" A light went off on his face. "Riza! Professor Efraim mentioned you a few times. I was his teaching assistant. I meant to come here a while ago and clear everything out. But letting go of someone who inspired you so much is hard. Which, you know, I-I'm sure you understand!"

Riza ignored his unnecessary attempt to save face. They wanted this person who was more up than the sun to go away. But someone who had worked with their father may know some things a dead office wouldn't. And this one was chatty. "Can you tell me what my father was like? Up until he died."

"Yeah. Sure! I don't have to teach until this afternoon." He sat on the desk with his legs spread out like a true teaching assistant. "I'm sure you know he was a serious person, but he was never harsh with us. He always had one eye in his own world. We all knew he was separated from his Partner—ah, uh..."

"Go on," Riza said.

"Right. Anyway. He became more distant one day. Literally changed in one day. He wasn't sleeping or eating much. He missed a few classes, and I had to fill in for him a lot. A few of the scholars and I got worried, so we decided to check on him. I remember the floor being covered in paper. Crumpled pages everywhere. He was sitting at his desk, and I guess he was throwing the stuff he hated away. He was working on a poem. Said it was the most important work of his life. We felt we were close enough to him, so we told him to take a break. That we were worried about his health. But he told us he couldn't stop until he finished."

Their father was definitely intense when it came to work, but he never neglected the people he cared about. Riza recalled many evenings reading with him—and Riza's twin sister. He never ended story time without teaching them something about the Plane, about its many cultures, and how important it was for them to keep an open mind.

"Then I guess he did finish eventually. And just like that, he changed back to his old self. He was back to teaching regularly and keeping his diet up. But he was friendlier! He invited me and the other scholars to his home to share meals. We'd have book discussions. The last class he taught... In retrospect, it made sense. It was like he was saying goodbye. He gave us this lecture about university being 'the last bastion of new thinking.' It was all very...final." He stopped. He searched for more to say but found nothing.

Riza latched onto one thing in his story—the poem. Its completion was the turning point in his whole spiel. "Did he ever read the poem to you?"

"No... I don't think he did. At least I never heard it. Now that I think about it, none of the other scholars ever mentioned hearing or reading it. I guess it was a personal thing."

"Okay, thanks." Riza turned their attention back to the bottom row of notebooks.

"No problem! I'm always glad to help any relative of the professor's!" He came off the desk. "If you want to take anything of his, feel free! Those are all his personal works. The poem may be in one of them."

Riza reached for the first book, then stopped. His personal works would be charged with his emotions. "Are there any boxes I can use?"

"I'm sure there are in the storage closet. Be right back!" He went and returned in a flash. He was resourceful, if Riza had anything good to say. Must have been teacher's pet. "I can pack them for you if you'd like? Least I can do for not cleaning his room sooner."

Perfect. "Yeah. Thanks. His diplomas, too."

He packed the books neatly, wasting no space, and put the diplomas on top. He handed the box to Riza. "Do you want the door plate too? I need to remove it before the new professor comes in next term."

Riza looked at it for a second, then back at the assistant. His face was eager. "Keep it."

EIGHTEEN

YUNAI

Yunai cut the oranges into uneven slices, then synced them into the fruit bowl. As she reached for the next orange, the smell from the pan on the stove tingled her nose. She kept cutting. She could cut one more orange before she had to flip the fried plantains Estefania insisted they make for breakfast. Estefania was supposed to be helping her anyway, so she should have been at the stove.

"They're burning!"

Yunai turned to the stove, dropping her knife. Estefania ran to the stove from the other side of the kitchen and contained the smoke, syncing it up through the vent. "I said they shouldn't take long to fry! Agh, these are the last we have!"

"I was cutting the fruit," Yunai threw back. "You could have flipped them."

"I was getting the plates out."

"And I was already *doing* something."

"Then pay better attention next time!"

"*I'm trying!*"

The stove exploded. Fire from all the burners raged, joining into one inferno. Estefania scrambled back until she fell flat on her bottom. Yunai froze in place. She stood frozen even as the flames singed her braids.

Before she realized where it came from, water soaked her, snapping her out of her daze. She caught her breath and faced Ignacia, who still wore her nightwear, face scrawled with early morning disdain. Ignacia made a come here gesture, and the pan synced into her grip from wherever it flew from. Then Yunai noticed the cadets piled in the stairway.

"Not again..." Raki murmured, her eyes fixed on the frying pan.

"Estefania, are you alright?" Ignacia asked. She kept her attention on Yunai.

"I didn't burn to death if that's what you mean." Obi helped Estefania up.

"Yunai." It was a question and a demand.

Her panicked mind didn't know where to go—the wet stove, the pan kissed with charred plantains, Esera mouthing "blame her" while pointing to Estefania, or Ignacia, who was ready to throw the pan right at her face.

Words failed Yunai.

"Cadets, get ready for the day," Ignacia said, still holding the pan upright. "Breakfast is grab-and-go and leftovers today. Raki and Esera, meet me in my office before you leave."

The cadets ran back up.

"You don't know how excited I was for plantains this morning..." Estefania griped as Obi pushed her upstairs.

"Yunai." Ignacia headed back to her office. Then she turned around and set the frying pan on the counter. And *then* she went back to her room, shaking her head.

Drawing on nothing but obedience for her scoutmaster, Yunai moved her legs in Ignacia's direction. She lowered herself into a chair in her office-bedroom. Ignacia sat before her, no desk between them, and put her head down in her hands. Letting a moment pass, she lifted her head back up and rested it on clasped hands.

"Yunai, I want to help you, but the stove is how we eat."

"I-I'm sorry," Yunai blurted out, eyes and nose running. "The resident I'm with hates me, and I don't know how to control myself, and I failed last night during the fight—"

"Stop," Ignacia said. "You have to zero down before something floods somewhere else. Take a breath."

Yunai didn't take any breaths but managed to settle herself before Ignacia continued.

"I heard about last night. Raki mentioned the fight to me early this morning. When she thought I was fully awake and ready to be talked to."

Yunai glanced at the entrance where Raki tried hiding behind Esera. Esera shoved her forward, and the two stood behind Yunai.

"Let's start there. You three fought a former scout? Did you get a name?"

"Yes and no," Raki answered. "She said she saw human zonbi in the crowd. But we didn't see a thing. Then someone tranquilized us and she was gone."

"We didn't stop her," Yunai said, voice still unsteady. "She killed two people..."

"Don't give in to pity." Ignacia unclasped her hands and lifted her head. "Three cadets versus a fully trained scout is not a fair match. But this is concerning. Very concerning if a scout has broken their Word. And she sounds like the man who claimed he saw blood on the memorial."

"Yes," Yunai said.

"Niesh should be aware of this already since it was a public incident." Ignacia went quiet for a few seconds. "I don't know what to make of all this, the seeing things and the tranquilizing. There've been several incidents of people seeing things in the past few weeks... Regardless, you three did well to track her movements. That's very good scout work, excellent initiative."

"That was Yunai!" Raki squeezed Yunai's shoulders, a dimple rising in response. The praise restored some of her confidence.

"Can we pursue this further? Help the scoutmasters find the defector?" Yunai was riding the high of Raki's and Ignacia's praise. If she could help bring an unnatural man to justice, she could help with this scout, too.

"No, no. You three did great, but this is a Cathedral-level issue. Trust me, they're on it. You did your part by identifying the threat and reporting it. And you have your own assignments and training to worry about."

"Yes, Master." Yunai was deflated but not defeated.

Raki took Ignacia's cue and left for her service. Esera, who was silent the entire time, left seconds after Raki.

"Yunai, take a few minutes to reset before you go, and make sure to talk to Estefania at some point today. I'll send a note with one of the base cats to let the hospital know you'll be late. And I'll look into replacing the stove..."

Yunai nodded and got up when Ignacia did.

"Keep a straight back against those residents. The medics don't like our presence there, but you can't let it affect your work. Think of it as extra training for keeping zero."

Yunai thanked her scoutmaster, then went up to the quarters, thinking how she could still help solve this mystery on Taisala on her own time.

Nineteen

RAKI

Raki followed her scoutmaster escort into the orphanage. She was late. Again. She wondered if they would penalize her for her lack of punctuality, but Paloma was away from the orphanage's office. The scoutmaster directed her to a note on her desk before taking off. Paloma had taken the children from Toya's room out to the city for the day—leaving Toya alone with one of the caretakers until Raki arrived.

She entered the room and spotted Toya scrunched up on her lower bunk. The caretaker read a book to her from a chair. As Raki got closer, she saw that the caretaker was reading quietly to herself. Toya just sat there.

"Good morning," Raki said.

"Oh, good." The caretaker got up and closed the book. "I have other children to look after. She's been quiet as death this morning." She left in a hurry.

Raki approached Toya. The child didn't react, not when the woman left, not to Raki's presence. The space between them was heavy, and Raki didn't know how to make it lighter. "How are you doing?" she said.

Still no response. Figured. The answer to that was too obvious.

Raki spent the rest of her first day playing her shadow. Sitting with her during tutoring sessions and activities and getting her what she needed when the caretakers asked. Small talk on Raki's end and none on Toya's. But she needed to connect with her somehow. This child needed help.

"Why..." *...are you here by yourself while everyone else is out in the city? Nope. Rephrase that, Raki.* "Where did the other children go?"

Nothing. Her eyes barely shifted.

Raki moved to sit next to her on the bunk. "I know the other day was—"

"Adults can't sit on beds. It's creepy."

Raki got back on her feet awkwardly. She didn't consider that, but at least it got her to talk? No. That sounded creepy, too. Moving on.

"Sorry. I'm just trying here."

"Don't. Just stand there and leave me alone, and you can get your credits." Toya scrunched up more and twisted her head further away.

"I'm not here for credits. I'm here to help."

"I don't need your help."

"Then why are you here alone when everyone else is out?" Damn. The words slipped from her tongue anyway.

Toya sprang out of bed and got away from Raki fast. Cursing herself, Raki went after her. "Wait! That's not what I meant!"

Toya raced out of the bedroom, through the office, and into the garden. She ran all the way to the Cathedral's back entrance and stopped at the locked gate.

"All I meant is there's a reason you're here," Raki stated when she caught up to her. "If you tell me why, we can work together so it doesn't happen again."

Silence.

Raki ran a hand over her face. Being responsible for one child had sounded perfect, but if things were going this badly this fast? She wondered if it was possible to get a new placement. The hospital was her preferred choice. She could deal with conceited residents.

Raki dropped her hand when she heard sniffling. Toya still stood there, but she wiped tears from her face.

Okay. Raki had to keep trying. Too soon to call it quits, and Raki was no quitter. "Alright. Tell me what you want me to do. What do you want from me?"

"I want you to let me leave. There's someone I want to see, and I don't want to be here anymore."

"Even if I wanted to, the scoutmasters wouldn't let you pass."

Toya turned to the brick wall and threw a hand in its direction. "Just move the roots and bricks and move them back!"

Raki crossed her arms. "Or you can sync them yourself."

"No."

Raki couldn't believe this child.

"Why on Lemana's Plane won't you sync? I get the other children are too young, but you're definitely old enough. Not syncing, that's like...like...not breathing! Or not eating!"

Toya spun around. "You don't even know how old I am!" She stormed back to the orphanage, ignoring Raki's bewilderment.

Raki was getting sick of all this shouting and walking away. They were going to get somewhere today, dammit. She synced the metal doors of the orphanage shut with a tug of air before Toya reached them. Hopefully, none of the caretakers had plans to leave anytime soon.

"Let me go in!" Toya fumed.

"Thirteen? Fourteen?"

Toya didn't react to either.

"Twelve?"

Silence again, but her face twitched.

"I'll open the door if you tell me why you refuse to sync. And why you were left here."

Toya stared her down. Raki stared back. The seconds that passed between them felt like minutes. Raki's arm started to cramp, but she refused to let it show.

"Because I didn't want to go, okay? Because who wants to be around a bunch of babies who make fun of you and adults who won't *do anything about it?*" Toya paused, gathering up her voice when it slipped between the cracks. "Because I don't want to get yelled at when I get mad and the zonbi come after us! And who cares about syncing? The caretakers do everything for us anyway."

Sudden darkness was their only warning.

"I don't want to be here, *and I don't want to be on this island!*"

Winged zonbi engulfed the root dome. They squeezed their heads through the small holes, body parts that didn't fit tearing off and falling to the ground. Raki unclenched her hand. Toya looked at the infestation, her body tense but her face unfrightened. Raki wouldn't even think about taking this many on by herself. The Cathedral scoutmasters were going to have to take this one.

"Get inside!"

But Toya didn't move. Instead, the tension seemed to drain from her body.

"Hey!" Raki's scouting instincts told her to grab the girl and haul her inside—but the zonbi did not advance. It was similar to what she heard of the zonbi attack on the hospital.

Caretakers emerged from the orphanage as the zonbi began to burn from the outside. The scoutmasters had come swiftly. Toya snapped back to reality as her mind caught up with what her eyes witnessed.

Raki ran up to Toya and placed her hands on the girl's shoulders. "Are you okay?"

Toya gulped, her body resetting to a neutral position. She faced Raki. The tears in her eyes shimmered when the sun filtered through the root dome again. Words perched on the edge of her lips, but they retreated as she did, back into the orphanage, pushing past caretakers and children.

"That child." Raki heard the voice of the caretaker who had watched her earlier. "We wouldn't be getting these attacks at all if she weren't still here."

Raki chewed on her comment as she chased Toya down. She found her back on the bed in the same spot, in the same position. "Are you alright?"

Toya remained silent.

Raki was not interested in putting this question-silence bit on repeat. "Have the zonbi acted like that before? We should have been eaten alive!"

Toya surprised Raki by meeting her gaze. The tears had vanished, and the petulance had softened into sadness. "They stop like that sometimes. I don't know why."

Raki stared at her. Zonbi never stopped attacking, not until they tore their target apart. She wanted to ask Toya if she had anything to do with them stopping, but she didn't want to antagonize her into silence again. What could anyone do to influence spiritless creatures anyway? Raki wanted to ask her a whole lot of questions, but better to start at square one.

"What if I took you out the days I'm here? We can try rearranging your schedule."

"Why?"

"Well, getting permission is better than breaking you out. Not to mention you're too old to be hanging out with the younger children. Getting away from them and this place can help with the getting mad thing. And if it's just us, we can get to know each other better."

Toya shifted her eyes away, avoiding hope. "Paloma would never go for it."

Raki wasn't sure about that. It was obvious Toya wasn't wanted here. "I'll talk to her when she gets back. I was assigned to mentor you, so it wouldn't be right if I didn't try to make this work."

Toya shrugged her shoulders. "I don't want to learn syncing."

Oh, she was going to learn, but Raki would introduce that in time. They needed to build a relationship first. "We'll just focus on getting to know one another. Deal?"

Toya loosened her body. "Fine."

Success! Raki smiled, relieved. That first hurdle was hard to clear, but Raki knew it would be worth it.

She convinced Toya to play board games with her until everyone returned. They spent most of the time in semi-comfortable silence. All the while, Raki wondered how Toya ended up in the orphanage and why she was adamant about not learning to sync.

TWENTY

ESERA

Esera synced the trick chains around his training partner's ankles and wrists. He hog-tied them as they lay on their stomach, their head turned to the side.

"I think they're still loose," they said. They synced a piece of gravel toward them with an awkward hand motion. "I can still sync."

Niesh had instructed them to sync their partners' chains tight enough to cut off circulation so they couldn't sync with their hands or feet. Esera didn't feel any particular way about this training—he'd take it over learning bloodletting any day—but he still hesitated to tighten the chains.

"Hurry before Niesh walks over," his partner whispered.

The threat of her presence forced Esera's hand tighter. His partner yelped. They tried syncing again, but the gravel only tumbled over on itself this time.

"Better."

Esera unsynced the chains and set them on the floor. It was his turn to play the captured. But he knew—didn't want to at all but knew—he had to follow up with Niesh about last night, whether she already knew or not. Coming in late gave him an excuse not to speak with her first thing, but he couldn't delay for too long. Better to approach than be approached.

Esera told his partner to wait and walked up to Niesh, who was advising another pair. He saluted, indicating he didn't come over to waste her time. "I have something to report about last night."

Niesh walked to the back of the vault, and Esera followed. Anger and apprehension twisted in his stomach. He knew skipping leftover breakfast was a good idea. He hated this woman, hated that he had taken the initiative to report to her. But he couldn't afford to slack off. He recapped last night to her, focusing on his role—and left out the part about seeing bloody roots.

"We couldn't stop her," Esera said, finishing. "Someone tranquilized us, and she was gone when we woke up."

"No trace?" Niesh asked. "No trail or anything that could help us find her?"

"No." Esera pretended not to notice Niesh's dissatisfaction. He was just a cadet, and Ignacia stated this was Cathedral-level work. Niesh couldn't expect him to be successful this early in their training.

Niesh eyed him. "Esera. You're one of the diversions."

"Yes." Esera started to itch.

"You have your first mission. Find any information about this defector and who they escaped with."

She paused. Esera failed to mask his confusion.

"I realize you've only started training, but I don't think a little detective work is above your head. The people expressing unnatural thoughts have been civilians, but a rogue scout who has killed two people already—that we can't take lightly. This scout would know to avoid my scoutmasters, whether they're on duty or not, so a cadet has a higher chance of catching them off guard."

He wanted to scream. He wanted to fight. He wanted to implode.

"Okay."

"Good. I expect reports every week. I'll send word to Ignacia that you've taken on extra work to support my scoutmasters." Niesh looked beyond him. "You and Matagi are from the same cabin, so he'll be your comrade. The scout knows your face, so having a second to take point is necessary."

Esera's body temperature spiked. If Niesh noticed, she didn't mention it.

"Dismissed."

Esera saluted, then returned to his partner. He wanted to saw his stupid, obedient arm off and slap himself with it.

TWENTY-ONE

YUNAI

If Yunai wasn't stewing in shame, she would have been boiling in indignation. Braulio, along with his companions Siaka and Mirta, performed surgery on a golden iguana. Farid, donned in surgical attire, assisted them by observing the iguana's coloring in case it started to pale. And Yunai, wearing her regular uniform with only a mask to protect her, was relegated to standing in the back of the operating room...guarding the door.

She did exactly what Ignacia and Niesh taught them—to take initiative, to be prepared to fight in any circumstances. And this resident had punished her with non-work. It was impossible to stop an animal from going zonbi once they started to fall, so what was the point in delaying the inevitable? If Yunai had felled it right there, it wouldn't have smeared itself against the back door. It wouldn't have posed a threat.

"At least let her observe, Braulio."

Mirta's whispers brought Yunai back to the present. She kept her eyes down and picked up her ears. She heard nothing from Braulio in response.

"She didn't know what you were trying to do. We don't even know if your theory makes any sense."

Thank you! Yunai grinned under her mask.

"That's why I had to try?" Braulio snapped. "How do we know it doesn't if we don't take a chance? Aren't you tired of watching innocent animals fall?"

They paused the conversation while they continued their work. Yunai looked up. Farid kept up his watch as Braulio and Mirta focused on the iguana's belly. Siaka, whom Yunai learned was Odomi's adopted Son, had been silent the whole morning.

Yunai was curious as to how Braulio arrived at that theory. Moreover, she wondered why he entertained it in the first place. She couldn't imagine the same hospital that also served the cadets supporting his research. Cadets and scouts were trained to fell zonbi, no matter where they were in the process of falling.

"The zonbi that have been attacking the hospital act differently," Braulio said after some minutes. "They don't immediately go after people. It's almost like they're drawn to something."

What does that have to do with your theory?

"What does that have to do with your theory?" Mirta asked. She was quickly becoming Yunai's favorite person.

"It shows a level of sentience we never see. Almost like they're making a choice."

"How do you make a choice when you're brain-dead?" Siaka speaking up surprised Yunai. He looked like he had no interest in their back-and-forth. "What's changed that would switch up generations of behavior?"

Right, Braulio, your theory can't hold water.

"I don't know, Siaka, but I wasn't expecting you and Mirta to be this critical. Why are you both pushing back this hard?"

"Because they're right."

Seven eyes greeted her.

Oh...did she say that out loud? Yunai's face grew hot.

Mirta smirked with her eyes. The residents and Farid turned back to the iguana. "Right about what?" Braulio asked calmly.

Yunai knew what she wanted to say but waited for someone else to speak up on her behalf. She felt she had no right to insert her opinion after Braulio shut her down last time. But she also refused to let this man define her time here. "I just mean they're right to ask questions."

Siaka eyed her curiously. Braulio closed the iguana's belly, and Siaka started cleaning when he finished. Mirta directed Farid to roll the surgical table the iguana was on out of the operating room.

Braulio turned to Yunai and faced her directly. "And why would a cadet care about asking the right questions when your job is to hack and slash?"

"Because if the right questions aren't asked, people can get hurt." Yunai cupped her flesh elbow with her root hand.

Braulio's gaze lingered on her arms before he removed his surgical attire. "And what would be the right questions to ask?"

"I would ask..." Yunai didn't have an actual question. She hoped playing the root limb card would be enough to make her point that not felling zonbi on sight was risky. Yunai was learning, though, that Braulio held to his convictions as much as she tried to hold on to hers. "...I would ask why these patterns are happening in the hospital in the first place instead of jumping to theories."

"Then do that."

Yunai got out of the way when Braulio walked toward the door, pushing it open with his back. Siaka followed him out, sparing her no attention.

"Do that?"

"He wants you to do his dirty work." Mirta dumped her soiled gloves in the hazardous waste bin. "Which means you're right, but he's too proud to show it."

"Oh no, I was just suggesting—"

"Hey. I heard how he went off on you. Don't miss this chance to prove your worth." Mirta herded Yunai out of the operating room and into the sanitizing room. Braulio and Siaka finished washing their hands and left as the young women entered.

"I don't need to prove myself to him."

"I meant to yourself. I can tell he rattled your confidence." Mirta motioned for her to wash her hands.

"Does he—"

"Always act like an animal whose tail got stepped on? Yes. All the time. Don't take it in your veins. Some people are like that for no reason."

Yunai felt a lightness in her chest as she scrubbed her arms. It took less than fifteen minutes for this spirited young woman to turn her week around. Could she be reassigned to Mirta? And never breathe Braulio's frigid air again?

"I have some time before my next appointment," Mirta said as they exited the room and walked out into the main hall. "How about I help you with your new assignment?"

"It's...s-sure. I would love that." Yunai figured Braulio used their q-and-a as an excuse to get rid of her, but she wouldn't pass up a chance to learn from a resident who welcomed her presence. Or pursue this new problem.

Yunai stopped and looked up. She had been too distracted by her breakfast blow-up to notice the repaired glass ceiling. Then she looked at the door where the goat zonbi ended itself. The door had been cleaned and sanitized, and neither incident left injuries.

"So why do you think these patterns are happening, Yunai?" Mirta asked.

Yunai had never seen this level of activity during her past visits to Taisala. She ran through every unnatural encounter she experienced since arriving. The couple's painting on that side street, the men at the memorial, the scout at the concert, the goat—but there was no common thread. Unless all of them happening in the same time-frame was the denominator. Which meant two things—she had to assess the hospital situation on its own, and there was something—or someone—bigger at play that connected everything.

"If the zonbi aren't going after people, then maybe they're going...somewhere," Yunai said, facing the back door.

"The pharmacy and greenhouse are that way," Mirta said.

"Can we check them out? Am I allowed back there?"

"No, but I am." Mirta did a quick sweep of her surroundings. "I can take you, but we have to be quick."

Mirta led her through the door. She acknowledged a man sitting in a window with a wave. "This is the pharmacy. Nothing back here but the hospital technician and the store of harvested plants and medication."

Yunai flashed a half-smile at the technician and gave the place a once-over. She couldn't imagine what zonbi wanted to do with this quiet place. "You said there was a greenhouse?"

"This way." Mirta led her past the pharmacy and to another door. She pushed it open, the early afternoon sun warming their skin. Down a marble pathway was the greenhouse, nestled on a cozy, uneven lawn. Yunai could see the back of the cabins from where they stood. "The scoutmasters have been here already, and I doubt we have better senses than them."

Yunai followed Mirta down the pathway. She stuck up for her and now took her somewhere restricted. And Yunai barely knew her. "I don't mean to be rude, but why are you helping me? I thought the hospital didn't want us here."

"We don't," Mirta replied. "But there's no point in antagonizing you all without good reason." Mirta grabbed the greenhouse's door-knob. She turned around. "You seem pretty insightful for a cadet. Braulio, Siaka, and I...we like to question things too. Braulio's theory is a stretch, but it's not totally baseless either." Mirta turned the knob and pushed the glass door open, allowing Yunai to step in first.

Yunai entered a castle of green, serenity washing over her. The greenhouse reached far down the lawn and held several shelves of plants. A root chandelier hung in the middle, and a statue of the legendary healer, Raíz, was erected underneath it. Yunai didn't see anyone else in the building.

"We're not fans of the Scouthood, and neither is Odomi," Mirta said, closing the door behind her. "Your Grand Scoutmaster is trying to protect us, but she's doing the complete opposite."

The "your" was targeted, but Yunai took no offense. Mirta didn't seem the type to misfire her spite. Not like *Braulio*. She walked deeper into the greenhouse. "I think she doesn't want to leave room for people to get hurt."

"I think she lacks direction. She's pretty much running the Cathedral headless."

Mirta's comment lacked the hatred of the man's from the memorial, but it still set off an alarm through Yunai. If a scoutmaster had been around, they would have given her a warning.

"I'll take a look around," Yunai said quickly.

"Go for it."

Yunai strolled among rows of potted plants, many she had never seen before. The scoutmasters likely limited their sweep to people who were in the greenhouse at the time of the attack, so they probably didn't check the physical area as thoroughly. Not that there was much to check. Aside from the plants and the roots, the only thing that stood out in the greenhouse...

Yunai's root arm tingled. Startled, she slapped her flesh arm on it. It had never done that before. She looked at the statue of Raíz a few feet away from her. The longer she looked at it, the odder her arm felt.

Yunai moved closer to the statue and stuck her flesh arm out—the surrounding air was cold. She reached over the nest of roots at the base of the statue, the air growing colder. She ran her hand across the statue, then stood on her toes, moving her hand up to—

"Agh!" Yunai fell back on her behind, hitting her head on a table. She stared into a form with no name, chained to the statue. The bare torso was human, the multiple legs tentacled, the head canine, the top of its skull exposed. Zonbi didn't amalgamate with human parts, but more terrifying than its human form was its immobility. Its body was chained, and the head didn't move. It stared, needing no eyes to bear down on her.

"Yunai?"

Yunai scampered to her feet, flesh hand on the table for support, root hand trembling. With all her defense of felling zonbi on sight, she was sure struggling with syncing water from her water pouch. The form let out a sound, a low rustle of night noise that sounded lonely. Was this creature responsible for the strange zonbi activity?

"What happened?" Mirta asked. Yunai let Mirta help her to her feet when she appeared. "Are you okay?"

The low rustle increased to a groan, not at all dog-like. Only one of them saw and heard this thing...which meant one of them was unnatural.

"I-I...I just tripped..."

"Gotta be careful with these roots," Mirta said.

Yunai's dizzy eyes jumped from Mirta to zonbi. She wasn't sure who to focus on.

"Don't know why Odomi refuses to move them."

"Mirta?"

149

Siaka's voice. Mirta walked Yunai away from the table and back toward the entrance. They met Siaka halfway.

"Woman, what are you doing?" Siaka demanded. "Mom said not to bring anyone here."

"Relax, just helping your boy with his theory. If Odomi doesn't find out, there won't be an issue. Right?"

Siaka's eye lingered on Yunai. He looked into the space behind them before looking back at Mirta. "Our next appointment moved up. Get the cadet out of here before I tattle."

Yunai looked between them. Mirta smirked, and Siaka's features softened. Mirta whisked her away from the greenhouse and the monstrous nightmare.

TWENTY-TWO

NIESH

Niesh watched the cadets play syncing games with the children in the orphanage while the caretakers watched. The cadets synced roots horizontally at the giggling children as they tried to jump over them. How innocent they looked, shielded from the complexities of the world. She turned her attention back to her Sister. Paloma leaned against the orphanage's wall, her shoulders drooping.

"Where's the problem child?" Niesh asked, scanning the crowd.

"Inside. She doesn't like to join these days."

Good. If the child could self-regulate, it would make her scoutmasters' jobs easier. Her recent outburst had almost been her last. Luckily for her, the zonbi had stopped their advance—like the infestation on the hospital's roof.

"Her cadet is taking her out the next time she's here," Paloma said.

Even better. One thing taken care of.

"And how are you?" Niesh gripped Paloma's forearm.

Paloma's chest inflated, then deflated along with whatever words she wanted to get out. She focused on the children. They were the only thing stopping the tears from running down her tired face.

"We may have a lead," Niesh continued. "I have people on it.

Whoever is causing this unrest in the city, whoever aided in killing the Saint... Whoever robbed his body, they must lead back to one source. There is no way these are isolated incidents."

Paloma squared her shoulders and pushed herself up. She hooked a lock of hair behind an ear. "Who?" A pause to maintain composure. "Who stands to benefit from the pain of others? From my pain?"

Someone whose ambition eclipsed any logic or consequence. Someone who believed their pain was worth more than the Saint's life.

"I have to head to the hospital. The zonbi activity there has been strange. Too many of the animal patients keep falling, yet they never go on full attack mode." Niesh gave Paloma's forearm a squeeze before she let go. "My scoutmasters have been on top of things, but I need my eyes on that place now. Nothing in that hospital moves without me knowing."

ODOMI

"You still haven't explained exactly why you need me."

"You still haven't told me your name.

"I don't trust you."

"And I'm making sure I can trust you."

Odomi had observed several people in her search for the spirit she needed. All were critical of the Cathedral, but none had matched their actions to their words until now—even if it cost two innocents, or whatever Odomi made the scout see. Thankfully, her prospects avoided capture by the scoutmasters. The woman who threw herself onstage at the concert only received probation for disorderly conduct.

Odomi took the plate and cup from the woman and set them aside. They sat at the kitchen table in her home, but the scout made Odomi's home her own by propping her feet on the chair next to her. Odomi only allowed Siaka to sit like that, but she was too wound up to correct her.

"Been sitting in your house with nothing to do," the scout said. "Please tell me how that's ensuring trust."

"Everything in my house is intact. Nothing stolen. Food not overeaten. What greater test of trust is there than allowing someone in your private domain?"

The scout tched and turned her head away, one cheek forcing itself up past her attitude. "So what's next then? Fetch your mail? Water your plants?"

"Tell me about yourself." Odomi tried to relax back in her chair.

"You want to know why I abandoned my Word."

"Yes. But I want to know *you*. That's equally, if not more, important."

The scout took her feet off the chair and crossed her legs in her seat. She eyed Odomi for several seconds. "I got sick of high-and-mighty scoutmasters telling me to uphold morality when they barely held it with one hand. I don't like hypocrisy, so I left. Skipped the termination process, screwed my contract, and left."

Odomi continued to wait before speaking. She needed more from this story, more from this woman who went back on the Word of the Scouthood and turned her back on the Cathedral. Scouts did not quit early in their careers without backlash from society for abandoning their duties.

"I can tell you want more than that, but that's it," the scout said. "And for me, that was enough."

"Every organization has its corrupt. I've overseen more malpractice hearings than I can remember."

"That's nice, but I wasn't interested in...being told to throw an unnatural family out of their home while I knew my Master in Command treated his own family less. And that was the first instance. I got reassigned a few times. The faces changed, but the attitudes didn't. So I struck out on my own. I believe in the mission of the Scouthood, but I don't need to be bossed around to do good in this world. I get paid behind backdoors, and people get the help they need."

Her anecdote had promise. But much like her Word, that promise could be broken. And a scout, bound to a contract or not, still had ties to the Natural. Trusting her would be risky. "But I still don't know about *you*."

"Listen, lady—"

"Thousands of scouts have come before and after you, so you aren't the first one with those thoughts. What made *you* leave?"

The scout pulled her legs apart and put her feet on the floor. "How about I take an intermission, and you tell me what you want from me?"

"Not until I hear all I need to know."

"You'll hear nothing if I don't get something!" The scout synced the metal of the chair's arm up and snapped it off, forging it into a stake. She jumped onto the chair and dove at Odomi. Her expertly forged stake stopped right between Odomi's eyes. "That same attitude the scoutmasters have. You have it too, medic."

"And I know a scout never forgets their arrogance." Odomi had commanded the roots in her house to track the scout's movements from the moment she first entered her home. Odomi now trained their ends on every vein and opening of her guest. Her body would find out what her roots contained if she were foolish enough to hammer the stake.

The scout threw the stake back to the chair, forging it back into an arm. She didn't move the rest of her body.

"I need someone with a righteous spirit," Odomi said. "A leader. A revolutionary. Someone whose convictions are their very heart and blood."

"You love drama, don't you?" Minding the proximity between her body and the roots, the scout retreated to her seat. She sat upright, feet firm on the floor. "So you think I have all of that?"

"I think there's some potential. Whether it can be realized or not...I'm not sure just yet."

"Hmph. And you don't plan on telling me what for just yet. What's stopping me from walking out of here right now?" The scout monitored the roots still aimed at her body. "You won't torture or kill me without good reason. And I don't see you turning me into the Scouthood."

Odomi checked out her clothing and hair, clothing she had given her and hair that was silky. The night she found her, her clothes were worn and had a stench. Her hair looked like it hadn't been properly washed in ages, either. "I don't see too many individuals paying for a service they can get free from the Cathedral."

The scout bit the inside of her lower lip. Odomi knew the woman didn't have much bargaining power, no matter how much she puffed her chest. Odomi commanded the roots back on the wall.

"If you truly hate the Scouthood, then I believe you won't have a problem with my proposal," Odomi said. "We are going to change the Plane, make it better, and that includes getting rid of the Scouthood."

"We?"

Odomi smiled. "Change is never a solo effort." She stood up, took the cup and plate from the table, and walked to the sink. "If we can get to a point where you're not threatening me with my furniture, I'll tell you everything."

The sound of synced water against dirty dishes filled the air for a while, giving both women a reprieve. Odomi set the clean dishes on the drying rack and reached for a towel to dry her hands.

"Galu."

Odomi stopped drying and turned her head slightly toward the scout.

"My name. Galu."

RIZA

Riza heard rapid knocking on the door, but their mind and body did not have the energy to answer. It eventually stopped. They heard glass clang on the ground outside, then footsteps walking away. If they couldn't muster the energy to care, they could at least have the sense to not get caught.

Riza rolled off their new couch and stumbled to the door in the darkness of the house. They opened it and looked down at a small box at their feet. They grabbed it with purpose to avoid looking suspicious, then slammed the door. They turned back to the couch where they had been lying the whole day, then decided the kitchen would be better. Braulio had helped them purchase new furniture, furniture without their father's lingering emotions. Being on the couch made existence less arduous, but they didn't want it to be the only place they could stand to be.

Riza opened the box and looked at its contents—two bottles of rum. They poured some of the rum into a glass and stashed the rest in a bottom cupboard Braulio would never check. They sat at the kitchen table, where the box of their father's books had been since they retrieved them. Riza stared at the box, time of no essence.

It was never easy, doing the one thing a person wanted to do after waiting for so long. They grabbed the glass and took a swig. Took another until its chemicals worked on their nerves. Finding a dealer who sold alcohol through backdoor channels had been surprisingly easy for Lemana. Forget what Braulio thought. It was too hard, listening to the memories whisper through the air.

Riza pulled the first book from the box, a thin red notebook. This one had little emotion. Hints of sadness, of longing. Nothing strong enough to make them open it. Riza figured they'd save time finding their father's poem if they read the emotions of each book instead of flipping through them. His last poem would generate strong feelings, no matter what else he had written in the book. And reading his words in addition to his emotions would push them over the edge, even with liquid strength.

They grabbed the next one, this one thicker. A sensation slithered through their chest, straight to their gut. Riza twisted their lips and tossed the book away. They really didn't need to read their father's more...salacious thoughts.

After taking a cleansing gulp, they looked at the next one, a violet notebook with its cover coming off. Riza grabbed the book, and they—

"Shit."

—dropped it back on the table, knocking over the glass. They stopped all movement. But it was too much.

The rage.

The bitterness.

Emotion strangled their heart with claws. Forced a fist down their throat. Made ice of the rum. They took several minutes to zero down, eyes closed, breath controlled. When the space felt safe, they opened their eyes. The book acted like a magnet to their sight. They inched a hand toward it. Their father's emotions felt raw—this had to be it.

Riza took shallow breaths. They placed their hand on the cover

—and the liquor formed spikes. They opened the book and frantically flipped, each page soaked in anger. They flipped until the anger ran cold. The page they stopped on seized their hand. Riza's hand dragged itself down the paper. They wanted to rip the page out and burn it to ash. Drawing on every shot nerve, they yanked their hand away, using the other hand to calm it down.

This was all too much.

Riza leaned their head in and made out the words at the top of the page:

still water, skin

Riza didn't understand poetry, and their mind was too smothered with liquor and emotion to analyze the title. They kept reading, stepping through the words with caution.

forgetting how to speak
with waves
begged me to see that
I can no longer live like this

my body, my home
have become my knell

Riza didn't realize their shirt stuck to their torso until they started shaking. They had broken out in cold sweats, and their breathing was more strained.

They slammed the book shut. They didn't want to find out what finishing the poem would do to them. These cold chills, this hopelessness...was this how their father felt? No. He must have felt worse. Riza only felt the remnants of what he experienced.

Riza snatched the glass and took their desperation to the cupboard. They needed a lot more rum to remove the taste of death the poem left in their mouth.

ODOMI

"That cadet...is smart..."

Odomi checked the greenhouse to make sure nothing was out of place or taken. She held off on checking during the day to avoid stoking the suspicion of that cadet Siaka warned her about. Anyone was a potential threat. Niesh's scoutmasters searched the greenhouse when the zonbi broke through the roof, but that didn't mean she could rest easy. She spun back to Leonardo. "Did she say anything?"

"...who would she talk to..." A rough air seeped out of his mouth. "Whatever you conjured...to mimic me..."

Odomi ignored his comment and took stock of her immediate area. The greenhouse saw the least amount of traffic of all the buildings in the hospital. To reduce the chance of someone disrupting the plants, she only allowed the pharmacists, a few of the senior medics, and her three residents in. She never blocked the entrance in case of emergency, but it was an understood rule that anyone wanting access had to get Odomi's permission. It was the best place to hide Leonardo, away from her home, but at a place she frequented that she kept under her watch. That cadet was indeed smart.

But now Niesh hovered around, and that woman was smart, curious, *and* fiercely determined. The Grand Scoutmaster spent all morning shadowing medics and sitting in on appointments and animal surgeries. If she intended to spend more time in the hospital, then Odomi needed to push her timeline up. That required making a firm choice—try draining Leonardo one last time or letting Galu into the movement. Maybe she could ask some of her comrades in the movement for support? But they were busy. Or maybe Siaka could step up...

"...you seem agitated."

Odomi hated when Leonardo spoke up when she wasn't paying attention to him. No one wanted to be caught off guard by a voice that sounded like dead leaves.

"Control your emotions."

Of course that was the one thing he managed to say without losing his breath. Odomi almost snapped back, then checked herself. She turned back to the worktable where the journal was. She needed to breathe in its waves before her stress, and this fool, got the better of her nerves.

"Wouldn't want your curtain...to drop..."

Had it been a mistake to fake the Saint's death? Some of her comrades were strongly against the plan.

It's too risky.

There's no going back.

It's not necessary.

There are other ways to achieve our goals.

But how could they realistically achieve their goals under the Saint's thumbprint? How much could they actually change within the institution of repression?

"...imagine Paloma's face...seeing her Partner like this..."

Not much, and history proved that. Their movement was fragmented, a collection of ideas with no unifying voice. Taking the Saint's vibrancy would give them the power they needed. Only his sacrifice would unite the Revivalists.

"Imagine failing...and seeing the disappointment...on the face of your son."

Now she *would* snap. Odomi commanded the roots to sink their teeth into Leonardo's nerves. He would have howled if he had the energy. If he still possessed Lemana's gift of life, it would turn on the chandelier's root lights. Theoretically, traces of his power would be left in the roots, but Odomi had never captured that energy.

That was about to change.

Odomi commanded the roots deeper. Agony wrung Leonardo's face and twisted his limbs. They targeted his heart during the attack on the induction ceremony, so Odomi had to be careful not to strain him too much, or this death would be more than clinical.

Deeper.

She focused her attention on the roots above. No light, not even a little glow. Even a small snap had the power to illuminate the whole chandelier. It made no damn sense.

Deeper.

He choked. His veins bulged, making a map of his body. She didn't let up. He *needed* to give her something. *He* needed to pay for all the harm he and his predecessors had caused.

His head bobbed forward. Odomi stared at him as her frustration grew. Before it spilled over, she released the roots. Leonardo sagged against the chains. Odomi inspected a root. This was the longest she ever commanded the roots to drain him—but nothing. She felt no emotion, saw no glow or spark, and saw nothing that indicated his power had been siphoned. She grabbed a root and ripped it open—nothing but common root tissue.

Odomi's frustration surged. She had tried taking blood samples and experimenting on nerves, both of which allowed people to synchronize with the Natural world. If she couldn't get anything from either, then the solution was above her well of knowledge.

Nothing to do but go home and re-strategize before her emotions attracted zonbi to the hospital. Better to work out her emotions in the safety of her home.

TWENTY-THREE

RAKI

R aki rolled her eyes when Estefania told her to scoop more fried plantains onto Ignacia's plate. The platter of plantains was right in front of Estefania, and she had been hovering around Ignacia all afternoon. Raki piled a healthy serving on Ignacia's plate and sat back down.

"Twenty-three looks good on you!" Moraima said, continuing the conversation. "I never would have guessed."

"Your youthful looks are a thing to behold!" Umaru held a quarter of an orange upright as if it were a metaphor for Ignacia's age. "We should all be so lucky after our time as scouts."

"Thank you," Ignacia said, biting off a plantain. "But I promise my joints are older than what you see."

The cadets were gathered around the kitchen table. Laughter and conversation passed over plates and bowls of food—rice and beans, fried plantains, sliced oranges and grapefruit, tamales, and flan. Raki listened to Esera, Sega, and Obi debate the best comedy acts of the last cycle. Yoel and Matagi ate in silence. Yunai, who limited her interactions to smiles and nods, brought another platter of rice to the table from the new stove. Ignacia and her partner, Lulu, a woman with roots in Fa'atasi, sat at the end of the table. Her partner fed her a spoonful of rice and beans, a few grains falling into Ignacia's lap.

The birthday dinner reminded Raki of home. Her parents laying jokes on each other. Her grandparents making sure everyone was fed, and the young ones ensuring their elders rested.

Raki needed a day like this... *Toya* needed a day like this.

"My cadets have never cooked for me, much less celebrated my birthday," Ignacia said after swallowing a bite of food. Then jokingly, "Feels like a setup."

"You binge on plantains when you're stressed," Estefania said. "I know being our scoutmaster stresses you out, so we thought a dinner would be a nice breather."

"We?" Matagi said dryly.

"Fried food isn't enough to bail you out of 'Aute's House." Yoel sipped his coffee and glared at Estefania from behind his cup. "You're so transparent."

"This isn't a bribe, *Yoel*," Estefania said. "And how can you see me clearly when you're as bitter as your coffee is?"

"My coffee is black, and it's still sweeter than you."

"Okay, okay, you two." Ignacia made a settle-down gesture with her hands. Her partner kissed her on the cheek and whispered something into her ear that made her chuckle. Ignacia was glowing.

Raki was still wary of her teaching style—but Ignacia cared. She admitted, it was nice coming home after a rough day without worrying about whether her scoutmaster would go off on her for leaving a dirty dish in the sink. She heard horror stories from the other cadets about their scoutmasters—some had been punished and dismissed for the smallest infractions.

Which took her back to the orphanage. The way the caretakers treated Toya. The way Toya must feel under all her attitude.

Toya needed an Ignacia.

Raki needed to be an Ignacia.

"IT COULDN'T HAVE BEEN anything else but a zonbi," Yunai said, "but it had a human torso."

Raki, Esera, and Yunai lounged outside in front of the cabin. Esera hooked a mini radio into roots on the cabin's wall. He played a station that ran lo-fi bamboo music, which complemented the hot twilight. Cadets hung out on their porches, and the cabin cats prowled around the courtyard. Raki stared into the faded red sky, ignoring her slice of half-eaten flan and trying to pay attention to her companion.

"A human zonbi. That only you saw." Esera kept his tone neutral, but Raki detected the doubt in her Brother's voice. "Should you be saying this out loud? Where scoutmasters sleep?"

"I have to tell someone, and I trust you two," Yunai said. "Braulio, that resident, he's trying to see if he can stop zonbi from falling if he calms them down. I don't think it's possible, but I suggested there may be something in the hospital that's affecting how the zonbi act, and he told me to investigate. What if what I saw is that something? My root arm shook, too, when I got close to it. It never does that."

"So you're listening to him now." Esera never missed a chance to take a shot at someone when they deserved it, but the way he homed in on Yunai's interaction with Braulio... He had been acting off ever since they started their service assignments.

"Yunai, you should just report that to Ignacia," Raki said, pulling away from the sky. "You can get in serious trouble if you don't and something happens."

"But what if I do and the Scouthood thinks I'm unnatural? That's why I want you both to come with me. It won't be suspicious if other people verified what I saw. This zonbi could answer a lot of questions about all the strange activity happening."

"I'm not trying to get sent home." Esera tinkered with the roots when the radio started going in and out. "And I can't play detective, anyway. The Cathedral is...making me help out the scoutmasters in town. I don't have the space."

Yunai shuffled her feet across the dirt and threw her eyes everywhere. "I understand. It's a lot to ask..."

Raki had a child to mentor. She couldn't get caught up with Yunai's assumptions. But she also didn't have it in her to let her go alone. She hesitated but eventually said, "I'll go with you. But just to observe, and we report right back."

Yunai's spirit returned. "Thank you, Raki. I'd really appreciate the companionship."

"Don't thank her just yet." Esera turned the volume up as the trio watched the silver of the moon put the twilight to rest.

BRAULIO

Braulio synced a bit of orange onto his canvas. He painted a stylized wheel with a finger, one eye on his work in progress, the other on Riza, who sat across from him. Riza's eyes were dead, their canvas and paints untouched.

"It's either this or I drop you at 'Aute's House," Braulio said, both eyes back on his canvas. With another finger, he synced up yellow paint. "They have art therapy there, too."

They sat on the rooftop of a near-empty art restaurant. Few were left in Lemana. The Cathedral had shut down several in the last cycle for violating Natural laws, or whatever foolishness. They were one of the few public venues Braulio enjoyed.

Riza shifted in their seat and leaned to the side, head resting in a hand. "I talk about my father's last thoughts, and you toss jokes around."

"It's not a joke. It's a next step. You can either stay in that house and become a zonbi, or you can process your emotions—and his emotions—on that canvas so the Scouthood doesn't...you know." Braulio indicated what "you know" meant with a click of his tongue and a tilt of his head.

"And how do you process something you don't fully understand, Braulio?" Riza shifted up slightly as the waiter approached with glasses of water. They waited for him to leave before continuing. "He wasn't that far gone. I know he wasn't."

A thick silence followed. Braulio acknowledged it by not rushing to fill the space with empty words. He continued with his wheel, moving on to green.

"There was no point in coming out tonight, was there?" Riza said.

"Like I said, you need to deal, and that means me not cosigning everything you believe."

Riza huffed. They picked up the menu both had been ignoring, then just as quickly threw it back down. They could go long periods without food, but Braulio wished Riza would eat something.

"Now I remember why I stopped writing you," Riza said.

Braulio let his canvas fall to the table. It was either that or throw the thing at Riza. "I'm just trying to protect you. Lemana is the last place someone like you should be."

"And before Lemana?"

Yeah. Should have just thrown it. "Riza. I have my own life here. A job. I know I dropped the ball with you, but I'm carrying a lot more than just your stuff."

More silence. At least this time the waiter came to take their orders during it. Braulio gave his order and shook his head at the waiter when Riza didn't speak up. He used the timeout to reset the conversation. The break between them wouldn't be bridged in one night. No need to force it.

"What are you expecting to discover with this poem?" Braulio asked, picking the canvas back up.

Riza flicked their canvas and tapped their fingers on the table. Were they ignoring him or just lacking answers?

"Riza."

"That he didn't take his own life. That he was another victim of the Cathedral, an *unnatural* who they hounded down and slaughtered. That the only reason they told us he killed himself was because the university needed to avoid a scandal—an unnatural teaching the next generation to ask questions."

Braulio looked up and straight into their black amber eyes for the first time that night. Those were eyes of determination, eyes that refused to accept any other reality. Riza's explanation was plausible, but what proof did they have? Feelings from a poem they didn't even finish reading? Braulio searched for ways to support their mission without letting his opinions create a murkier bog between them.

"I'm not expecting you to understand," Riza said, answering the question in Braulio's head. "You get to be normal, so these aren't thoughts you're saddled with. But I get to distrust people who kill people like me."

The next scene punctuated their conversation perfectly.

Braulio stood up when he picked up on a struggle nearby. He walked over to the railing and looked out into the plaza, Riza following suit. A man with a scarred face and a viridian scarf dragged a girl out into the middle of the plaza by her hair. Bystanders, human and animal, encircled the two.

"You're getting a live demonstration tonight!" The scoutmaster gave the girl a yank. He threw a radio to the ground, smashing it to pieces.

Another man broke from the circle and stared the girl down. "I'm sorry, I tried to warn her. I never wanted that music in our house!"

The scoutmaster spared the man a glance, then addressed the crowd. "Hey! If you heard music that talked about taking mind-altering substances, how do you think you'd react?"

"I-I-I was just listening, I don't want to, I-I w-wouldn't—"

The scoutmaster turned the girl's words to screams with another tug of her hair. The crowd started hurling insults at her, questioning how she could *ever* listen to music like that. Braulio felt the bile rise in his throat.

"Saint's dead and somehow people think they can do whatever they want now," the scoutmaster said.

Riza strangled the metal railing. "I can get her out of there."

"What, so you can see your dad a lot sooner?" Braulio forced them back with a firm grip. He knew Riza could in their unique way, but he questioned their emotional stability. "Don't. You're too raw right now, and we're in public."

"So I just—"

"Yes. You just. Use the canvas." Braulio pulled Riza away from the railing and led them back to the table. He had witnessed several run-ins between scoutmasters and citizens, but none so showy or brutal. One thing he and Riza did agree on—the Scouthood was a menace. Maybe their father did fall victim to their surveillance.

The uproar from the crowd shielded both from whatever terror the scoutmaster visited upon the girl. Braulio watched Riza turn all the way inward until the only way they could release their anger was through art that was indifferent to their emotions.

TWENTY-FOUR

RAKI

Raki followed Toya off the train and into the city streets. The child was quiet and sullen the whole ride. She wanted to visit Maogatai University to see someone whose name she refused to tell her, but Paloma instructed Raki not to let Toya go there. She didn't give a reason, and Raki didn't bother asking. Spending a day in town would be better for Toya, anyway.

Regardless, getting Toya out of the orphanage should have switched her mood up, but no. Still silent. Still petulant. These things took time, didn't they?

"We've got the whole city to ourselves!" Raki said, putting her hands on her hips in triumph. She sneered when someone bumped her arm.

Toya just looked at her, then looked away.

Raki dropped her arms. "Sooo, what are we feeling today? Shopping? Parks?"

Toya walked away from the platform. Raki caught up to her when she realized Toya would only keep going.

"What do you like to do?" Raki asked, matching her pace.

"Whatever the caretakers make us do."

"Okay, but what do *you* like to do? For fun?"

"Nothing's fun in an orphanage."

Most of the children *were* much younger. Raki couldn't see Toya playing animal syncing games when most others her age were learning to sync themselves or going to parties. She was learning that getting through to Toya required striking from different angles. "How about before you got here? What did you do then?"

"I don't know."

"Oh, come on, there—"

"Can we go in that store?"

It was less of a question and more of a heads-up. Toya bolted into a trading post, breezing right through the woven cane mat hanging in the door. *Patience, Raki, patience.* She followed her in, acknowledging the shopkeeper.

Raki found Toya poking around the different wares on display—clay pottery, turquoise jewelry, and intricately designed figurines. She kept a close eye on Toya as the child picked up a turquoise ring and slid it onto a finger. She held it up to the light, the ring's color casting a glow on her skin. Raki peeked at the price on the shelf—and silently begged Toya to put it back. The ring cost more than a cadet made in a month. A scout, even.

Raki was grateful when Toya set it down. Toya brushed her eyes over the next shelf, then turned to the exit. "We can go." Another heads up because Toya was on her way out before she finished her sentence.

They walked down the market street for half a minute, then Raki followed Toya into another post. This one housed all sorts of goods from around the Plane, from clothing to cleaning concoctions. Toya scanned the store from the entrance, then buzzed right over to the clothing racks. Raki relaxed when she saw the affordable prices. Then she looked at Toya's clothing—a faded red shirt and brown shorts, both old but in good shape. One of her sandals was missing a strap, a root replacing the missing piece. Raki wondered how Paloma would feel about her buying Toya a new closet.

Toya picked up a traditional print dress made by the nomadic peoples and put it against her body. Its prints were in a different style than what Raki and her family normally wore. Toya put it back on the rack and moved to another set of dresses. She grabbed one imported from Artemisa, with a floral pattern and puff sleeves, and smiled. People occasionally wore the traditional clothing of people from different backgrounds when appropriate but tended to stick to the garb of their own heritage.

When Toya moved to put the dress back, Raki quickly said, "You can try it on."

Toya glanced at her shyly, then looked back at the dress. Raki caught her burying a smile under her bitterness as she made her way to the dressing room. Raki waited by the door.

"It's a cute dress!" Raki called. "Maybe you can wear it out next time." She heard shuffling, then a bump on the wall. "You okay?"

After a minute, Toya opened the door. Raki fixed her mouth to appear delighted—but she wanted to cringe. The top of the dress squeezed against Toya's torso, the sleeves ready to scream open. The skirt part was free, but showed her shins awkwardly. And the extra bows and buttons and frills made her look like an overgrown dress-up doll.

"Is it supposed to fit like this?" Toya attempted to adjust her body into the dress.

Raki took a harder look. She wasn't super familiar with traditional Artemisan clothing, and didn't think Toya was either, but this dress obviously wasn't for someone Toya's age. "Yeah, that one's not for you."

"Is it the wrong size?"

"No, I mean that's for a child. Like younger than you."

The switch from bashful to disdainful was instant. Toya stormed back into the dressing room and slammed the door.

"Toya, it's fine! We can find ones for older children!"

The sound of Toya breaking out of the dress was her only response. She threw the door open, left the dress on the floor, and blew out of the post.

"Toya! Agh..." Raki grabbed the dress, ran it back to the rack, then flew through the door. "Toya!" She found her further down the street. Raki pushed through the crowd. When she almost lost sight of her, Raki crouched down on all fours and boosted herself into the air, leaping over heads. She spotted Toya from above and landed right in front of her. Before she darted away, Raki grabbed her.

"Leave me alone!"

"Will you calm down? It was a mistake!"

"You let me look stupid!" Toya tried to fight off Raki's hold. "You're supposed to be *helping* me!"

"I was—I am. It's just shopping, it happens. It happens to everyone!"

"I don't know how to shop."

"You just...try things on and pay for them? How do you not know how to shop?"

"Because *I don't. Know!*"

Raki luckily caught the zonbi from the corner of her eye. She threw Toya behind her, punched her fists into the ground, and pulled out spiked gauntlets. The crowd scattered. Raki launched her gauntlet at the zonbi, boring her fist clean through the creature. Its remains hung on her forearm like a thick bracelet. Raki looked away as she lowered her arm to let the carcass fall off. Guts soaked her arm. Excellent.

"I knew this was a bad idea. We should have gone to the university like—"

If Toya kept on, more zonbi would attack. One arm around Toya's shoulders, the other scooped her up by the backs of her legs. Then Raki leaped Toya away from busy city streets, hoping she wouldn't challenge their brusque exit in midair.

TOYA COLLAPSED ONTO A BENCH, dizzy. Raki took off her shirt, cleaned her arm with it as much as possible, then burned the ruined shirt. She pulled an extra top from her backpack and put it on.

"That was awful!" Toya cried, clutching her head. She didn't notice the zonbi guts Raki had gotten on her. "Why would you do that?"

"I was hoping it would settle your anger." *But it looks like nothing can help that.* Raki bit back the thought. She needed this child to zero down and open up. They'd get nowhere if they accomplished neither. "Toya. What was your life like before Lemana? Did you do things with your family? With companions?"

The anger that sat so easily on the surface broke into small cracks. Raki saw the sadness in her coal eyes, the tremble at the edge of her lips. Toya looked away, trying to mold the anger back over her face.

Raki crossed her arms, pondering the best way to bridge the gap of understanding between them. "When I was around your age, or maybe younger, I went shopping with some companions from school. They were a lot more developed than I was. I was barely in bras. We went to the mall after school one day to try on dresses for a party. They all tried on these shapely dresses, and I did too. I knew none of them would fit me properly, but I was so eager to fit in that I—"

"I don't have stupid memories like that! I don't know how to shop or dress myself or have companions! And I don't know how because I don't *remember* how! I don't remember c-coming to the orphanage or what m-my life was like before it or who my parents were or wh-where I'm from!"

The sadness flooded around them. Tears flowed from Toya's eyes. Raki checked for any sign of zonbi, and thankfully none came. A part of her was glad Toya didn't sync—reactions from the Natural on top of zonbi would have been too much to deal with. She sat down next to Toya, who yanked away from her when Raki tried to rub her back. Better to wait until her emotions descended from their peak.

"When I try to remember, I get nightmares, and I can't even remember those when I wake up. The other children remember their lives, but I don't. The caretakers tried to help, lots of people tried."

"I'm sorry, Toya... I don't know what to say."

They sat in silence for a while, but this time the silence was easy.

Raki felt stupid for trying to relate to her with a prepubescent shopping story. It sounded like something a parent would try. Esera always told her she tried too hard to act like one.

"All I know is that dumb orphanage," Toya said. "I hate it. I hate it so much. No one wants to adopt someone like me."

"I'm sure there's a parent or a family out there for you. There's someone for everyone." Raki wanted to tell her about Esera's adoption but decided against it. No more relating for today.

171

"I can't remember anyone who cares about me, and no one I know wants anything to do with me."

"So what am I?" Raki asked, slightly offended.

"A cadet who needs credits, like all the others who came before you."

"Toya. There are no credits. I'm not a scholar. Yes, I'm here on orders from my scoutmaster, but that doesn't mean I can't care."

Toya shrugged.

"Then I guess I have to prove it to you." Raki jumped back up. "We'll go out every day I come. There's no better way to relearn life than to live it. It may jog some of your memories, too."

"I guess..."

"Also, Toya, you...you have too many outbursts. Which I understand why now. But you're going to have to learn how to sync if you want to stay safe. I won't always be around to look after you, and a scoutmaster may not make it in time the next time a zonbi attacks." Raki watched the "no" bubble up and pop in Toya's throat. If she had managed to sway her opinion on syncing, then she wasn't doing a bad job at all. She still didn't understand why Toya was against it, but that was an answer to uncover another day. "Here, let's start with something easy."

"Now?"

"Yes? I know we had an eventful morning, but there's still a whole lot of day left."

Toya groaned as Raki crossed her legs on the ground. Toya kneeled in front of her.

"So syncing is basically connecting your blood to the Natural world."

"I *know* that," Toya snapped, looking at Raki like she was stupid.

"Just listen, alright?" Raki held up her hand, palm facing Toya. "It's easy. You just let the dirt stick to your hand." Raki placed her palm on the ground. A thick film of dirt and gravel stuck to her palm.

Toya stared at her hand, unimpressed. Raki widened her eyes, signaling to Toya to try. Toya slapped her hand on the ground and raised it. A little dirt and a few pieces of gravel stuck to her hand.

"Okay, there's a little there," Raki said.

"Or it's sticking to my sweat. Jeez." Toya rubbed the dirt off. So much for the positive approach.

"Maybe don't slam your hand down. Take your time. It's your blood doing the work, but your body has to connect too."

Toya raised her hand and lowered it to the ground. Deep breath in. Deep breath out. She lifted it. A thin layer of dirt covered her hand, with little skin showing.

Raki clapped. "Yes! There you go. See? Easy."

Toya cracked out a grin. Raki watched her eagerly sync with the other hand. Less dirt this time, but still a success. Toya couldn't hide her glee now. Raki continued to show her simple exercises, the rest of their day passing with relative ease.

TWENTY-FIVE

ODOMI

"What's been up yours?"

As she ran downstairs and into the kitchen, Odomi paid no attention to Galu, who read a book on her couch with shoes on. She opened her freezer and snagged a concoction. She popped the top off, thawed the bottle slowly in her hands, and downed its contents. Knowing how tiring performing her hospital duties and executing her plans would be, Odomi had prepared a few energy-boosting concoctions for the days her aging body couldn't keep up. Today was gearing up to be one of those days.

She heard Galu enter the kitchen. "I know shit's happening, so why don't you just tell me what it is."

Odomi turned to face her. "We need to move things along."

"Cool. I mean, I have been saying that."

"Niesh wants to meet with me personally."

Galu's face remained neutral. "Doesn't she meet with senior staff regularly?"

"Ibrahim meets with the medics regularly and does one-on-ones when necessary, and with advance notice."

"Still not following. The circumstances are different now?"

Odomi eyed her intently, then moved past her and back into the living room. Galu didn't know about her captive in the greenhouse, but her nonchalance still aggravated her. That cadet getting too close to Leonardo—with Mirta's assistance—unnerved her. Siaka wasn't sure what the cadet or Mirta saw, if anything, and if the cadet had uttered a word to her scoutmaster...

Galu trailed her into the living room. "Hi. Scout here. I know there's information you're withholding aside from what you're already not telling me. Why does a meeting with the GS matter so much?"

"Because there are things she can't find out."

"Things you can't tell me?"

"Yes." Before Galu had a chance to push back, Odomi continued. "You'll be spending the day with my Son."

"Why? Is this meeting a house call?"

"No. I'm covering my bases. Niesh is relentless. If she can't find anything at the hospital, she'll find her answers somewhere else. There's no reason why she won't show up at my doorstep at any moment."

"Hmm, I actually like her, but she's definitely a hard ass. Okay. Fine. Whatever you say."

"I'll send him over after our meeting. He'll have questions for you. Keep your head down and stay out of trouble."

"Yeah, yeah." Galu plopped back on the couch and returned to reading.

Odomi grabbed her bag, double-checked to make sure the journal was still in it, and left, securing her home with the roots.

NIESH

The cadets in the water tank felled the shark-turned-zonbi without a fight, but the fact that they had to fell zonbi in a hospital at all...

The Board would never stand for it if they found out.

Niesh watched the cadets haul parts of the zonbi out of the tank in the sanctuary and through the back door to burn. The residents synced the contaminated water out and through one of the drains in the floor.

If the zonbi here weren't out for blood, they were here for another reason. And Niesh was going to find out today.

ESERA

"Begin!"

Esera and the other cadets dove into the water from the driftwood platform. They propelled themselves through the ocean as far as their bodies allowed. Humberto was training them to dive at deep levels. Deep-water diving wasn't new to Esera, but he savored every moment he swam through blue space. The ocean was the only place he felt whole, safe, and at ease.

Some cadets turned around when the pressure bore down on their lungs. Esera kept diving, the water growing darker. More cadets conceded to the ocean's strength. Esera looked around. No one around him—except for Matagi. Esera ignored his presence and focused on the depths ahead of him. But he couldn't help thinking of their assignment tonight. Esera knew why Ignacia picked him, but he wanted nothing to do with this hunter business. He wanted nothing to do with Niesh and her half-assed plans. They had nothing to go on, no clues, barely any information.

The pressure became too much for Esera. He could have gone deeper, but his thoughts interfered with his ability to ignore the strain in his chest. He stopped and turned for the surface as Matagi continued deeper into the dark.

ODOMI & NIESH

Odomi sat. Niesh stood.

"How often do you pay attention to who comes in and out of the hospital?"

"We keep logs of every visitor, patient, animal, resident, medic, technician, scoutmaster, cadet, and support staff who comes in. A senior medic reviews them before and after every shift change."

"And no one suspicious has ever entered?"

"No. Not since Leonardo's passing, no."

A pause.

"What are you looking for?"

"Have you heard the rumors about Leonardo?"

"...yes. Ibrahim is a gossip. His body was robbed."

"That's it?"

Hesitation. "Something about his body being swapped. It's disgraceful."

"What I don't understand is how they did it. Replacing his body with another corpse. To breach a place so well-defended without being seen. There's no explanation that's Natural."

"The unnatural are getting bold, indeed."

"Bold—and discreet."

Both waited.

"The cadets are doing a good job handling zonbi outbreaks. Though I've heard from some of the medics that you believe they deserve dignity in their felling."

"Brutality goes against the medic's oath. And felling with grace keeps my patients and staff safe."

"And what about their behavior? I've seen no effort from your end to find out why they're behaving differently."

"They're not harming anyone, so I don't see why I need to."

"You're not curious at all? You don't find it unnatural?"

"They're already unnatural, Niesh." A smile. "It's only important that they're felled, right?" Another pause.

"Thank you for your time, Odomi."

Odomi remained seated. Niesh left.

SIAKA

"They let residents train with one eye?"

She was blunt. He could work with that.

"Eh, only need one." Siaka sat across from Galu on the train. Odomi gave him the day off to stage this little play with her new comrade.

"How'd you get it? Zonbi attack?"

Siaka grinned. "Torture."

The coolness escaped from her face when his grin didn't falter. "Oh. That's a story worth hearing."

She wasn't the first person to ask about his missing eye, and she wouldn't be the last. The question used to rankle him, but the need to repress his emotions had quickly changed that. "How about a trade? Your story for mine."

"Hmph. Your Mom said you had questions for me."

Siaka only needed one moment of vulnerability. Naturals' emotions were tricky to latch onto, and a trained scout would be harder. If he successfully revealed her true emotions, the journal Odomi had entrusted him with would react. She would be the spirit Odomi needed to unify the unnaturals.

Galu jumped off the train when they reached their stop. "Why the personal approach? No one who's ever wanted anything from me has been this...intimate."

"Think of this as an interview," Siaka said, following her. "If you're not the right fit, we'll send you on your way. No strings attached." He wasn't sure if that was true or not, but he needed to say something to ease any concerns she had.

Siaka led her to a quiet park. They started down the overgrown grass, away from listening ears.

"I don't have some sort of memoir if that's what you people are looking for," Galu said.

"Honesty is the only thing we can work with."

They walked deeper into the park before Galu started.

"I was raised on Fa'atasi, in a lively city far away from any wilds or wastelands or roving zonbi. Sibling is a dentist. Parents work for the local council. I was a well-behaved child. It was a boring, simple, easy life, the kind you don't know is good until it's gone."

Siaka glanced at her, his attention roused.

"Don't get excited. I say gone because I left. I didn't realize how good our governance was until I came here. Or at least until I saw how the Scouthood ran things, even while the Saint was still alive. The bootlicking, the disregard for humanity. My scoutmaster was one of the better ones, but even she compromised her morals when it suited her.

"I saw their behavior for myself when I was sworn in as a scout. My first Master in Command was a known abuser. Masters make good money, and he made sure he kept every coin for himself. While his children starved and while his Partner struggled to keep their house together. I reported him to the Scouthood, but my grievance disappeared as soon as it left my mouth. The only reply I got was an offer to change Masters. Guess they were trying to shut me up. But I took it because it was better than working for someone who didn't care to protect their own family.

"The next was the tipping point for me. I was reassigned to the unnamed continent during an extra bloody period of the conflict over there. If you know anything about that place, then you know the zonbi there are ferocious. You know scouts aren't supposed to get involved in government conflicts—but the Saint himself gave direct orders for us to get involved. He commanded us to support the soldiers with the removal of unarmed, suspected unnaturals from territory the soldiers claimed didn't belong to them. But we didn't physically remove them. We were only told by the soldiers to round up all the zonbi we could find from our latest mission and bring them to the soldiers. I didn't think they were going to release them on people we only suspected to be unnaturals until I saw it myself. They didn't even have a chance to scream. Again I complained, and again nothing was done."

Siaka found his mind easing away from her words. He felt little from her and found it hard to connect emotionally. That unnamed continent was Odomi's original homeland, so he knew the horrors unnaturals faced there. But Galu's story wasn't the moving narrative he assumed it would be. Not that it *had* to be, but her pain felt secondhand. Not like the grief Odomi carried every day. But he trusted his Mom's judgment, so he had to make this work.

"Were you the only one who spoke up?" Siaka asked. He stopped walking when Galu did.

"I'm sure I wasn't, and I know I'm not the only scout who ever has."

Siaka scrutinized her face, the way her lips cut her thoughts open, the strict steadying of her eyes. He knew this was as deep as Galu's story would go—which meant this was his chance. "Becoming a scout only to realize they're not as upstanding as everyone believes they are. I'd be pissed."

"I felt disgusted." Galu broke herself open upon saying those words, revealing hostile body language. "How are we letting these people continue to protect our world? Why does no one question anything or keep anyone accountable? I returned to Taisala to help out when I heard about the increase in zonbi. I hoped the Saint's death would have changed the Scouthood's thinking, but it's only gotten worse."

He felt it. Her resentment leaked through her repressed wall, a crack in the dam. Her emotions caught Siaka's waves. He pulled her into his dim emotional pool, its soft current beckoning her spirit deeper.

"I only hate that I didn't leave sooner." Galu's voice grew hotter, her movements wilder. "Why in the world did I think switching or speaking up would do anything? I was an idiot for thinking I could change things!"

Siaka felt her move deeper, their emotions riding the same wave, though at different heights. He stole a peek at Odomi's journal in his bag. If Galu was the one, the journal would let him know—but it told him nothing.

ESERA

Esera entered the top floor of the abandoned building where they had fought the scout. Matagi followed him in, veering to the right to inspect the area. The journey into the city was predictably silent, only necessary questions asked and answered. If they could maintain that level of exchange during this pointless mission, Esera would breathe easier.

He needed to say something introductory, at least. "This is the only lead we have. So it's this or nothing."

Matagi aimed for a shattered box near the middle of the room, the box the scout used to forge her stakes. He kneeled and scanned the debris, picking up a stake and turning it around in his hand.

While Matagi focused on the scout's traces, Esera concerned himself with whoever knocked them out. He didn't know what they would have left behind. They didn't use darts, so the sedative must have been synced in. Esera felt the area where he had been shot. The residents who checked them afterward said the sedative wasn't concerning. It was a standard concoction that posed no threat. Anyone could have made it or gotten their hands on it.

Esera inspected the back area. He didn't see anything of note, no shoeprints or medical items or suspiciously synced walls. He looked at Matagi, who had moved to the window where the scout sniped her victims. Esera needed to think at a higher level. They were not going to find any physical evidence here. If they couldn't rely on physical evidence...

"How did she kill two people if there were three of you?" Matagi asked.

"She was a fully trained scout," Esera fired back, keeping himself in check. "It's not like we stood a chance. And we were knocked out."

"I ask because I want to know her level of skill. In case we find her and have to take her down."

"Niesh told us just to observe."

"She'd prefer if we did the dirty work."

"She does?" Esera flexed his fingers. "Because that's not what she told me."

"She wants any unnatural dead. No sense wasting time going through the chain of command if we can do it ourselves." Matagi turned to face him. "Or is that a problem for you?"

"It's a problem for me if we disobey orders from the freakin' Grand Scoutmaster, and I get sent home because of it." Tempting heat enveloped Esera's senses. Damn him, Matagi wasn't going to make this decision. "I'm not here to bulldoze my way through the Scouthood." *Like you.*

"Neither am I," Matagi replied to his unspoken words. He angled back to the window. "I have a family to take care of. I don't have time to waste playing nice when I have a future to secure."

Esera tched. He didn't have a decent rebuttal against caring for family—and it actually annoyed him. He didn't want to feel anything close to empathy for Matagi.

"Forget about this scout." Matagi walked away from the window. "You were sedated without a dart and were out for a while. That's expert-level syncing. Something only a skilled medic, or an assassin, would know how to do without leaving a trace." He made for the door.

Now Esera burned up. He didn't care how immature he felt, that was his part to solve! "Where are you going?"

"Don't we have to report to Niesh? We're done here." Matagi left.

Esera unleashed the heat gathered in his body, turning the room into a sweltering bath. Once he was sure he expelled most of his fire, he followed Matagi out, kicking the door on the way.

TWENTY-SIX

YUNAI

"**A**re you sure you want to do this?"

Yunai hiked up to the hospital from Lemana, Raki trailing her. The dead night amplified the sound of their steps. Yunai had convinced Raki to spend the evening in the city with her. She wanted to make sure the hospital's evening staff had gone home, as fewer people worked the overnight shift. Leaving the cabins for the hospital in the middle of the night would have appeared suspicious, and the fewer people with eyes on them, the better.

"If *we* get caught," Raki continued between breaths, "we can get sent home, especially you, since Ignacia told you not to push that thing with the scout. You know that, right?"

"I know." Yunai kept walking but picked up her pace. They walked in hard silence until they reached the hospital's entrance. Yunai got halfway through signing in when the scoutmaster on duty stopped her.

"What's your reason for coming here this late?" he asked.

Yunai looked up at him. She must have looked like a rodent caught digging through garbage.

"Anyone not on staff needs to list a reason for visiting after hours. Including cadets and scouts."

Shoot. Yunai didn't know about this requirement. She scrambled for a reason. "Records. Patient records. My resident, Braulio. He told me to double-check his records for signatures or missing info. Something about an audit coming up." A scoutmaster wouldn't know if the hospital had an audit coming up, right? She heard Raki take a deep breath behind her.

"This late?"

"I didn't finish, and the audit is coming up soon. There were a lot of files." Yunai turned to Raki, turned back, then added, "He said I could bring a companion to help. She's a cadet too."

The scoutmaster glanced at Raki, then back at Yunai. He tapped the sign-in sheet. When Yunai realized he signaled for her to continue, she finished writing, then passed the pen to Raki. Yunai gave the scoutmaster a wobbly half-smile, and the two entered the hospital.

Yunai zipped straight for the sanctuary. She averted eye contact from all sides, hoping no one cared enough about her to greet her.

"So who should do these files while we look for this zonbi?" Raki said. "Because I thought you wanted me to confirm what you saw."

Yunai turned to Raki. "I had to say something. Paperwork takes a while, so we'll have plenty of time. And that scoutmaster has no reason to check on us." She continued walking.

"And how much time *do* we need? We can't stay here all night."

"Not a lot. We're just observing, remember?"

"Alright."

Yunai felt the friction and knew Raki felt it too, but she chose to ignore it. She led Raki to the back of the sanctuary, then to the rear exit leading to the greenhouse. Yunai lit a torch bright enough to guide their path but small enough to prevent revealing their presence. They took the marble path down.

ESERA

"We're here under special orders from the Grand Scoutmaster," said Esera. "She sent a messenger cuckoo ahead with information." Esera and Matagi, who stood off to the side, watched as the scoutmaster guarding the entrance to the hospital unlocked the cabinet behind him.

"Lotta cadets here late," the scoutmaster said, going through documents. He picked one out, read it, then put it back. "You're good to go. She doesn't want you to sign in. The staff knows you're here to grab medical supplies for Ibrahim."

"Thanks," Esera said. He and Matagi went in. They stopped at the entrance. Esera swept his eyes over the area. *Lotta cadets here...* He really hoped this wasn't the night he'd see Yunai in these halls.

"We should split up," Esera blurted out when he saw Matagi start to speak. "This place is big." Matagi walked off, heading for the sanctuary. Esera rolled his eyes. The main hospital was his then.

Esera barely finished giving his report before Niesh directed them to investigate the base hospital. There were dozens of medical facilities in Lemana, not to mention pharmacies, but she was certain the sedative originated from *this one*, and this one only. How she arrived at that conclusion, he didn't know. And now he and Matagi had to go on another wild chase looking for evidence linking back to the identity and whereabouts of the scout.

Whatever. He was here to take orders and feel nothing and avoid getting punished and sent home. No need for questions.

YUNAI

"What am I looking for?"

Yunai and Raki stood before Raíz's statue. Raki walked around the statue while Yunai stood frozen—either she couldn't see the zonbi anymore, or it was no longer there.

"It was here. *It was right here.*" Yunai's torch flickered. She took a couple of steps forward. She lifted her root arm, but it didn't tingle. "It was chained to the statue, so it couldn't have escaped."

"Then someone must have felled it," Raki said. "If someone else saw what you saw, they probably burned the thing. Which would help prove you're not unnatural."

Yunai turned to Raki. "Then why couldn't Mirta see it?"

"Maybe she's the suspicious one? I don't know, Yunai. There's no zonbi, so why does it matter?"

"Because I need to know why I saw it in the first place. I need to know why certain people are seeing things others can't! If you were in a position to stop something bad from happening, wouldn't you do everything in your power to help?"

Raki turned her head away and shook it, moving her lips in silent thought. "You're right. There's a child who needs my help. I'm sorry. I can't risk being here right now. I have to go." She walked away.

"But—"

Raki disappeared faster than Yunai could get her words out. She sighed, turning back to the statue. This was important. Raki might not think that his mattered, but Yunai did. She didn't want to be anything like the recruits who hid in their rooms while they fought the tentacled zonbi. She wanted, *needed* to be someone who acted. She had to prove herself. And prove herself right to her parents.

Yunai weakened her torch flame when she realized it had grown too big. Any bigger and she'd burn her face. She jumped when she heard that rustle of night noise. It sounded quieter this time. She stared at the statue, waiting for the zonbi to appear. Nothing. She thought for a second, turned around, paused, then turned back. Still nothing, but she heard the noise again. If the zonbi wasn't in front of her, then...

Yunai glanced up, raising her torch. Clouds blocked the silver of the moon, leaving the greenhouse dark, so she increased the flame. The noise intensified. Yunai took off her shoes and synced with the glass wall of the greenhouse, using one hand and her feet to scale the wall. She made it to the space above the statue where the root chandelier hung and reached her root hand out. She touched a cold face. She expected it to feel like the canine head she saw before, but the shape of it felt...human. She moved her hand over it. She didn't know what—or who—this was.

Faces flashed before her, all the possible faces of people who could have been trapped here. The unnaturals she had encountered, that scout, any of the patients she had seen, the—

"Ah!"

Yunai's shock detached her feet and hand from the ceiling and snuffed her torch. She stuck her hand back before she hurled to the ground, hanging in midair, and relit a smaller torch with a snap of her fingers. She brought the torch up before her—and looked into the wilted violet eyes of a Saint the Plane thought dead.

"Tried to call you..."

Yunai shivered. His voice was more unknown than the night.

"...you're smart...cadet..."

His body faded into view. He was chained to the ceiling by his legs, arms, and torso. He barely resembled the youthful man Yunai had seen in newspapers and artwork.

"What are you doing up there?"

Yunai followed that other voice to...Matagi? Back to the Saint. Back to Matagi. He forged his metal teeth into claws. "Do you see this?" Yunai asked.

"I don't see anything." Matagi tapped his claws on his thigh. "Nothing but you."

Yunai's torch went out when common sense woke her up. Matagi wasn't here to check on her. Why was he— "You really don't see—"

"Unnaturals have been seeing things. And so have you."

Yunai let her hand go and fell, forging her ice spears as soon as Matagi launched his claws at her. She deflected the metal with one of the spears, its tip breaking. She landed in front of Matagi and jumped back. She suppressed the urge to retaliate. Her focus was on protecting the Saint, not engaging in combat with Matagi.

"Why are you attacking me? What are you doing here?"

"Just following orders." Matagi synced his claws back onto his hands from the ground. He pointed one claw at her chest. "And I should ask you that."

"I'm trying to figure out why all these unnatural occurrences have been happening." Yunai checked her emotions when one of her spears started dripping.

"That's not your job."

"But it's yours?"

Matagi sighed. "Yes. So tell me why you're in this exact hospital. In a greenhouse cadets don't have clearance for. At this late hour." He set his outstretched arm in an upright position.

"Because why wouldn't I do something if I knew something bad was happening? Why wouldn't I investigate if I knew it could lead to something?"

"Vague, rhetorical questions from the heart don't answer—"

The room turned pitch black. Matagi and Yunai looked up.

"Zonbi," Matagi said.

Neither noticed them gather. A thick coating of zonbi was pasted to the ceiling, like the cat zonbi that had stuck to the sanctuary's ceiling. They didn't attack, and their eyes stared at nothing, the Saint a ghoulish centerpiece.

"Matagi!"

That was Esera's voice? What was he doing here?

"Zonbi rushed over here and I saw you head here, so I alerted the scoutmasters on patrol." Esera appeared before them. He locked on to Yunai, then looked at Matagi. "What..."

"Esera!" Yunai pointed a spear at the Saint. "Can't you see who's on the ceiling?"

"...am I supposed to?"

"Only you...see the truth..." The Saint's dying voice regained some life.

"Yunai, what am I looking at besides the zonbi?"

"There's nothing there. Your companion is a suspect."

Everyone's voices desperately aggravated Yunai's emotions—

"...don't bother saving a dead man... Bring Odomi...*to jus—tice.*"

—until the zonbi broke through the glass.

They rushed into the greenhouse. Yunai broke her spears into shards and shot them upward in a hail of ice. Pieces of zonbi parts broke off and fell while Matagi sliced off heads that charged his way. Esera barrel-rolled away from a human-sized chunk that crashed to the floor, ending up next to Yunai with nifo'oti drawn. The zonbi surge knocked pots to the ground and reduced tables to raw material.

"Yunai," Esera started. He and Yunai jumped back when the zonbi pooled around their feet. "This doesn't look good. At all. You know that, right?"

With no water left, Yunai shot at the zonbi with fire bullets using her flesh hand. She held her position even as zonbi swallowed what little standing space she had left. She needed to finish this and get the Saint down from the ceiling's frame he now hung from by a root.

Esera synced with a root hanging from a loose beam and used it to swing over to an intact table. "Yunai, get out of there!" He swung the root at Yunai.

Yunai ignored Esera's cries and the root. He obviously couldn't see or hear the Saint, so this had to be up to her. She continued firing, but her one hand wasn't fast enough to keep up with the infestation.

A zonbi arm grabbed her leg and pulled her down into their mass. Esera swung back to where she made her stand and tried pulling Yunai out. But the zonbi shackled his legs too. Then both their arms and hands. The zonbi dragged them deeper into its body until they had to hold their breath against the rot.

...pressure...

...darkness...

...relief came when Yunai felt the zonbi mass slip off her body. The greenhouse was bright with torch flames. She released her breath and gathered her senses—and wished the zonbi had dragged her under instead.

Surrounded by scoutmasters who got to work felling the zonbi, Braulio stood over Yunai and Esera. He had snaked a root around their wrists to pull them from under the zonbi.

"Using my name to sneak in. You like to cause trouble, don't you, cadet?" Braulio's voice was unnecessarily calm. "Well, don't just sit there in a daze. Try doing your job."

But Yunai just sat there. Esera got up, ignited his nifoʻoti, and aided the scoutmasters and Matagi. Impending doom settled in when Siaka and the scoutmaster who had questioned her earlier showed up. The scoutmaster must have figured out her audit excuse was fake, and Siaka...

Yunai got up when she remembered that the Saint stated to bring Odomi to justice.

The zonbi quickly fell to the scoutmasters. The shattered greenhouse was secure, and emotions had zeroed out. The scoutmaster turned to Yunai. "Someone want to tell me what part of an audit involves raising the dead?"

"Question the girl," Matagi said.

Esera averted all eyes. Yunai glanced up at the ceiling's frame without moving her head—and saw nothing. She faced the scoutmaster, her fate waiting somewhere between his question and her response.

TWENTY-SEVEN

ODOMI

Odomi watched her Son sync hot water into her teacup. Siaka pulled the tea bag from the cup once it finished steeping, then Odomi heard him toss it in the trash behind her. He sat down and leaned back in his chair, crossing his arms. After a while, Odomi raised her head. The look Siaka gave her told her he was the adult right now, and she was the child who failed to listen.

"The entire greenhouse is compromised," Siaka said. "You have to stop, Mom."

Odomi sipped a little of the tea to test the temperature, then set the cup back down. She blew chill air over the cup. "Were you able to get anything from Galu?"

"No, I couldn't. Her emotions weren't enough. The journal didn't do anything."

"Then we don't stop." Odomi tried the tea again. It tasted cooler this time. "Either we find a suitable spirit, or we claim his power. It has to be at least one."

"I don't think you know just how close those cadets were last night. I'm pretty sure the same one who was with Mirta saw him."

"Do you have proof? Did specific words come out of anyone's mouth?"

"No one has to say anything *or* be specific."

Odomi slammed the cup down. *"Then we don't stop."* Tea splashed out of the cup, evaporating before droplets hit the table.

Siaka remained unmoved. Odomi wasn't looking at him, but she knew he mouthed something that indicated he was fed up with her.

"I know dealing with your son's death hasn't gotten easier, but I can't let the Scouthood find you out." Siaka leaned forward and cupped his hands over hers. Odomi didn't realize her hands were shaking until she felt the steadiness of his. "You saved my life when you adopted me. So I'm going to do whatever I have to do to protect you. Even if you don't want me to."

A knock at their door. He got up and left the kitchen.

Odomi closed her eyes. The steam scalded her face. She reopened them minutes later to an empty cup.

BRAULIO

Braulio stepped back when Siaka opened the door. "Well? What does she plan on doing with the cadets?"

"I didn't ask," Siaka said, closing the door. "She's more stressed about the greenhouse. That's a lot of medicine destroyed."

Braulio huffed. It would cost more, but they could get plants delivered from private greenhouses in Lemana easily.

What Braulio needed more was these cadets—*this* particular cadet—removed from the hospital. He was grateful the scoutmaster sent him a message that she signed in after hours using his name. And to pull a fake audit out of her ass? The gall of that cadet, the sheer *impertinence*. If they did anything less than ban her from the Scouthood...

But. *But.* And Braulio hated buts.

He never forgot Siaka's appearance in the greenhouse last month. His not signing in, the other voice he *knew* he heard. He heard the zonbi that attacked the greenhouse acted similarly to the cats that had infested the sanctuary. His theory that zonbi falling could be stopped may or may not be unfounded, but something was going on in the hospital. That cadet may have come close to cracking the mystery wide open.

And whatever was going on in the hospital, Siaka was involved.

"What could she have been looking for?" Braulio asked as they walked down the street to the nearest station. "I thought she and Mirta already tried looking for answers."

"Don't know. But you should have just let her join in on the surgery. Then she wouldn't have raised hell in the greenhouse."

"Are we meeting Mirta at the station?" Braulio asked, choosing to ignore that battle. No need to agitate Siaka further.

"She's at the cabins. She let Yunai into the greenhouse in the first place, so she has to report."

YUNAI

Yunai shook. She didn't try to stop. She shook all night in bed, shook in the shower, shook all the way downstairs, and shook as she pushed the door open to Ignacia's office-bedroom. Ignacia sat at her desk. Mirta sat in a chair across from her—she gave Yunai a small smile—and Matagi stood off to the side.

Niesh stood right in the middle of the room, making sure she was the first person Yunai saw when she entered, even if Yunai acknowledged her last.

"Have a seat." Ignacia nodded at the chair next to Mirta.

Yunai closed the door, and that's when she noticed Esera leaning against the wall next to the door. He made no move to greet her.

Raki was nowhere to be found.

"Yunai," Ignacia started as Yunai sat, "do you acknowledge that I spoke to you very recently about not pursuing Cathedral-level issues?"

"Yes." Yunai looked Ignacia straight in her eyes. Niesh's glare felt heavy on her back.

"So please tell us why you lied to a scoutmaster to sneak into the greenhouse during the dead of night."

"I thought...someone was trapped there. I couldn't—I couldn't walk away."

"I let her tour the greenhouse," Mirta said. Her voice was companionship to Yunai. She was surprised to see her here but grateful. "I understand it's off-limits to all Scouthood personnel, but I thought if zonbi are endangering the hospital, then more people should be familiar with where we store our medicine."

The lie came out so naturally. Yunai almost believed her.

"Mirta, was it?" Ignacia asked. "Are you her supervisor?"

"I'm not, but I take any responsibility from our end. I know Odomi will have words for me, too."

Back to Yunai. "Yunai, who did you think you saw there?"

Yunai opened her mouth, then bit her lip. *The Saint's trapped there, he's alive, we have to get him out!* It sounded ridiculous in her head and would sound even more foolish out loud. It was absolutely the Saint. Who else on the Plane possessed burning violet eyes? The new one hadn't come forward, so it made sense. But she could have been seeing things, like the scout or the man at the memorial. He had been caught and taken away, his fate decided.

"I...I'm not sure." Yunai clenched her pants. "Just a person chained to the statue. Then moved to the ceiling. They were in a lot of pain."

"Mirta, did you see this person too?" Ignacia asked.

"No, I didn't." Then, "My companion, Siaka, Odomi's adopted Son, came and got me when my next appointment was moved up." It wasn't a lie exactly, but it sounded like one. Why was Mirta risking her good standing by defending her?

"Yunai, you saw this person during the day," Ignacia continued. "And you chose to go back instead of reporting what you saw to your supervisor?"

Yunai searched for words that would make her choice make sense, but she found none. Ignacia picked up on her mental roadblock and shifted to Esera.

"Esera, you and Yunai are companions. Did you know she planned to go there during the night?"

"Yes."

Yunai snapped her head toward Esera. The word came out fast. She heard Niesh shift her body in his direction.

"I told her I couldn't go because I had my own service to do," he said.

"And Raki? We saw she signed her name, but she wasn't there last night."

He hesitated. "She knew too. But she didn't go."

Yunai could only stare. Esera didn't see her there, but she *did* go. Raki said—*in front of him*—that she would come with her. And she still didn't understand why he and Matagi showed up.

"She must have changed her mind," Ignacia said.

"Companionship is important in scouting, but it can also blur one's vision." Niesh's voice commanded the room to zero.

Ignacia glanced at Niesh, then turned to Matagi. "Matagi, what's your assessment of what you saw?"

"I saw a cadet somewhere she had no business being, seeing things that weren't there. Her actions were in line with the unnatural behavior the island has been seeing. And they caused a great deal of damage to the hospital's source of medicine."

Yunai shook harder. Somehow, Matagi's words sickened her more than Niesh's presence.

Esera came off the wall. "She was probably scared she'd be taken away if she reported something that wasn't there."

"She was seeing things," Matagi retorted. "You and I saw nothing there."

"*She's not unnatural, you—*"

"Stop." Niesh's command dampened Esera's anger. He swung around and rubbed his hands over his face, taking deep breaths.

Yunai felt Mirta's hand on hers. She forgot about her entirely.

"Yunai." She thought Ignacia said her name. Mirta squeezed her hand, and Yunai turned to face Niesh when she realized she was speaking to her. "I assume you were with Esera when he fought the renegade scout."

Yunai swallowed then nodded, unsure what that had to do with this.

Niesh looked at Mirta. "Mirta, you seem responsible, even if your good intentions were misguided. I can trust you to ensure Yunai remains with her assigned supervisor while she's performing her service?"

"Yes," Mirta replied congenially.

"Boys, you did a good job last night. I'll follow up the next time we meet."

Yunai glanced at Esera. Helping out the scoutmasters meant more than he had let on.

"This meeting is over. Head to where you should be."

The cadets and resident filtered out of the office at different speeds. Mirta shut the door.

Mirta hugged Yunai, then whispered, "You're not unnatural. We'll meet soon." She smiled and hurried through the cabin door.

Matagi sped upstairs, and Esera just...headed for the door.

"How can you just...hang me out to dry like that?" Yunai threw the words out.

Esera stopped, slumped his shoulders, then turned around. "You said it was a zonbi. Not a person."

"Because it *was* a zonbi."

"And then it what? Turned into a human? Look, I defended you as much as I could. But I have a job to do."

"*What job?*" Yunai controlled her voice, remembering the Grand Scoutmaster was a few feet away. "Are you and Matagi Niesh's personal cadets? How—why did you say Raki didn't come? She came with me and left before you showed up, you heard Raki say she would come with me!"

"Just be lucky Niesh didn't send you home. Or worse." Esera sighed and pinched his forehead. "It's pretty clear to me you can risk getting sent home. But I can't. And I need my Sister here."

"I thought I was your companion!"

"That doesn't mean we have a bond."

Any words she wanted to say crumbled against that declaration.

The tears stinging Yunai's hazel eyes stoked her anger. She brushed past Esera and ran out of the cabin before she had another outburst.

ESERA

It was a fact. He didn't mean for it to come out like that, but...it was a fact.

Esera let Yunai brush past him. No point in stopping her. She was someone who made the execution of others her personal mission. That job would fall on him as a hunter, a mission he chose not to walk away from. But he felt no pride in ending another's life and had no love for anyone who did.

Matagi came back downstairs and headed for the door. And Esera decided he wasn't finished. "You know she's not unnatural."

"I don't." Matagi kept walking.

"She's our cabinmate."

"That doesn't mean we have a bond."

Quakes were rare but not unheard of on Taisala. This was... No. This was anger. Rage. Hurt.

This was Esera.

Matagi stopped. Turned around. "Zero down, or you won't be able to call her your cabinmate for much longer."

Esera thought of Raki, Raki's parents, Afato, all the people who had ever been there for him. And he fought back images of those who had shown him how ugly he could become. His teachers. His old relatives. His father.

The quaking subsided.

"Like I said, I have my own family to care for," Matagi, perfectly calm, stated. "Whatever your issue is, settle it instead of using me as your outlet for whatever you can't deal with."

Esera's foot traced a crack in the floor as Matagi left the cabin.

IGNACIA

"Ignacia."

"Niesh."

"Pardoning her should not have been an option. Punishment or expulsion. Not pardoning."

"Then why didn't you?" Ignacia asked. Niesh's decision was out of character. She had expelled plenty of cadets as a scoutmaster for much less.

"She was instrumental in finding that ex-scout, which is one of the few leads we have. And her actions may lead us to some other answers I'm searching for. But just because I didn't doesn't mean you couldn't have."

"I needed to understand why she did what she did," Ignacia said. "Don't forget she reported that man at the memorial. She's a good cadet. Why would I immediately dismiss someone without giving them a chance to explain?"

"Don't forget she omitted details with that incident." Niesh tched. "As soon as you learned her emotions put everyone in that hospital in danger—sick and vulnerable people and animals—you should have sent her packing. But if I even couldn't teach you that as your scoutmaster, what hope do you have?"

Ignacia caught herself on those sharp words. Niesh's blunt tongue was not out of character, but... This had to be stress. All of her decisions had to be influenced by stress. Too much responsibility and not enough time.

"Teach your cadets what it means to be a proper scout. Or cadets won't be the only ones under threat of expulsion."

The ground shifted beneath Ignacia. She had a tight rein on her emotions—so this was someone else. She and Niesh looked at each other until it stopped. She felt quakes before—and that was no normal quake.

Niesh didn't release her eyes from Ignacia for a while. Then she left without saying another word.

TWENTY-EIGHT

NIESH

Niesh and four of her scoutmasters marched to the greenhouse. She stood at the front of the damaged building, two scoutmasters on either side of her. Residents and technicians removed the last of the salvageable plants and carried away the statue of Raíz, leaving the greenhouse nothing more than a heap of broken glass.

Niesh gave it a quick once-over, her gaze lingering on the middle of the ceiling. She snapped her fingers. Each scoutmaster took a corner. They ignited big torches in their hands and set the remains of the greenhouse ablaze, making ash of secrets and subterfuge. One scoutmaster moved to the middle and blew a breath of fire up, torching what was left of the ceiling. Niesh wasn't taking chances. If there was someone up there she somehow couldn't see, they were no more. The unnatural could not be underestimated.

After the scoutmasters smothered the fires and synced the smoke upward and away from the hospital, Niesh ordered them to guard. She walked through the burned space. She dragged her boot over the charred pieces of broken wood.

It wasn't enough. She needed the whole hospital to burn. It had become a haunting ground for unnatural activity.

"What's going on here?"

Odomi. She also needed this woman brought in. The hospital was only as damned as the person running it.

The medic appeared before her. Some of her locs curtained her face but didn't do enough to hide the puffiness under her eyes and the redness in them. "Why wasn't I, the damn director, made aware you'd be starting fires in the hospital? *Why* are you starting fires in my hospital?"

Niesh dismissed her scoutmasters. As soon as they were out of earshot—she made sure to herself none of them had enhanced hearing—she responded. "I got a tip this morning concerning the Saint's missing body."

Odomi made no movement nor made a snap rebuttal. But their immediate airspace turned *slightly* colder. Anyone with less training would never have noticed. Niesh didn't know if Odomi was behind the Saint's grave robbery, but natural reactions never lied. She didn't know who this supposed person trapped in the greenhouse was either, but she needed to probe for the Saint's missing body.

"Why would you think that?" Odomi finally said. "What reason would I ever have to rob a grave of its spiritual leader? And, if so, why on Lemana's green Plane would you attempt to set his corpse on fire?"

Niesh focused on Odomi's eyes, not their tiredness but their resolve. Eyes never lied either. Odomi had the eyes of someone not angry that their authority had been sidestepped, but of someone determined to see a plan through. Odomi was a senior medic with more than enough experience with the human body. She could have easily put the Saint in a death state. She had full access to the Cathedral—and the mausoleum. She had the means and the opportunity. The only thing missing was a motive.

Niesh was tired of questioning and suspecting and inspecting. She had enough evidence. It was time to blow this conspiracy wide open. "Take me to your house."

"Excuse me? I have work to—"

Niesh walked past Odomi. It was time.

ODOMI

Damn this woman. No respect for anyone's time or words. Odomi cursed Niesh under her breath, then trailed her.

Siaka had a simple checkup right now... He needed to get home before them. The hospital's root system was intimately familiar with Odomi's blood. She could use it to contact him. Focusing on the roots connected to the sanctuary, Odomi commanded the roots running alongside its backside to communicate in the special code she and Siaka used to reach each other in emergencies.

Odomi hoped he would see it as soon as it reached him. He needed to get Galu out of the house and out of the parish. And she needed to make sure Niesh didn't discover the Saint's new hiding place.

SIAKA

Siaka stopped writing when he saw two root ends on the room's wall curve into C shapes. They moved toward each other and stopped short of overlapping.

A heart.

"I'm going to reassign you all to another resident, just for today," Siaka told his elder patient. He had come in with his trogon companion, who perched on his shoulder. "I'm sorry. I just remembered I have a personal thing to take care of."

Siaka shot out of the room and scanned the sanctuary hall as he rushed for the stairs. No sign of Odomi. Or Niesh. He saw her enter with a group of scoutmasters and figured he needed to be on guard.

He blew out of the hospital as inconspicuously as he could.

ODOMI

Odomi unlocked the roots on her house door, then crossed her arms. Niesh looked at her.

"I unlocked it," Odomi said with raw acidity.

Niesh narrowed her hardened brown eyes away and pushed the door open. Odomi took a shallow breath and went in. Niesh stopped in the middle of the living room. She swept her eyes around the

201

room. Aside from a few carved masks on the walls and wooden figurines in a couple of corners, there wasn't much for her to see.

"Do you need the grand tour?" Odomi asked, tone still dipped in acid. She flexed her fingers, ready to weaponize her roots. She knew a hundred ways a person could die, and she could inflict a hundred deaths on this woman. It would end all this instantly. But having a dying Saint and a dead scoutmaster in her home would be somewhat inconvenient.

Niesh ignored her and entered the kitchen. She opened all the cabinets and the fridge and moved everything around on every surface.

"I promise, the utensil drawer is not where I'd hide a dead body," Odomi said. The woman putting her fingers all over Siaka's clean kitchen would have offended her if she weren't so exasperated by her pointless searching.

Niesh closed the fridge. She walked out of the kitchen and through the living room, turning for the stairs. Odomi, again, followed her. Niesh trudged up and threw open the first door she came across. Siaka's room.

"I'm assuming this isn't your room?" Niesh asked as she again opened doors and moved objects.

Odomi didn't move from the doorway. "My adopted Son sleeps here sometimes."

"Does he have a partner?" Niesh tugged on a piece of fabric peeking out of the bedside table. She pulled out a pair of red under-wear that was definitely not Siaka's.

"He has an active social life," Odomi said, swearing in her head. Underwear shoved in haphazardly? This child. Siaka did well getting Galu out in time but failed to cover her tracks. "Niesh, this is a waste of time. What are you expecting to find by opening the drawers?"

Niesh threw the underwear on the bed. She walked out. Odomi grew tired of walking behind someone else in her own home. "I don't know the kind of stress you're under, with Leonardo gone and the strange activity in the city, but you're not thinking clearly. And I don't think you're aware that you're not."

Odomi snapped the roots on her bedroom door locked when

Niesh extended her hand to open it. Niesh balled her hand into a fist, setting it on her chest.

"Making a scapegoat of my hospital, flooding it with scoutmasters and untrained cadets. You're an excellent scoutmaster, Niesh. Why these snap decisions and senseless actions? Has the Board yanked your spine this hard?"

Odomi synced a root off the wall and slapped it on Niesh's wrists, tightly cuffing them together as soon as Niesh synced her metal armbands down her arms. Her blood cut off from her hands, Niesh flexed her forearm and forged a crude axe blade on its underside. She lifted her forearm and swung it at Odomi, aiming for her hands. Odomi rapidly heated her free hand and caught Niesh's axe by its side. She hissed on contact, blood rushing from her palm. She turned up the heat higher, Niesh's weapon bending against her hand.

"I know they're ones to fear." Odomi steadied her legs. Restraining Niesh and attempting to break her weapon put tremendous stress on her body. "But fear cannot be the reason that drives any decision you make."

Odomi stumbled when the axe forged back into raw metal. It slinked around Niesh's arm, a part of it turning into a small blade that sliced her wrist. Blood trickled down her arm—and onto the root. Niesh gained enough control of the root to sync it off her wrists. Odomi whipped the root away before Niesh had a chance to use it against her. Niesh forged a long blade in her hands. Locked eyes.

Step.

Swing.

Black.

...Odomi still felt her lungs expanding. She opened her eyes. Niesh's long blade touched her throat as she inhaled.

"For the people I gave the Scout's Word to protect. For my Sister, whose Partner was taken from her—" Niesh gripped her weapon tighter. "—you are going to tell me where the Saint is, why you took him—and why you're in league with a renegade scout."

"You have no proof of any of that. And I don't know anything about a renegade scout." Odomi synced with a root on the wall, unlocking the door to her bedroom. "But feel free to prove me wrong."

Niesh forged her weapon back into armbands. She pushed the door open but didn't go in. She raised one arm and swung it toward her chest. The resulting wind lifted the curtains and opened all the doors before her. With the other arm, she forced out all the items in the closet, the drawers, the shelves. Niesh scattered them around the room in a whirlwind, then dropped her arm, everything falling after. She lifted one leg and brought it down, the house moaning down to the earth beneath it.

Odomi bit back words hot and nasty. She steadied herself through the house shake, fuming when she heard objects fall to the floor downstairs and waves lapping against the house.

"You're right about one thing. I am an excellent scoutmaster. And my scouting senses rarely fail me." Niesh whipped around and pushed past Odomi into the hallway. "I'm far from done with this place. Expect eyes on you at all times. Everywhere."

Odomi stared at the aftermath in her room, her mind beyond all reason and emotion. She flinched when Niesh slammed the door.

Minutes passed. Curtains billowed.

Odomi eased the tension out of her shoulders and jaw, then moved into the hallway, stopping in the middle. She looked up at the confluence of roots on the ceiling and commanded them apart, revealing nothing to the naked eye. No damage she could see from Niesh's leg stomp. No need to check on the Saint yet, not with Niesh lurking indefinitely. As long as her house roots stayed injected in him, he'd stay quiet. She never wanted to hide him in her home, but hopefully, his new, more secure hiding place would give her enough time to figure out what to do next.

TWENTY-NINE

SIAKA

"Where are you taking me now?" Galu asked, trying to match Siaka's pace. "The last time we took a walk, I ended up feeling awful. And are you gonna tell me what you two brought upstairs in the middle of the night?"

"Niesh is probably at the house by now," Siaka replied, doing his best to avoid people as they walked through the city. He stopped after a few seconds and scoped out the area ahead of them— Maogatai University.

Galu stopped next to him. "And my second question?"

Siaka shelved her question, focused on where they needed to go. He spotted the faculty building in the distance and headed there, Galu following.

"Ugh, I can't stand scholars." Galu groaned.

They entered the building. Siaka walked down the hallway, checking the names on the doors. He stopped when he came across one with no roots and no plaque. The waves coming off the room were faint, but Siaka felt the rage deep in his body. He hesitated to bring Galu here at first out of a lack of trust, but they were running low on time. He opened the door and stepped in.

"What is this place?" Galu walked in and checked out the table and shelf. Siaka closed the door after her. "Is this where I'm staying now? You know, I'm getting really tired of being jerked around. One of you needs to—"

"Still water, skin." Siaka breathed out, diving deep into his memories.

"What?"

Coming back up, Siaka walked to the shelf, running his hands along the book spines. He exhaled the rage as it cleansed his body. "The name of a powerful poem. The professor who wrote it, who this room belonged to, was considered unnatural."

"So, what, they killed him?"

Siaka hesitated. "Yes. He was known in certain circles for denouncing the Natural. He wrote about it. Lectured about it. I was lucky enough to hear him speak before his murder."

Galu sat on the dusty desk. "Keep going. All the way."

"There are a lot of people around the Plane who believe the Scouthood is the reason the Plane is dying. That their corruption is poisoning the land and making zonbi of life. They want to abolish the Cathedral. Turn the Natural inside out. Free what they call unnatural. You were a scout. You've seen just how terrible it is out there."

Galu tilted her head to the side. "So has your eye, too, I'm assuming."

Siaka smirked. "There's a lot of energy and movement to accomplish all this—but no one to bear the flag."

Galu set her head upright and leaned back. "Your movement needs a ringleader. I got that."

"It needs someone with complete dedication and no doubt. Mostly, someone with the kind of anger blind to anything else."

"Is that what you were trying to get out of me? Were you trying to make me angry?"

"I was trying to bring it out, yeah."

Galu furrowed her eyebrows. "I felt strange... What did you do exactly?"

"Something unnatural," Siaka said with an easy smile.

"Okay..." Galu jumped down. Looked Siaka straight in the eye. "Odomi killed the Saint."

"She didn't." Siaka pursed his lips. No point in hiding it. "But she was part of the plot."

Siaka watched Galu's face pass through contemplation and then arrive at a conclusion. Guess she knew they had dragged Leonardo upstairs in their home.

"How do I become this leader you need?" Galu asked.

Siaka pulled the journal from his bag. He made sure it was locked before handing it to Galu. "This is a memento of...someone who was very important in the movement."

Galu took the journal and brushed her hand over its chains without pricking herself. "Someone? No more secrets. All the way, remember?"

"I don't know, I promise. Odomi does, but there's a lot she doesn't tell even her own Son."

"Fine," Galu said. "So what do we do with this? Obviously not open it because these are trick chains."

"If you're good enough to be our leader, the book should react to you somehow. And I don't know how either, but we'll know it when we see it."

"Why not try someone who's already in the movement? Or why not either of you? Makes more sense than trying an ex-scout."

"Trust me, we have. But most people have their own agendas or think Odomi's plan is a crapshoot. They don't see the bigger picture. As for us, Odomi has more sadness than anger, and I'm just not the right person." Galu searched his eye. Some part of her probably thought this plan was inane, too.

"Tell me what to do," she finally said. "I already told you my story, though, so I don't know what more I can do."

"Try focusing on the emotions connected to your memories. And this room will help me with what I need to do."

Galu rolled her shoulders. She jumped back onto the desk, crossed her legs, and closed her eyes. Siaka let himself ride the waves of rage coursing through the room. They took him further out, carried him across time and space to where his deepest pain floated beneath the surface. He waited for Galu's emotional signal in the distance. After a while, he felt a blip, a small lap of water struggling to hurdle deeper depths. There was anger, regret, but neither strong enough to dive deeper. The journal didn't change. Galu wasn't enough.

"Anything?" Galu said after some time.

"No..." Siaka sighed. "This is pointless. No offense."

If this was the extent of her true emotions, there was no way she was the one. And people of the Natural couldn't fully ride waves anyway because they were too emotionally repressed to feel anything true. Which meant Galu would never be a suitable host. Which meant she would never be what Odomi needed.

And Odomi couldn't find a way to take Leonardo's power.

All their planning started to feel hopeless.

THIRTY

IGNACIA

Ignacia, small torch in hand, stood atop one of the hills between the city and the base. The fading silver of the moon peeped between passing clouds. She watched her cadets, paired off, spar on uneven ground and slippery mud. The day's intermittent showers cooled the air, a balm for Ignacia's mood. Thankfully, her cadets got the hint that this was not the time to bicker or annoy her. They mostly kept quiet or stayed out of each other's way. Even Umaru stuck to making only one observation throughout the day.

Speaking of Umaru, he and Moraima fought the closest to her, Moraima's roots against Umaru's shields of ice. With the ground soaked, Umaru had the advantage of reforging his shields whenever Moraima cracked them. Moraima was skilled in using her roots for sneak attacks, and the night gave her cover, but she still held back. Ever since her first match with Matagi, she avoided decisive strikes or changed tactics that would have injured her opponent at the last second. Or maybe she was just like this, cautious and considerate. And it made Ignacia wonder how she got into the Scouthood.

Her feelings blunted her actions.

It was unacceptable.

"Take the opening when you see it!" Ignacia called out to her. "A missed chance in a night fight can cost you your life!"

Moraima jumped back from Umaru at the sound of Ignacia's voice. She synced her roots back up her sleeves and waited for Umaru to approach headfirst, as he typically did. With one shielded arm up, he rushed Moraima—then slid feet first on the slick grass in an attempt to trip her up. Before he could, Moraima jumped high in the air, flipped over Umaru, and landed on—

"Ah!" Moraima slid but regained control of her legs before she fell. Ignacia focused her eyes for a better look—Umaru had iced the ground during his slide. Good strategy.

Moraima took measured steps to steady her footing. She almost jumped again but decided against it. Probably thinking Umaru iced more patches of ground in the darkness. Instead, she released her roots and—again—waited. A better choice, maybe. Melting the ice would have taken her too long.

Umaru caught on and stood in place as well. He threw one shield at Moraima. She caught it with a root and threw it to the side. Then deflected a hail of ice with the other, losing some of her balance. And used both roots and her arms to block Umaru when he launched himself at her, shield first. He broke her footing, sending her to the ground. Umaru landed upright, one hand on the ice.

"Move, Moraima! Control the night!"

But even after getting on her feet, Moraima didn't move from her spot—a spot Umaru was still synced with. With his hand on the ice, Umaru forged a cactus prison around Moraima, tall ice stalagmites with spikes sticking from their sides. Moraima moved to use her roots, but the spikes bullied her from all sides. Umaru was tired, even if he refused to show it, so Moraima could have taken advantage of the moment to break free or make an attempt to strike from the prison.

But she did neither. Ignacia had seen this over and over. A fellow cadet was vulnerable, and that meant Moraima had to give them grace.

Ignacia was tired of watching. And allowing.

Or cadets won't be the only ones under threat of expulsion.

"Umaru! Moraima! Guard!"

Umaru melted his prison and ice floor and mustered up enough energy to stand guard. Moraima forced herself up slowly, then lit a torch. Ignacia slid down a nearby root and landed before them. She noticed her other cadets cease their matches but didn't bother redirecting them. She wanted them to stand at attention.

"Moraima."

"Y-yes, Master?" Her torch faltered.

"On your first full day here, what did I say you needed as scouts in order to succeed?" Ignacia threw a hand up when Umaru's mouth moved.

Moraima stared at her, then searched the air for the word. It was neither in her actions nor her vocabulary.

Ignacia dropped her hand. "Umaru."

"Initiative, Master," he said quickly.

Shame crawled over Moraima's face.

"Moraima, I made a point of saying that the first day, before any training started, to lay down what I expected of you. Of all of you. It makes no difference if you can fight or not—if you care about your comrades or not—if you can't do what's needed in the moment."

"I…" she tried. But the meek girl knew she had no explanation to counter with.

This felt like Yunai all over again. Ignacia tried to ignore the churning in her stomach and Niesh's voice in her ear that was turning into her own. But she couldn't.

"A recruit who isn't ready to fight today will be dead tomorrow. And a cadet who can't remain at zero can never be a scout."

"Yes, Master…" Moraima's voice sounded like a train had run it over.

Ignacia saw the sadness in Sega's eyes. She continued anyway. "You're dismissed. Pack your bags tonight. You're going home to Artemisa tomorrow."

Moraima stood frozen in silence as the tears poured down her face. Her torch dimmed until it went out.

"Everyone." Ignacia paused and looked away from the ex-cadet. "We're done for the night. You have your dinner assignments." She turned around and headed back to base, listening to feet slosh against the ground and whispers rise against the night's end.

THIRTY-ONE

RAKI

R aki paid for her and Toya's meals at the food cart, then returned to their table. Toya sat with her legs crossed in her chair, sporting the new sandals Raki bought for her, and flipped through the book Raki also bought for her earlier in the day. Toya turned the pages quickly. Raki wasn't sure if Toya knew how to read, but she knew better by now than to ask something like that outright.

"Any good?" Raki asked, taking her seat.

"It's okay." Toya closed the book. "The main characters are annoying. Why are they chasing after the same boring, brooding guy when the world is in danger? That's stupid."

Raki chuckled. "I'm glad you're at least reading it."

"I know how to read," Toya snipped.

Raki put her hands up. "Never said you didn't." But she was relieved she didn't have to ask.

The food cart worker brought their baskets of akara to the table. Toya took a large bite into one of the spicy bean fritters while Raki picked at one mindlessly until the beans peeked through its fried skin. She skipped breakfast and needed to eat but couldn't find her appetite.

"Why are you so sad?" Toya asked. She laughed. "Did some

boring, brooding guy play with your heart? Is that why you got me this?"

"Hardly." Raki left the akara alone and pushed her basket away.

"Do you want me to ask you what's wrong? Am I the adult today?" Toya sneered. "Finish your meal! I didn't waste two hours of my life cooking so you could waste two minutes of yours staring at my food!"

Raki arched an eyebrow at Toya's parody of the caretakers. The staff at the orphanage did tend to sound like they regretted their entire lives. "No. I'm fine. No adulting from you."

Toya shrugged and returned to her food.

Thoughts turned in Raki's head on an endless loop. Yunai's obsessive need to solve everything, Moraima's sudden dismissal, and Ignacia's overnight coldness. She hadn't found time to air her concerns to Esera—he was too preoccupied with his own business lately—and there was no one else she trusted enough to talk to.

Either way, she couldn't focus on any of that right now. Sticking her nose where it wasn't needed would get her in trouble. None of it mattered to her, anyway. Her focus was this child.

"Hurry and finish. We need to start practicing."

"Yeah, yeah," Toya said, scarfing down the last of the akara. "You're the adult. I get it."

~

RAKI AND TOYA stood waist-deep in the calm ocean. Raki brought her to one of the quieter beaches where rarely anyone hung out except a few locals. If Toya lost control, few would witness it.

Toya synced up balls of water and tossed them at Raki, who punched at them with her fists. Toya was doing well, very well, and her effort surprised Raki. For someone who supposedly never synced before, Toya had grasped the basics quickly.

"Can we do something else?" Toya asked. "I know how to make these balls without thinking about it now. I don't need to keep doing it."

"You don't stop practicing something once you have it down,"

Raki replied, punching a ball of water. "You keep practicing until it becomes second nature."

"Whatever." Toya rolled her eyes but kept syncing with the water. She tossed another ball. Then another. She grinned. Paused for a second...

"What are you doing?"

She synced a small, fast-moving wave at Raki. Raki ducked under, swam to Toya, and popped up in front of her. "Don't do that again!"

"At least I know how to do it." Toya backed up.

Raki put her hands on her hips and stared the child down.

"Fine, okay. Just give me my space back."

"I need you to listen today, alright?" Raki backstroked back to her original position. She sighed. "Look. If you want, you can toss two."

"Gee. Exciting." But Toya did as Raki told her. She synced two balls up and threw them at Raki. "What's with you today? You're acting like...one of the caretakers."

Raki continued punching the balls. Steam rose from some of them when she made impact. "I'm allowed to have bad days."

"Just asking."

"Just concentrate."

Minutes passed. Raki appreciated the silence, and it also irritated her. Toya started blasting jets at her in quick succession when she grew bored with forming balls. Raki didn't complain.

"Is all that steam normal?" Toya asked.

"No, it's not." The steam formed a fog that hovered around Raki's airspace.

"Isn't that what happens when you lose control? Can't you draw the zonbi here?"

"Don't worry about me," Raki snapped. "You're the one who needs to be controlled."

Toya's last jet broke before it reached Raki. "What does that mean?"

"The zonbi aren't going to come because I'm having an off day. They only come when people are wildly out of control. Like whenever you're having one of your fits."

Toya said nothing. Finally.

"I have to make sure you know how to control yourself before I move on. You'll just keep inviting trouble otherwise, and no one will adopt you then. You may even end up at one of the rehab centers if you don't get better."

"No one will adopt me..." Toya repeated her words in a daze. "Why did I think you were any different..."

"What are you talking about?"

"*Why did I think you were any better?*" Toya threw her fists down on the water. Sparks of ice shot everywhere.

Raki synced an arc of air in front of her, protecting herself before the sparks struck her. "Listen, you little—"

No. She wasn't in the mood for her attitude, but she didn't need to start cussing little orphans out.

"You're all the same! You treat me like some...some project you have to fix to get your credits."

"How many times do—look, I have a goal. We all do. We're not assigned to places to sit around and do the bare minimum. It's called community service. We serve people. And that means I'm going to do my best to make you a better person."

"What if I don't want to? Why can't people just accept me? Why do I have to learn syncing or be Natural to be a better person?"

"You're actually crazy!" Raki threw her hands up. "It's normal, Toya! It's what people do. Syncing is normal. Not syncing is not normal. It's unnatural!"

Toya pointed at her. "The waves are getting stronger. You're going to drown us!"

Raki looked down. The waves lapped up higher, slapping her thighs. "We won't drown. Our lungs can take it."

"So *I* need to be controlled, but *you* can create tidal waves and somehow that's normal?" Toya waded out of the ocean.

"Where are you going?"

Toya kept walking. She made it to the beach and snatched her sandals up.

"Toya!" Raki ran out of the water and grabbed her bag. The sand and rubble grew hotter beneath her feet with each step. Hissing, she dropped her things. She grabbed a foot and synced wind over her feet to try cooling them, blowing off the broken shells and rocks that stuck to their soles. When she looked back up, Toya was gone. And her feet started heating up again.

"Dammit!" Raki fell back on her bottom. Too many thoughts. Too much responsibility. She needed to calm down. Needed to return to zero. She turned her vision away from the world and up to the sky.

THIRTY-TWO

YUNAI

"Steady...almost there..." Braulio said.

Yunai forced her focus on her footing but stole glances at the young, coral whale shark resting in the giant orb of water. She, Mirta, Braulio, and Farid held the orb up as they navigated to the only available pool in the sanctuary. After the greenhouse, Braulio grudgingly agreed to let Yunai provide support again. He had been even-headed with her since the greenhouse disaster, and it made her nervous. Regardless, helping him, Mirta, and a few of the medics recover the sick whale shark from its shiver in the ocean had taken her mind off everything else—including the growing tension in the cabin since Moraima's dismissal.

"Unsync and get to the other side," Braulio said to Yunai. "Be ready to resync so we can lower her carefully."

Yunai let go of the orb and ran to the other side of the pool while the others held the orb like a three-legged chair. Water sloshed out, and the whale shark let out a cry. Yunai resynced when she was in position. They lowered the whale shark into the pool, getting on their knees to bring her down as gently as possible. She let out another cry when she realized they weren't carrying her anymore and rested at the bottom of the pool.

Mirta took a bottle from the utility pouch around her waist and unscrewed the top. She poured its powder into the pool. The whale shark fell asleep within minutes.

"Underwater surgery is tricky but fun," Mirta said, observing the animal. "But only people with strong lungs and excellent syncing can perform it successfully."

Yunai watched the whale shark sleep at the bottom. She had never seen a creature so pacified. Since Niesh burned the greenhouse down, the animals that came to the hospital showed less agitation. There had been no new infestations either, but it was also too soon to tell if removing the greenhouse—and that person—made any difference. Yunai had to be mistaken about them being the Saint. Niesh would never have eliminated him.

"Taking the tumor out shouldn't take super long. Stand guard and walk around the pool. Signal us with a root if anything happens." Mirta and Braulio took concoctions from their pouches and swallowed them. Braulio passed one to Farid. Yunai assumed it was something to neutralize the effects of the anesthesia they poured into the pool.

Mirta and Farid jumped into the water, but Braulio turned his attention to Yunai. "You're having dinner with us tonight."

Yunai was taken aback. "What? Dinner?"

"Braulio and I want to chat with you more about the greenhouse," Mirta said before she dove after Farid.

"Meet with Mirta in the main hall when your shift is over. I have to leave early to cook." Braulio jumped into the pool.

Yunai forgot to blink. The torture was never-ending.

RAKI

By the time Raki made it back to the orphanage, she ran out of breath and sweat soaked her braids. High jumping from the beach all the way to the Cathedral grounds had killed her knees and burned her lungs. She was not looking forward to waking up to the pain in the morning.

"Paloma!" she called out as soon as her scoutmaster escort let her into the building. She crouched, steadying herself with hands on thighs, and took several breaths. "Paloma!"

"Yes, yes!" Paloma ran out of her office. "Raki? What's going on? Where's Toya?"

Still struggling to breathe, Raki met Paloma's eyes. "She didn't come back?"

"No? I've been at my office all day. I would have seen her. What happened?"

"We got into a fight." Raki summoned a burst of energy in order to stand up straight. She put her hands on her hips. "I thought she would've come back here."

Paloma's face changed from worried to oddly relieved. Raki wasn't sure which part of what she just said inspired the change. "You know what? Don't worry about her."

"What? I'm sorry, don't worry? Are there scoutmasters looking for her?"

"Oh no, we wouldn't waste resources like that. Honestly, between you and me, Niesh has been wanting to get rid of her, and I'm inclined to agree. She's brought nothing but trouble since she was brought here."

Who were these people? Raki couldn't believe what she was hearing, what this woman, this weepy-looking woman in charge of the well-being of these children, said with actual human words.

"The zonbi haven't come around since you started spending time with her. But no, the scoutmasters have more important duties. A child like Toya isn't..."

Raki blocked out the rest of this woman's words. She sped off back to the city. She took shallow breaths, her ears and stomach crying in pain. The other children and the caretakers were awful, but for the director to undermine any integrity the orphanage had?

And then there was herself, the one person who made it her job to help her—and she broke the girl back to the moment before they met. A sad child cornered by bullies.

Raki felt like the evilest bitch.

YUNAI

"I sent a message to Ignacia letting her know you'd be spending the evening with us so we can get to know you better. I promise I'm not inviting you to your funeral." Mirta and Yunai walked out of the hospital and to the resident apartments. They were situated in a circle like the cabins, but were much nicer, each three stories high.

"Why does Braulio want to have dinner with me?" Yunai asked. "I got the whole greenhouse destroyed."

"Yeah, that was pretty bad. But he's had some thoughts since then. So have I."

Mirta led her up to the second floor of her apartment building. She unlocked the roots from her door and pushed it open.

"You're his roommate?" Yunai stepped inside. The smell of herbs and spices tangoed with her nose. Her mouth watered.

"Oh no. He's way too particular and fussy for me." Mirta closed the door and locked the roots back. "I'm lucky enough to have my own place. Braulio!"

Mirta walked into the kitchen as Yunai looked around the living room. The space was...surprisingly sparse for someone with Mirta's sunny personality. Yunai imagined Mirta as someone who collected art from all cultures, who hung paintings of bubbly companions on stringed root lights, with books and papers scattered everywhere. The reality only included a table with chairs and a couch with a side table next to it. She noticed a set of shoes next to the door.

Yunai debated whether she should stand around awkwardly or gather up her watery guts and go into the kitchen when a young man appeared in the living room. Her eyes were instinctively drawn to his bare feet, which explained the shoes. He looked exhausted, and his dark brown hair toed the line between stylish and disheveled.

"Riza. They."

"Yunai," she replied, making a mental note to adjust her language. Mirta said she didn't have a roommate, so this was probably one of her companions. "Are you a resident too?"

"No." Riza nodded their head at the kitchen, then entered the room. Yunai followed when she realized they were signaling her to come.

"You shouldn't leave guests floating by the door," Riza said.

"I didn't," Braulio replied.

Mirta pulled Yunai into the kitchen when she got to the

entrance. Riza opened the fridge and peered inside. Braulio picked up a pot from the stove with heated hands and poured its contents into a serving bowl. He acknowledged Yunai with a glance and a little "Hi."

"Pathetic," Riza said, walking out with a pitcher.

Braulio rolled his eyes. Yunai smiled. And that's when she noticed the rainbow alligator hanging on the kitchen's back wall. It was shaped from gold wire, its body parts out of proportion. The rainbow colors bleeding into each other reminded her of the wheel that pair had painted on the side street. The painting that resulted in a stay at 'Aute's House.

Yunai didn't ask about it. She was done being a busybody.

"Help us set everything out," Mirta said, squeezing her hand.

Braulio brought the bowl out to the living room. Yunai helped Mirta with the bowls, cups, and spoons. She still felt out of place around these people she barely knew, but helping took her mind off the discomfort. They gathered around the table and passed bowls around.

"Riza is my companion visiting from Artemisa, our homeland," Braulio said after a moment. "They may or may not be interested in what we have to talk about."

Riza said nothing as they poured water into their cup. Yunai was curious about them, but she got the sense that they didn't share personal details off bat.

"Why did you invite me here?" Yunai asked. "I thought you hated me. I almost got the hospital destroyed."

Braulio ladled the soup of potatoes, corn, tomatoes, yuca, and green plantain, which Yunai recognized as ajiaco, into his bowl. "We don't like scouts. We think the Scouthood is more destructive than people are willing to admit."

Yunai's face grew hot. It didn't bother her when Mirta expressed the same opinion, but Braulio saying it irked her.

"You should have been expelled after what you caused," Braulio continued, pulling no punches. He passed the ladle to Riza. "But that's not my call...and you may have actually solved our zonbi problem. So why did you go snooping through the greenhouse, Yunai? Be honest."

Because you made me? "Because..." Yunai stared down at her unfilled bowl. "I thought I saw someone trapped there."

"Who?" Braulio asked.

"The..." Yunai eyed Braulio, then looked back at her bowl. He always looked so serious. She couldn't imagine anyone playing him for a fool. "You wouldn't believe me."

"Try me."

"You wouldn't believe me!" Yunai cried. She spooned ajiaco into her bowl with haste when Riza passed the ladle to her. She started eating, needing the distraction and not wanting to be rude.

"We've seen things you wouldn't believe."

Yunai stopped her spoon halfway up and turned to Riza. They leaned back in their chair, cup in hand. Yunai returned to the safety of her bowl. She didn't want anyone's eyes on her when she gave her answer.

"...the Saint."

"Ha!" Mirta slapped her hands on the table. "I knew it wasn't some random person! You owe me!"

"We don't know if it's true," Braulio snapped. "I need proof before I fork over any money."

"It's *so* true! I knew he wasn't dead. That's why there's been no new Saint yet."

"You believe me?" Yunai was awestruck. Anyone else would have chained her and hauled her off to the Cathedral for judgment.

"*I* do," Mirta said. "It makes the most sense."

"Is that why you defended me?"

Mirta slurped a heaping serving of ajiaco. "I didn't want you to get in trouble, and I could tell you were hiding the truth. Remember, we don't like scouts, and that especially means the Grand Scoutmaster."

"You were right next to me when I saw him..."

"I didn't see what you saw, and I'm definitely not trying to get myself hanged. But I believe you. If he was trapped, he for sure would be in his emotions. That combined with his power would definitely lure zonbi."

"We believe in things the Natural doesn't want to believe in." Braulio put his spoon in his empty bowl, pushed his chair back, and crossed his arms. "We don't like accepting things just because someone with a capitalized title told us to."

Riza set their cup down. They got up and disappeared down the hallway.

"Are we that annoying?" Mirta asked.

"They're fine. What I want to know is how you saw what you saw."

"I'm not sure," Yunai said. "But I know it was him. His eyes were violet. He looked almost dead, but it was definitely him."

Braulio looked at Mirta. "Odomi?"

"Odomi?" Mirta huffed and pushed her half-full bowl away. "What, you think she's the one who trapped him? Why?"

"It's her hospital. And Niesh already suspects her."

"But *why*?"

"Siaka's been acting funny too. That's why I didn't want to do this at my place."

"*Why* would she be involved, Braulio? What grudge could she possibly have against the Saint?"

"M-maybe she's unnatural!" Yunai blurted out desperately. The discussion turned into a race, and Yunai struggled to keep up. "The Saint told me to bring her to justice, and only someone unnatural would target him. If she kidnapped him, we have to tell the Cathedral!"

"Slow down, Yunai," Mirta said. "We don't know that she is."

"And even if she was," Braulio said, "we wouldn't be quick to turn our mentor in. She's like a Mother to us, unnatural or not."

"They'd also think you played a part or would certainly think you were unnatural if you were the only one who saw him," Mirta said. "And after that last meeting..."

"Right... I couldn't tell them the truth."

"And Niesh already sent the firing squad to the greenhouse," Mirta continued. "If he were there, he isn't anymore."

"Unless he was moved," Braulio stated. "We've seen no zonbi come or fall since then, so he can stay gone for all I care."

Yunai flinched. "How can you say that? How can you walk around knowing he may be in danger somewhere?"

"I *don't* know anything, actually," Braulio said. "All we have is the word of a cadet too eager for her own good."

"You invited me here. And I have a duty to..." Be a busybody? She just told herself she would stay in her lane. Instead, she circled right back. If she pushed her boundaries again, no way Ignacia—or Niesh—would let her off, not with what just happened to Moraima.

And Yunai refused to be sent back to parents who wanted nothing to do with her.

"Look, I'm not trying to be mean. I don't care for the Saint. I care about the people and animals I'm supposed to care for. I think you get that. I'll be back." Braulio got up and went down the hallway.

"He's an ass," Mirta said, not quietly, "but he really does care for the people he cares about. And the animals probably more."

"What about everyone else? What am I supposed to do? I can't say anything to anyone, and it's frustrating." Yunai ran her hands through her hair, then pulled on her ends. "My cabinmates are avoiding me. Ignacia dismissed one of our cadets, and everyone's blaming me for it. I feel like I have no companions or comrades." Yunai let go of her hair before she pulled it out.

"Forget about them. They'll come around or they won't. But, unlike Braulio, I do think this Saint thing is worth checking out. This is too much of a scandal to let go of, especially if Odomi is involved."

"But—"

"I'll talk to her. Like I said, I'm not plotting your funeral, and you should take time to settle down."

Yunai felt her body relax. Mirta was consistently the bright sun of what often felt like a long cycle. "I don't deserve your help. We're not even companions."

"When someone invites you for a meal, it means we're companions." Mirta gave Yunai that smirk that let her know everything would be okay. "And if an Artemisan says she'll help you, you better believe her."

BRAULIO

"What did you think bringing me here would do?" Riza asked. Braulio found them sitting on the railing of Mirta's balcony, one leg hanging down, back against the wall.

"A little company can't hurt, Riza," Braulio said, tempering the judgment in his tone. "Honestly, I was thinking you'd be interested in the stuff going on around here. It's definitely relevant to you."

"You were hoping someone else's problems would make me forget about mine. Just because unnatural things are happening with other people, doesn't mean I have to get involved."

Braulio braced himself, ready for a fight. "I haven't seen much of you since you told me about your father's poem. Have you read the whole thing yet?"

"Yes." They didn't go on.

"And?"

Riza laced their fingers together and fiddled with them. Their expression went blank. "When I finished it, the room smelled like rotten meat. I could smell it in my throat."

"Rotten meat?" Braulio watched Riza's fingers and connected the dots. "Like a dead body."

Riza clutched their hands together. They started to speak but faltered. After a minute, they tried again. "It was definitely a poem about death. I didn't understand all the words, but..."

Braulio didn't press them to go on. Their silence sounded like acceptance. Braulio considered himself lucky—he had never lost anyone he shared a bond with. He couldn't relate to what Riza was experiencing, but he hoped reading the poem and experiencing their father's final emotions would give them some peace. The Plane was a cruel place for anyone, especially the unnatural.

If Odomi was unnatural and the one behind the Saint's death, he wouldn't hold it against her.

"I'm going back to his office one last time," Riza said, hopping off the railing. "I don't want his things to be felt by anyone else."

"Do you need me to go with you?"

"No. I'll be fine." Riza went back inside.

Braulio lingered on the balcony. He walked up to the railing and peered into the night. Looking down, he spotted Yunai walking back to the cabins—and Mirta heading into the city.

THIRTY-THREE

ODOMI

A scoutmaster posted at the train stations she used to travel between work and home. Scoutmasters posted along her path home. More surrounding her home. Every day, Odomi ignored them all as she went about her business. The excess of scoutmasters was wild, but was there any use in pointing this out to a woman so deep in her schemes she couldn't employ logic?

She locked back the roots to her front door and went straight to her bedroom, passing Siaka's unoccupied room. She instructed Siaka to stay at his apartment until Niesh ended her surveillance and told Galu to stay away as well. She hadn't been able to check on Leonardo since Niesh invaded her life, either.

Was there any point in keeping him alive now? All her efforts to drain his power had been unsuccessful. Galu was a dead end, and she couldn't look for anyone else to try with, not without a scoutmaster executing her on the spot. Was there any point to anything she did?

Odomi closed her bedroom door. The tears came as easily as she collapsed onto her bed. She failed her son's memory. Of that, she was certain.

SIAKA

Siaka hoped to spend the evening with his companions, but as soon as their shifts ended, they made themselves scarce. No big deal. It happened. So he found himself heading back to the office to check on Galu and decide what to do with her. He gave her a lot of trust and received nothing in return. Not her fault, but the ex-scout knew too much about their plans. Siaka wasn't sure if they could trust her to keep their secrets if he let her go.

As he approached the faculty building, he spotted a child walking up the steps. She appeared unaccompanied. Siaka slowed his pace and followed her into the building. She wandered through the hallway, standing on her tiptoes to read the plaques on the doors.

"You lost?"

The girl stumbled off her toes, her face caught between surprise and fear. Her features appeared Artemisan, dark eyes and brown skin.

"Don't worry, just want to help."

She made herself small, but her stature did not minimize her anger. Hesitated to believe him but wanted to all the same. "I'm looking for Efraim. He said I could come here if I ever needed help."

Interesting. What was the connection between this lost girl and the professor? "My name is Siaka. What's yours? And be honest," he added with a smile.

"Toya."

"Nice to meet you, Toya. I'm guessing you don't know the professor returned?"

"Returned?"

"He passed away."

"But..." She turned to look at the doors again, then turned back to Siaka. "He said he could help me."

"Where do you live, Toya? And how did you meet him?"

"I—I live far from here. I got to visit here a lot...with my companions..."

Not the full truth, but not a lie either. She was hiding something or was scared to reveal details about her identity.

"I-I don't know what to do. I don't want to go home..." Toya fought with her voice to keep it from breaking, but whatever hurt she was experiencing broke through her defenses.

And that's when Siaka felt it—small waves emanating from her being. She was visibly sad, but he sensed other emotions. He couldn't make them out. Maybe she was too repressed. But one thing was certain.

This girl was not one of the Natural.

"I knew the professor," Siaka said. "Well, my Mom knew him better. He helped a lot of people while he was alive. Maybe we can help you with whatever you need."

"I don't know..." She went silent.

Siaka had to think fast. He needed to speak with Galu, but he couldn't leave one of his own by herself, and he didn't want to bring her inside the office. She was young and vulnerable, but that didn't mean he could trust her. And bringing her home was out of the question, not with the neighborhood teeming with scoutmasters. But he didn't have a lot of options.

Damn. Time to make a hard choice. Galu could wait.

"Why don't I take you to my Mom's house? She has plenty of space, and she knows a lot of people. Maybe she can find someone to get you what you need."

Toya nodded. Siaka led her away from the university and hoped on Lemana he wasn't leading either of them to certain doom.

RIZA

"Who are you?" They asked the question at the same time. The woman shot up from the chair. Riza, box in hand, left the door to the office open, prepared to escape if needed.

"This is my father's office," Riza said. "Were you one of his students?"

"No. I'm meeting someone here." She eyed them cautiously. "Your father? Sorry about what happened to him. Heard he was an amazing man."

"He was." Riza didn't trust, didn't know, didn't care about this stranger. They moved to the desk and carefully took things from the drawers.

"These scoutmasters are heartless. They take life without considering its worth."

Riza stopped breathing. "What did you say?"

"I said the scoutmasters take life—"

"Who told you that? Who told you—" Riza slammed the drawer shut and dropped the box. They knew it. They *knew* it.

"The guy I'm supposed to be meeting told me. He said he and his Mom were close to him. Why? Is there a different story?"

"Where do these people live?"

"Don't think I can tell you that."

"You need to tell me! This was my father!"

"Zero down, alright? Their neighborhood is crawling with scoutmasters, so if you're anything like your father, you'll probably want to stay away."

Riza clasped their hands over their mouth and closed their eyes. After calming themself, they continued. "Is this guy still coming here?"

"Actually, he's pretty damn late." The woman ran a hand through her hair. "Okay, fine. I don't want to stay in this room anyway. I'll take you, but we need to be careful."

YUNAI

The temperature dropped when Yunai entered the cabin. Obi, Estefania, and Umaru were eating dinner. Umaru gave her a half-smile, then went back to his meal. The other two didn't greet her. Yunai tried to ignore them as she went upstairs. She made it to the top—and almost ran into Sega. Her eyes had something to say, and Yunai did her best to avert them. She moved past her, aiming straight for her bed in the empty quarters.

"I overheard Ignacia talking today."

Yunai kept going. She kneeled before her bed and opened the drawer, searching for her shower bag.

"They're thinking of putting in a curfew because of you."

Ignore. Keep zero. Shower. Bag. Where was her bag?

"A lot of things are about to change here because of you, and you don't even seem to care."

Found it. Yunai grabbed her nightwear, kicked off her boots, and headed to the showers. As she was about to leave the quarters, Sega threw herself in front of Yunai.

"Don't you care at all? You involve yourself with literally everything else, but your comrades don't matter?"

"We're not comrades." Yunai cursed herself for responding. She went around Sega.

"Apparently. You don't care at all that Moraima's gone. My companion was dismissed for being too nice, but *you* get to stay because you flooded the hospital with zonbi."

Indignation halted Yunai. Pride spun her around. And ego opened her mouth. "I got to stay because Niesh thinks I'm useful, even if what I did was foolish. Moraima was dismissed because she isn't."

Sega lunged. She brought Yunai to the floor, and Yunai fought back with a heated hand. They punched, grappled, restrained, fire and wind blasting everywhere.

"Stop!"

Yunai pushed her off. Sega almost tackled her again when Estefania forged chains from her metal bracelets and slapped them over Sega's wrists. Yunai lost hold of her senses and went in for round two when Raki appeared, blocking Yunai with her body.

"Are you two out of your minds?" Estefania used all her strength to hold Sega back. "You're lucky Ignacia's out with her partner tonight. You *both* would have been dismissed."

"That's what she deserves," Sega spat.

Estefania unlocked her chains when Sega wouldn't stop jerking around. "Let's go outside. You need to zero down." She pulled Sega downstairs.

"Are you okay?" Raki asked, stepping back. "What was that?"

"Why do you care?" Yunai grabbed her shower bag and nightwear and pushed past Raki. Raki grabbed her arm. Yunai tried yanking it away, but Raki was stronger than her. The fight with Sega, both verbal and physical, had worn her out too.

"Yunai...I'm sorry."

With those words, Yunai released a hard sigh. Not because she didn't believe her apology was sincere, but because she never needed to say it at all.

Yunai turned to face her. "Don't. I shouldn't have asked you to come with me. That was way too much to ask of you."

Raki gave her an easy smile. Then something sad and uncertain shaded her eyes.

"Is everything okay?" Yunai asked.

Raki shook her head. "I might be the worst person ever." Tears appeared in her gray eyes. Yunai pulled her away from the entrance. "I lost Toya. She never returned to the orphanage, and when I went back to see if she returned there, the director said to just forget about her."

"What? How can she say something like that?"

"I don't know, but I was awful to her first, and she ran off. And this island is so big, I wouldn't even know where to start looking for her."

"Can't you ask the scoutmasters for help?"

"I don't think they'll care. The director made that pretty clear. And it's my responsibility to find her, to make sure she's okay... I have to look for her." Raki walked off.

"Wait. I'll come."

"Yunai, I can't ask you to do that. You're already leaning over the edge."

"I want to. Even if it means I get sent home." *It probably is what I deserve.* "Don't think you can stop me."

"Okay... Thank you. But where do we even start?" Raki plopped down on the nearest bed, which happened to be Esera's.

"I think, in this case, we only have our scouting instincts. Does she have any favorite places you two have been to? Anywhere you think she would gravitate toward?"

Raki perked up. "The university. She asked me to take her there multiple times."

"That's a good start." Yunai put her shower bag away and put her boots back on. "We should go before Ignacia or anyone else comes home. I can't handle anyone else's judgment tonight."

THIRTY-FOUR

ODOMI

Odomi pulled the last of the passionflower the residents salvaged from the greenhouse from her medicine cabinet. She put them in her mortar and ground them with her pestle. She synced a little water into the mortar, though not as much as she usually did—this concoction needed all her ruthlessness.

She poured the concoction into a bottle and took it upstairs. When she reached the middle of the hallway, where there were no windows for scoutmasters to spy through, she pulled a needle from her pocket and transferred the concoction to the needle. It slid in thick. With one shot, she would put the Saint out forever, aborting a plan cycles in the making.

Odomi almost commanded the roots on the ceiling apart when she heard a knock at the door. She ignored it, dismissing it as a nosy scoutmaster. She commanded some of the roots to untangle when the person knocked again. Odomi moved the roots back and pocketed the needle. She needed to get rid of whoever rapped on her door this late.

Downstairs, she unlocked the door—and was surprised to see Mirta.

"I'm so sorry, Odomi. I know it's late."

Odomi stepped aside to let her in. She locked the door after her.

"What are you doing here? Has something happened at the hospital?"

"No. I came to check on you."

Odomi looked through her windows to see if any scoutmasters followed Mirta in or reported back via animal messenger.

"I know Niesh lost her mind on you. I just wanted to make sure you were okay."

"I'm fine, dear. You don't need to worry." Mirta, always the responsible one. Though this visit was odd, even for Odomi's favorite field surgeon in training. "Did Siaka send you? I hope that boy isn't using you for personal errands."

"No," Mirta replied, the immediate space flashing hot, then returning to normal. "I came on my own. Actually, there's something I wanted to ask you..."

"It can't wait?"

"It can't."

Odomi gave her resident a thorough once-over. Mirta's wits were always sharp. She knew something.

"Are you hiding the Saint?"

Odomi's world turned inside out. She grabbed Mirta by an arm and pulled her away from the walls. "Mirta. You're one of my best residents, a gift to the medical world. Be very careful about the things you choose to say."

"If it's not true, you wouldn't have pulled me away like this."

"Girl, have you lost your mind? There are scoutmasters leaking out of my ears. An accusation, doesn't matter if it's true or false, will get us both killed."

"Just tell me if it's true or not. Please."

"Why would you ever need a question like that answered?"

"The cadet I brought to the greenhouse wants to know if she's unnatural or not. She's afraid seeing things will make her a threat to the Cathedral. And I need to know if my mentor is a threat, too."

That cadet indeed saw him. Siaka had been right.

Another sound from the door, this time roots unlocking. Siaka stepped in—with a young girl.

"I'm allowed to enter my own home without asking questions!"

Siaka yelled behind him. He quickly locked the roots back. "Mirta? What are you doing here?"

"What are *you* doing here?" Odomi demanded. "I told you to stay away, Siaka! Who in Lemana's blue ocean is this child? Why would you bring her here?"

"She needs help. I'm sorry, I didn't know what else to do. She told me she knew the professor." Siaka gave her a look that told her the girl was more than a simple child.

Odomi pinched the skin between her eyebrows. Her simple night had suddenly tangled over itself. "Take the girl to my room and lock the door behind you."

Siaka winked at Mirta, then took the girl up.

"Mirta." Hesitation and a reflection. As soon as Odomi recognized Mirta's talent for surgery, she took her under her wing. Odomi hoped to somehow use her skills for their purposes. Letting that cadet into the greenhouse was a grave error in judgment, but Mirta always remained steadfast in her criticism of the Cathedral and the Scouthood. Perhaps clueing her in now wouldn't be a mistake. "Do you believe this reality is ours to shape? Do you believe the rejection of our humanity to be a curse upon this world?"

Hesitation. And a reflection. "Yes."

"Good. Follow me." Odomi took her upstairs. Finally, she commanded the roots apart, then synced the hidden ceiling open with a series of specific arm movements. The ceiling broke into blocks that shifted positions in and out, right and left. Old wooden stairs fell to the floor when Odomi finished the sequence. Kicking her shoes off, she led Mirta upstairs, lighting a torch when they reached the top. Mirta lit one after her.

"So many roots up here. And they're so green, they're almost blue. How—" Mirta gasped and dropped her torch. Odomi resynced it onto her palm before it hit the roots.

Leonardo was positioned in the middle of the attic like an ancient totem, roots holding him up from all sides. With his heart reciting the words of death, taking the roots out would have ended his life eventually, but she needed to ensure his entire body failed immediately. She couldn't risk him dying slowly and the ensuing emotions he would release.

"I can see him?" Mirta asked. "Should I be able to?"

"Anyone can now."

Odomi synced a couple of thick roots with her feet and peddled herself over to the Saint. She heard Mirta's shoes tumble to the hallway and roots shift and stretch. When Odomi reached the center, she took the needle out of her pocket. Death was close to dragging Leonardo away. His mouth hung open, his eyes stricken with red.

"...the end..." His voice barely a voice.

Odomi had nothing left to say. The roots stopped shifting. Mirta waited behind her, speechless.

SIAKA

"Wait here." Siaka closed the door to Odomi's room. He walked over to the windows and drew the curtains together. "Stay out of sight for now. My Mom should be able to help you when she's finished."

Toya sat on her bed. "What is she doing?"

"She's a medic. There's someone who—*shit*." Before he pulled the last curtain, he saw Galu and someone else approach the house. A couple of the scoutmasters stopped them, and they exchanged words.

"Stay here!" Siaka bolted out of the room—leaving the door wide open.

RIZA

Riza wanted no part of this stupidity. They needed to know what happened to their father. That's all that mattered.

"You have no right to detain us!" the woman from their father's office yelled. "Let us pass."

"Too many people are coming to this house," a scoutmaster stated. "Not one more is getting in without an explanation."

The woman was intent on arguing her case. But Riza had their own way of getting in. The waves of grief coming off the house gave them the opening they needed. "I'll just leave. Don't want any trouble."

"Where are you going?" the woman shouted.

Riza ignored her as they found a safe spot hidden from scouting eyes.

ODOMI

The needle touched Leonardo's skin when Mirta's voice cut through the air. "You shouldn't be up here!"

Odomi turned her head. The child stood at the top of the stairs. Siaka's failure to listen was repeatedly biting her in the ass tonight.

"Wh-who is that?" the child asked. Her breathing went into labor. "Is— Is that the Saint?"

Leonardo coughed, the roots shifting with his body. "...ah...one of...my children..."

Odomi turned back to him.

The Saint, straining against all physiology, gathered one final breath. "...my death means nothing...as long as my legacy lives on... my children, my orphans...removed from an unnatural life...placed into the safety of...the Cathedral to live a Natural one..."

"What do you mean removed?" Odomi demanded, gripping the needle.

"...the reach of the Saint is...far and infinite..." He coughed, grinned. "...the unnatural should not raise children...so I command their deaths...when we find them...to give our children...a chance to live righteously..."

"Y-y-you..." The child's body shook violently. "...you k-killed my parents??" She sank to the roots.

"...*my body, my home...have become my knell... so much that the only way...to live again is...to strangle the heart...of he who believes that...he has the right to air*...an unnatural damaged my heart with these wicked words...my retribution...has been my life's work..."

Her screams birthed terror to the night.

Roots tore from the walls, from the floor, pierced the Saint's torso, legs, neck. Dim waves crashed into the room, flooding the roots with their energy, drowning the Saint's dead body with their weight. The emotion overwhelmed Odomi, her mind and memories desperate to spiral. Mirta fell to her knees, the emotions having a weaker effect on her repressed state.

"*Mirta, grab her!*"

Mirta got up, synced her metal sleeves down to her hands, and forged machetes. She maneuvered through the wild roots back to the entrance, slicing and cutting when they obstructed her path. Odomi tried to command the roots to stop, but the child's rage was far stronger than her control. If she didn't stop, her pain would bring the entire house down.

Odomi stumbled over and through the roots to get out of the room. She jumped down to the hallway, using air to cushion her landing. The child fought for air in Mirta's arms, screams pumping out of her between each struggle. Everything in the home made from natural resources shook or broke or splintered.

"Odomi? What in the world?" Mirta didn't know what she was asking. "Why is your pocket glowing?"

Odomi looked down. The journal's violet light blinded her as the menacing sound of zonbi lengthened the night.

RIZA

Riza nearly fell to the ground after they exited the unstable house. Those lines...they were the last lines from their father's poem. And it wasn't a poem for a life he had given up—it was an elegy that summoned the death of the Saint.

Which meant their father didn't take his own life, and he wasn't just murdered. He had been executed.

THIRTY-FIVE

NIESH

"Commander!" The scoutmaster saluted Niesh. Niesh waved her into the conference hall, where she was having an informal meeting with Ibrahim. "There is a disturbance at Odomi's house. Multiple people trying to get in and what sounded like an explosion from the top floor, much like the one that killed the Saint."

Niesh stood up, preparing to depart. "Suspicions confirmed?" Ibrahim asked.

"Of course." Then to the scoutmaster, "Send a message to my hunter trainees. They'll be joining us in this fight."

RAKI

"Have you seen a girl wandering around, looking lost?" Raki asked the hundredth person on the university campus. "Really dark eyes, hair that stops at her chin?"

The scholar shook their head and walked away. Defeated, Raki returned to where she and Yunai agreed to meet at the top of the hour. Yunai sat on steps, head resting in a hand.

"This is impossible," Raki said, plopping next to her. "The campus is massive, and I don't know that she's even here."

"It's okay," Yunai said. "We'll keep looking. If anything, we can leave a report with campus security. Maybe she's here and we just haven't asked the right person."

"Maybe..." Raki noticed shadows passing over them. She looked up. A large flock of birds flew overhead, cutting into the light of the moon. But flocks of birds didn't normally fly at night...right? Raki took a closer look and saw that they were zonbi, their talons made from different animal parts. They moved too slowly to be on the attack—their movement reminded her of the zonbi that stuck to the orphanage dome. Her stomach sank.

"It's almost like the hospital," Yunai said, looking up.

Raki couldn't deny what their movement meant. They had reacted to Toya's emotions strangely during their argument at the orphanage. "That has to be Toya." Raki got up and ran in their direction, Yunai following close behind.

SIAKA

Whatever that explosion was pocked the pale silver night with zonbi. The scoutmasters fought them back fiercely, but combat mastery could only do so much against massive numbers. Siaka lacked the fighting ability to assist and wasn't about to lift a finger to help the scoutmasters, anyway. Galu looked back and forth between the zonbi and scoutmasters, unsure whether to help or not.

"We need to get out of here!" Siaka shouted.

"And go where?" Galu barked. "Back to the office where you were supposed to meet me? Or in your house that's currently a blasting zone? You people are done dragging me into your half-baked schemes!" She scratched the ground with both hands, forging spikes of earth, and shot them at the flying zonbi approaching them.

Siaka was about to try one more time to convince her—when the Grand Scoutmaster stepped onto the battleground. The way she casually walked through the mayhem toward the house without forging a weapon unnerved Siaka. Other people—cadets or scouts, he couldn't tell—filtered in in waves after her, their weapons drawn or forged. Galu was on her own. He had to get his Mom and Mirta out of here.

Siaka dashed back into the house, locking the roots, as if it mattered. Mirta rushed down the stairs in the same moment with Toya in her arms, Odomi right behind her.

"Niesh is here, Mom, we gotta go now!" Then Siaka saw it—the bright violet glow of the journal. He looked at Toya, then at Mirta— and that's when he felt the heavy waves, his spirit dimming in response. Relief and urgency twisted his stomach into knots.

"Mirta, I need you to go." Odomi took Toya from Mirta's arms. Tears ran down Odomi's face, the waves overwhelming her. "I don't want you to get caught up in this. Not right now."

Mirta let Odomi take Toya. Siaka wondered how much she saw —his companion was dazed.

"Forget about everything you've seen tonight. If anyone questions you for any reason, you were only here to check on me and then left through the back door. Nothing more."

Siaka squeezed Mirta's shoulder. "Mom, you need to go now, too. If that child is the one, you need to head to Vaiola. I'll stay." He ushered the women into the kitchen.

Mirta found her voice. "Siaka—"

"Niesh is at our doorstep, and she'll want a suspect. It can't be either of you, so go. *Now!*"

Odomi's face turned sick. She pushed down her words and bolted out the back with Mirta. Her ability would keep them hidden. Hopefully.

Siaka did not cower when the front door blew off its hinges. He turned to meet his challenge. Niesh walked up to the kitchen. She stopped in the space between the two rooms. Their eyes locked onto each other.

"Tell me where your Mother is, and I may spare your life."

Siaka weighed the choice to fight. He could not fight, but he could stand his ground using skills the Natural called unnatural— leaving Niesh to pursue Odomi if he fell, which was likely. That was a risk he couldn't take.

"She ran away. She saw me take the Saint's life using unnatural means, got scared, and ran away."

Niesh scrutinized him. "Am I supposed to believe you're behind all of this?"

Siaka's black eye burned bright. He grinned. "Feel free to check the attic."

ESERA

Esera struck down as many zonbi that arose from the lake as he could with his burning nifo'oti, but their numbers were staggering. Even the scoutmasters struggled. He watched one take a fatal blow to the head from a scaly creature with multiple wings and another lose an arm to a ferocious set of claws and fangs, both in the beast's mouth.

Matagi and the other hunter trainees were not faring well either. One on the lake stopped fighting due to sheer exhaustion—and a snake-like figure quickly pulled them under the water. Another who fought near Esera vanished when Esera checked on her after he felled the zonbi he was fighting.

He ignored it all. Their fates would not be his.

Esera drove the fiery hooks of his weapon into the visible neck bones of a five-legged zonbi, felling the creature. When he pulled them out, he saw someone familiar, neither a trainee nor a scoutmaster.

The ex-scout. He didn't understand her connection to this—whatever *this* was—but as a hunter in training, it was his duty to take her out.

Esera rushed up to her, nifo'oti primed. He lunged at her from her side, taking them both underwater. She fought off Esera's hold and sent a wave of pressure at him. He dodged the wave easily as she swam for the surface. Esera swam after her, catching up, and hooked his nifo'oti around her ankles. He didn't see that she had forged long icicles on both arms. She swiped them at Esera's hands, missing one but cutting the other. Bubbles boiled out of Esera's mouth as he hissed. She reached the surface, Esera resurfacing seconds later.

The ex-scout stood on the water, icicles still forged. "Seriously?" She synced smaller spikes from her bigger ones at Esera. He jumped back as they hit the water—and noticed a whirlpool circling his feet. She melted her icicles, then whipped the water from the whirlpool up with a sleight of hand before he escaped, sending him into the air.

She slashed him with wind from all angles, making shallow cuts in his skin. When the wind stopped, he fell to the water.

She raced to him on the water, coming in for the final strike—when she gasped in pain, falling forward. Esera had a little electric charge in him. As soon as she fell on him, he released his small store of electricity, shocking her into submission. He dragged her body to the shore, hissing at the sharp cuts all over him. He looked at her as she lay on her side—metal claws stuck out of her back. He looked up to see Matagi approaching them.

"I'm assuming this is our ex-cadet," he said, syncing his claws from her back.

Esera nodded, getting to his feet. Matagi forged his claws into chains to restrain the woman—but instead forged his claws back into teeth. Esera turned to see Niesh walking up to them. She stood over the woman, then kneeled, brushing the hair from her face.

"What a shame..." She stood back up, her attention now on both young men. Her eyes lingered on Matagi—then landed on Esera. "This wouldn't be the first life you've taken."

Esera shuddered. It wasn't a throwaway comment about the contents of his file that she must have read before recruiting him. It was a command.

He wanted to vomit.

Matagi stood at guard as Esera put his nifo'oti back on his belt. He cursed himself for using all his electricity to knock her out. It would have been the more humane way to...

He let the thought go. No point. No use. He was there to take orders and feel nothing—or suffer punishment.

Zeroing down as much as he could, Esera ignited a soldering fire on an index finger, the single flame almost blue. He knelt, facing the woman's back. His brain scrambled for the dozens of possibilities of where to drill the fire.

"Back of the neck."

It wasn't in his best interest to test Niesh's patience. He aimed for the middle of the woman's neck—and relived the horror of his childhood, a boy forced to become a man.

NIESH

The woman gargled her screams as Niesh walked back into the house. The scout looked familiar. She had seen hundreds in her time as a scoutmaster, but some faces stuck out. Regardless, that was one issue solved. She had no taste for killing people, but an ex-scout in league with the unnatural could not be allowed to bloom.

Niesh checked the ceiling to make sure Odomi's Son hadn't moved from where she detained him. Still out cold. Roots restrained him to the ceiling, and trick chains almost choked his neck. One wrong move and he was done. She almost dragged him under, but Niesh wasn't convinced he was the one behind all the unnatural activity. He'd be questioned in time.

She headed upstairs, then walked up the wooden stairs in the middle of the hallway, each plank creaking with each step. The attic was a jungle of healthy colored roots. The centerpiece—what was left of the centerpiece was the color of death.

For the first time since Leonardo's "murder," Niesh had to suppress a bout of emotions. This...even this was a lot to take in.

"Paloma...I'm sorry."

THIRTY-SIX

ODOMI

The girl's emotions disrupted Odomi's ability to conceal them, so she had instructed Mirta to take a different route back to base. The old woman didn't have the capacity to hide all three of them. Grief weighed too heavily on her chest. She needed to make it to Vaiola fast and think of a way to save Siaka. If Odomi lost another child, she would never recover.

When she finally reached the outskirts of Lemana, Odomi took a moment to collect herself. The child, whom she carried on her back, passed out a while ago, but her emotions continued to undulate even as she slept. The zonbi slowly flying far behind them in a straight line proved that.

Odomi looked beyond the hills to the massive roots of Vaiola. Still some time to go before they reached the safety of the swamp. She freed one of her hands, created a torch to light her path, and started walking again. The girl rustled in her arms.

"Where are we going?" she asked, her voice weak.

"Somewhere safer than where you were." Odomi rethought her response. Her life before the orphanage had been violently upended, forcing her to live under the manipulative thumb of the Cathedral. Better to inform the child of her choices and what Odomi planned to do. "Can you tell me your name?"

"Toya."

"I'm Odomi, Toya, and I believe we have a lot in common. I lost my son, and you your parents, to the Saint's machinations, and both of us carry that grief every day."

"I still don't know where we're going."

Odomi chuckled. "To Vaiola, the giant root swamp."

"Will I be safe there?"

"Yes." Odomi organized her thoughts. She needed to hit the right notes with this girl. They passed between two hills, moving deeper into the long stretch of green. "You were probably told, again and again, that you need to control yourself. That you need to *zero down*. That the way you behave is not okay. It may be a repeated notion, but that doesn't mean it's true.

"People who don't know true history teach us to reject our humanity, everything that flavors life. That makes the children of this world a dying species. And a dying species is difficult to revive. The Saint hopes we can be sustained by rejecting provocative art and silencing our emotions. But what he and the Plane fail to realize is that what he deems vices are the key to this world's revival. We are literally dying by righteous way of life."

"You're using too many big words," Toya said, the life returning to her voice. She tightened her arms around Odomi's shoulders. "Just say the Saint is evil."

"Hah, I get caught up sometimes." Toya's emotions inspired a poetry Odomi hadn't felt in a very long time. "I like you, Toya. It's not up to anyone else, myself or the Saint, to dictate your life. But I would like to give you an opportunity to help us change the world so people like him, and those who follow him, can no longer hurt people like us."

"Us?"

"People like us, we feel everything. And we can shape our world to be whatever we need. One of our old leaders was like you. Her journal entries are unapologetic, raw. She censored nothing and exposed everything. I think you're perfect to be her successor."

"I'm a literal child, lady."

"I promise you, that doesn't matter at all. But I need your

246

consent. Are you willing to bear the torch of our fallen hero? Will you help us revive this dying world?"

Toya adjusted herself again. She probably had the energy to walk on her own, but Odomi didn't want to risk her lagging behind, not with the zonbi still inching at their backs.

"If it means I don't have to go back to the orphanage, sure. Whatever I have to do."

RAKI

Raki and Yunai left the city and sped into the dark hills. They both lit torches and kept a watchful eye on the zonbi above.

"She can't be heading into Vaiola, can she?" Yunai asked. "She'll get lost or hurt for sure."

"I wouldn't put it past her." Raki jumped up to one of the hills and threw her torch ahead, giving her a better view of the landscape.

"See her?" Yunai called from below.

Raki peered into the night, aided by the torch's light. Even if Toya was straight ahead, she could have been walking in between the hills, outside her view, and she couldn't see where the zonbi trail ended. She extinguished the torch and lit another one in her hand. "We need to jump through! We don't have time to waste!" Raki's legs were still sore, but they didn't have the luxury of pacing themselves.

Yunai nodded and ran up the hill. She couldn't high jump, so she would have to catch up. Raki crouched and sprang up, looking down before landing on the next hill. She jumped to the next, then the next—

"Toya!"

—and nose-dived, fists first. She pulled up a gauntlet of earth on one hand and one of roots on the other. A woman held Toya on her back. She spun around to face her—Toya's eyes bugged when they met Raki's—then the woman turned back. Raki didn't see her sync with the roots, but the woman whipped two huge ones back at Raki, the roots coming at her in steep waves. She ran up one of them, using air to boost her ascent, then slid down its backside. She punched her earth gauntlet at the woman on the way down, aiming for her legs but missing.

247

"Stop following us!" Toya shouted. "I hate you!"

Toya's anger forced the big root's skin to splinter, tripping Raki as she slid down. She tumbled to the ground.

The woman kicked off her shoes, then synced with the roots beneath her. She started peddling when a bolt of ice speared into the root right behind her. Yunai caught up to Raki and shot fire bullets at the roots with her flesh arm, but the woman was too fast. The woman jumped off when she reached the roots' end, then ripped them out of the ground, slinging them back.

"Watch out!" Yunai pulled Raki out of the way, a root pinning Yunai to the ground with a slam. Most of the zonbi continued to follow Toya's trail, but a few circled down to Yunai as her fear leaked out. Raki got to her feet and watched Toya and the woman disappear into the night. She could catch up to them if she jumped—but her companion needed her more.

Raki scrambled to Yunai's side and, using her enhanced strength, lifted the heavy root with a strained roar. Yunai dragged herself out from under with her arms. Raki let go, the root crashing to the ground. She collapsed. Her body had endured too much today.

The zonbi that came close to them returned to the trail, bringing up the rear. Yunai was calm but injured. "Go..." she huffed out. "I'll be fine."

Even if Raki wanted to, her energy was depleted. Drawing on sheer necessity, she crawled over to Yunai and wrapped the bloody gash on her leg with the shirt on her back. She hoisted both of them up, Yunai's tall frame weighing against Raki.

Stop following us.

She walked herself and Yunai between the last set of hills, reaching the edge of Vaiola. Its awesome size was so incredible, it terrified her.

I hate you!

"I think we have to take this loss," Raki said, her voice breaking over the last word.

"I'm so sorry, Raki," Yunai said, struggling to stand. "There are cadets training in there now. Maybe one of them will intervene."

Raki held them there for much longer than she meant. When the last of the zonbi vanished into the horizon, they began the long walk home.

THIRTY-SEVEN

BRAULIO

B raulio stood out of the way of the scoutmasters who raided his apartment. He tried keeping his cool as they upturned furniture, opened everything without closing it back, burned the root locks, and rifled through his and Siaka's belongings. Still, he much preferred this to the interrogation the scoutmasters subjected him to earlier.

"*Are you aware your roommate is unnatural?*"

"*Are you in league with the people who have committed terrorist acts against the Cathedral?*"

"*Did you know about the plot against the Saint to fake his death and steal his body?*"

He wasn't aware of a single thing.

"This room is now under investigation," one of the scoutmasters declared. "If you have any essentials, like medication or important documents, you will be allowed to take them after we inspect them. Everything else stays."

Braulio bit his tongue and got to it. The scoutmaster followed him around as he gathered what he needed.

"If you don't have a place to stay, the Cathedral can arrange a room for you at a hotel in the city."

"No thanks," Braulio said, putting his items in a bag after the scoutmaster examined them. "I'll stay with a companion." Riza's place was out of the question...

"Are you sure you heard correctly?"

"I heard it myself. I don't know how...but he killed the Saint. And they executed him."

...so he'd stay with Mirta. Braulio was still confused as to how Riza ended up at Odomi's house. When they returned, their face was pale and they were unstable. Which meant their emotions were raw. When he saw the scoutmasters rush to the base, Braulio sent them home with the promise of checking on them when things calmed down. He couldn't risk being around Riza while the situation was hot.

Braulio quickly exited his apartment when he finished packing. He ignored questions and looks from the nosy residents who had come out of their rooms to see the raid. He bolted downstairs, straight for Mirta's, and banged on her door, half-expecting her to still be out. He was surprised when a young woman with dark brown skin and braids opened the door.

"Who's there?" The young woman stepped to the side, and Mirta came up to the door. Mirta pulled him inside and locked the door. "Did they do anything to you?"

"Aside from ransack my whole life? No. Not at all." Braulio was about to go off when he noticed Yunai asleep on the couch, one bandaged leg raised on a pillow. "Mirta, what on Lemana's Plane happened tonight?"

"A lot, Braulio." She moved back to Yunai's side. "Way too much."

"Oh...so you're the cactus." The young woman gave him a sour look before she limped down the hallway.

"She's Yunai's companion," Mirta said.

Braulio let go of whatever the young woman's comment meant and sat next to Mirta on the floor. "Where's Siaka?"

Mirta stroked Yunai's hair, tears streaming down her face.

RIZA

"still water, skin

forgetting how to speak
with waves
begged me to see that
I can no longer live like this

my body, my home
have become my knell

so much that the only way
to live again is
to strangle the heart
of he who believes that
he has the right to air"

Riza always admired their father for his passion, his courage in speaking out about the things that mattered to him. But what did that passion mean when it guided the words that murdered the Saint? And what did that mean for Riza? They had no personal feelings about the Saint or the Cathedral, but everything they knew, everything they thought they knew about their father...

Riza felt incredibly drained since leaving that house. Those explosive emotions had buried them, sending them to the deepest pit in their body. They didn't want to think anymore.

SIAKA

"Mirta." Siaka lifted his head when she walked up to his cell. That minor movement sent surges of pain throughout his body. The scoutmasters spared no aggression when they shackled his hands and ankles with trick chains. "They let you see me?"

Mirta kneeled and moved close to Siaka. Scoutmasters stood on either side of his cell. They shifted their stances, reminding both of their presence.

"They saw me come to your house last night. I had to come down to answer questions." A meanness took over Mirta's face, but her eyes retained their kindness. "I can't believe you... I don't understand how you could betray the Cathedral like this! I thought we were comrades!"

Siaka focused on the twinkle in her eyes, taking the hint. He knew of his Mom's interest in her skills, but he needed to be sure she could be trusted and recruited. "We damn the Saint like he damns us. He doesn't deserve the power that Lemana blessed him with."

"Was all this worth your life?" Mirta's face almost broke character. Her lips trembled. "You're going to be executed!"

Mirta's face nearly broke him. Siaka intentionally kept his feelings for her quiet. He couldn't let his true emotions come out around the Natural and risk her getting punished by association. But everything in him wanted to reach out and comfort her.

"We're the Revivalists," Siaka said. "My death will mean everything if it means we revive the spirit of this Plane."

Mirta stared at him, her eyes ready to betray her. "Just tell me one thing. How did you do it? Sneaking around the body, making people see things. That was all you, right? How did you do it, Siaka?"

Siaka grinned. Odomi's talent for revealing people's deepest daydreams was unmatched. "I only show people what they believe to be true."

THIRTY-EIGHT

NIESH

Niesh sat with Paloma on a bench in the Cathedral's garden. Niesh had told her everything, excluding the gory details. After the pain, the denial, the hysterics, and the resulting zonbi, her Sister had passed out in her lap. To experience the loss of the same person twice... Niesh understood losing family and almost welcomed the zonbi. She gazed out into the faded morning sky.

The Revivalists... In all her time, she had never heard of an organized name for any unnatural group. Nor had any been this successful. Niesh reminded herself to recall the scoutmasters who were searching for the next Saint. Now that Leonardo was truly gone, his successor would receive the power and emerge soon after.

Niesh didn't believe Odomi's Son for one second. Leonardo had been put in a death state, then robbed from right under her eyes. Tortured. Starved. Murdered. Those were the actions of a high-ranking medic with access to several restricted areas, not a resident. Her Son had turned himself in too easily. And Odomi was nowhere to be found.

The ex-scout's execution would set an example for the entire Scouthood. Interestingly, reports of people seeing things in Lemana had stopped after the ex-scout's appearance at the concert.

The Board... Niesh had no insight into what the Board would

think, so she had to write the best report, and they needed to accept whatever she gave them. Because she didn't want to be the next Grand Scoutmaster to entertain their displeasure.

IGNACIA

Ignacia put the memo on her desk. She dismissed the cat messenger without sending a reply. The sigh she released was strained with the weight of her choices.

Galu. One of her old cadets. Ignacia remembered her clearly—angry like Esera, an achiever like Raki, and over-eager like Yunai. She recalled rumors of her disappearance and assumed she had died in the field, her death unaccounted for. She would have never expected her to join the unnaturals, to kill two innocents for no reason.

Ignacia sat in the quiet of her office for most of the morning. She hoped her approach to training the next generation of scouts was not a mistake.

ACKNOWLEDGMENTS

No creative work is made without the support of family, friends, community, and professionals every step of the way. Shout out to my early beta readers, Cathy Andrews and Naomi Lee, for their first impressions and feedback that let me know this story was on the right path.

Big ups to my sensitivity readers, Stephanie Cohen, Sarah Clark, and Raven Kameʻenui-Becker. The work of improving representation in storytelling is an ongoing journey, and their guidance has been crucial in my growth as a marginalized writer who writes about marginalized peoples. Thank you to my editor Eliot West, whose sharp eye helped guide the editing process, to the wonderful folks at MiblArt for providing the fabulous cover art, to Book Brush for the beautiful chapter header art, and to Antoine Bandele for taking my manuscript from a Word doc to a professionally formatted book.

Thank you to my family for their love and support in all parts of my life. Especially my dad, who I get my love of writing and reading from and who continually pushed me to publish, and my mom, who never hesitates to encourage my dreams and remind me I am meant to thrive in this life. Thank you to the Cereal Crew for their support, to my closest and longtime friends Chelsea Dial and Verna Campos (aka The Triforce), and to one of my very first readers, Brayden Sotomar.

Last but absolutely not least, I want to thank our family's rainbow dog, Pepper, who taught me that joy, love, and inspiration can come from the simplest moments. I hope the treats are extra yummy in your forever field.

SHARE YOUR THOUGHTS

Enjoyed *Still Water, Skin*?
Share your thoughts in a review at one of the website below!

Storygraph

Amazon

Bookbub

Goodreads

ABOUT THE AUTHOR

Mariama Dumbuya, or Marie D, is an author, writer, and scholar. She has been writing on and (mostly) off for 20 years, that off time engaging with life the most crucial for developing her writing. Her past work has focused on mental health, self-development, and the trials and joys of being an introvert and has been featured in *Introvert Dear, Tiny Buddha, Global Voices, The Mighty,* and *Elephant Journal*.

Mariama holds her master's in intercultural and international communication from American University. Her academic research focused on the engagement among Africans and the African diaspora through the lenses of cultural exchange, global media, and popular culture. She enjoys spending time in nature, consuming art and media, volunteering and advocacy work, and traveling.

Still Water, Skin is her debut young adult fantasy novel.

LET'S CONNECT!

Learn more about Marie D and forthcoming books in the Record of Revival series at her official platforms below.

Official Website: maried.space
Instagram: @mariedspace
Threads: @mariedspace

Scan below to sign up for Marie D's newsletter!

SNEAK PEEK

The story of the scouts and the unnaturals will continue! Get a sneak peek of *An Iridescent Light*, the second book in the Record of Revival series, starting on the next page.

ESERA

E sera was short for sixteen, but never in his life had he felt so tiny. He stood next to Matagi before Vaiola, the sprawling swamp of roots on the two western isles of Taisala. The roots reached into the clouds, standing the tallest on the Plane. Looking at them filled Esera's bones with a primal anxiety. Vaiola was older than recorded time, a Natural mystery no one truly understood.

"The pair that came yesterday said they scouted the entrance," Matagi said, "so we should take one of the edges."

Esera still hated this guy, but he had no more realistic reason to argue with him. At least not with anger. "What if we took a less obvious approach?"

Matagi eyed him. "What do you mean?"

"I mean, what can we really find in the outskirts that the scout-masters haven't? If Odomi is supposed to be this experienced medic, and if she really is behind the Saint's death, whatever we're looking for won't be in plain sight." And he wasn't just saying that because Vaiola terrified him.

Matagi hmphed. "Okay. So where do you propose we look?"

"I propose weee..." Alright. So he hadn't thought that far ahead. His burgeoning scouting instincts only told him searching the outskirts would be a waste of time. Esera pivoted to his right. Ahead was the isle's cliff. "...check out the ocean."

Matagi looked in his direction. "The ocean." Then looked back at him.

"It's the only part no one has checked out. The other hunters will probably stick to the outskirts, so I say we look where no one else will."

"Fine." Matagi tilted his head toward the cliff. "Lead the way."

Esera walked the stretch of muddy ground out to the cliffside, Matagi in tow. The sound of waves crashing against rock intensified as they neared the edge. When they reached the end, Esera peered over the cliff. The drop down was harrowing. Not even Esera had the guts to take it. "Let's take a root down. The rock looks unstable."

Matagi and Esera synced with a root from the swamp and used it to rappel down the cliff face. The strong waves deafened all other sounds. When they reached the bottom, Esera signaled to Matagi that he was going to dive. Matagi waved a hand over his body, and Esera squinted at him, confused. When he got it, he shrugged. They didn't have their diving suits on them. Oh well. Next time.

Esera stripped his shirt and boots off. He synced out a cubby from the rock, set his things inside it, then plunged into the freezing waters of Yawi Yema West, the part of the world ocean between Taisala and Fa'atasi. Matagi jumped in right after, boots and shirt also stripped and metal claws forged onto his hands. Esera felt for his nifo'oti, his hooked clubs, on his back before picking a direction to scout. He swam to his left, keeping close to the rockface. In less than a second, Matagi overtook him with his enhanced speed. Esera puffed bubbles from his mouth but kept on. He possessed enhanced swimming skills but was not as fast as Matagi.

They swam past a rainbow of sea creatures as they scouted, not a zonbi in sight. Esera hoped they found something quick. He didn't want to encounter any ocean-dwelling zonbi. The octo-zonbi he and the other recruits fought on their first ship to Taisala had been a beast.

After several minutes, Matagi stopped suddenly. Esera stopped as well, then swam in front of him. He put on a questioning face. Then Matagi grabbed him and yanked him into a small opening in the rockface. Matagi peeked from behind the opening's wall, and Esera followed his lead.

Whyyy had he thought about zonbi?

It appeared as a small shadow in the distance at first. Then it grew bigger, bigger, bigger until its massive size swallowed all perception.

A zonbi whale.

Esera saw something fall from the creature's belly. Whatever it was broke off into several smaller parts, sinking to the depths below. Esera focused his eyes to get a better look—and made out long rectangular shapes with broken ends. Wood. The zonbi had swallowed a ship.

Esera got Matagi's attention. He jerked his head back, indicating they should retreat. But Matagi scowled, mouthing, "Your idea."

Yeah, well, I never said it was a good one.

The zonbi swam along the rock, heading away from the hunters. Matagi came out of the opening and crept along the wall. Esera, reminding himself to cut his tongue out later, followed him. They snuck along the wall, speeding up when they lost sight of the zonbi and slowing down when they thought they were in its line of sight.

The zonbi eventually slowed when it came to a large protrusion in the wall. It swam under it—then slammed into the ceiling. Esera and Matagi grabbed the rock tighter when the vibrations reached them. It slammed itself again and opened its mouth. Hundreds of smaller sea creatures escaped from inside it, all rushing up to the protrusion's ceiling. They ran into the rock, some back and forth and others once, splattering into the rock. If they were behaving like that, they were zonbi, not animals. And that was a whole infestation mere yards away from them. The chance of surviving that many zonbi was zero. But something attracted them, and Esera needed to find out what.

Esera looked at the space below the infestation. Zonbi normally went after people and animals, but otherwise remained passive. He remembered what...someone...said about the zonbi that behaved differently in the base hospital. The goat that ran for the door instead of attacking anyone. The glob of cats that stuck to the ceiling for minutes before breaking in. They were attracted to whatever had been in the greenhouse. He wondered if their fixation on the ceiling was similar. If so...

Esera pointed to the space below. Matagi looked at him incredulously. Then Esera held a finger to his mouth before sinking deeper. Matagi stared at him before he sank as well. The view above became blurrier the deeper they went, so Esera stopped before he couldn't make anything out. And from the angle they were at, it was hard to see. Esera floated to directly below the infestation. He dodged chunks of whale and more ship debris that sank as a result of the zonbi's slamming. Even then, its giant body was still in the way.

Esera swam up gently. He could see parts of the ceiling now. He made out...arched indentations in neat rows. In another clear spot, something round, egg-shaped. He unconsciously went up more when Matagi grabbed his arm. Matagi pointed a claw at a figure swimming toward the infestation—a person.

Matagi boosted straight for the person. Esera, stupefied by Matagi's stupidity, trailed him as fast as he could, desperation pushing him to match his speed. Matagi pointed again at the person. He made a grabbing motion with his hand and jerked his head in the opposite direction of the infestation. He was going to grab whoever that was, and they were both going to make a break for it. Too late for Esera to protest, so they had to act fast.

Matagi pierced the water like a bullet. While he aimed for the person, Esera got a better look at the ceiling. The indentations looked like fish scales, and there was another egg shape—a pair of breasts. Most of the smaller zonbi had destroyed themselves, and the zonbi whale had broken itself down to bones and muscle, giving Esera more visibility. The ceiling was a carving of a person. Or a fish? He couldn't tell.

He turned his attention back to Matagi, who was closing in on the person. Matagi reached a hand for their leg—but they blasted pressure in their direction, temporarily halting their advance.

And that alerted the zonbi.

Matagi grabbed Esera again and torpedoed for the surface. Esera looked back. The person swam for the ceiling but didn't make it far before the zonbi shredded them. Then the zonbi turned their empty eyes on them. Esera monitored the zonbi's movement but stole one more look at the carving. With the zonbi out of the way, he now saw that the carving was of a human, or what looked like a human. Long hair. Nude torso. A mask for a face and scales that started at the waist.

Esera's panic surged when the zonbi started snapping at his feet, and he couldn't use his reserves of electricity to shock them without hurting Matagi. He brought his legs to his stomach and looked up. The sun shone on the water, then blinded them when Matagi rocketed through the surface, blasting into the air. Matagi synced with a handful of rock on the cliff face, and Esera brought his legs up again when the zonbi leaped out of the water. Forgetting their shirts and boots, they scaled back up the cliff, relying on the rock this time.

Matagi threw himself on the ground when they reached the top. "That better have been worth it," he said, struggling for breath.

"It was." Esera gave himself time to catch his own breath. His heart was threatening to burst from his chest. "There was something down there."